Game of
Dog Bones

Center Point
Large Print

Also by Laurien Berenson and available from Center Point Large Print:

The Bark Before Christmas
Live and Let Growl
Murder at the Puppy Fest
Ruff Justice
Wagging Through the Snow
Bite Club
Here Comes Santa Paws
Doggie Day Care Murder

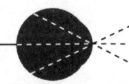

**This Large Print Book carries the
Seal of Approval of N.A.V.H.**

Game of Dog Bones

LAURIEN BERENSON

CENTER POINT LARGE PRINT
THORNDIKE, MAINE

This Center Point Large Print edition
is published in the year 2020 by arrangement with
Kensington Publishing Corp.

The text of this Large Print edition is unabridged.
In other aspects, this book may vary
from the original edition.
Printed in the United States of America
on permanent paper.
Set in 16-point Times New Roman type.

ISBN: 978-1-64358-708-0

The Library of Congress has cataloged this record
under Library of Congress Control Number: 2020942181

Thank you to Mary Miller for telling me all about judging the Non-Sporting Group at the Westminster Dog Show. I hope Aunt Peg does as good a job as you did.

My son, Chase, came up with the great title. Well done! As always, this book is for Bruce, who makes my life whole.

Chapter 1

Westminster Kennel Club Dog Show is the pinnacle.

For two days in early February, New York City is the only place for the country's best show dogs to be. This event is the American dog world's biggest stage. The top handlers, owners, and exhibitors are all there, eager to test each other's mettle as their dogs compete for the ultimate prize: Westminster Best in Show.

Throughout the year, there are dog shows with larger entries. And ones held at easier venues. There are certainly shows with better weather. But none captivate the imagination the way Westminster does. None possess its enduring allure.

The Westminster Dog Show is the second oldest continuous sporting event in the country. First held in 1887, it began before the formation of the American Kennel Club. The show has always made its home at Madison Square Garden, and over the years judging has had to persevere through such disruptions as blizzards and transit strikes.

Westminster isn't just the oldest dog show in the country, however; it's also the most prestigious. Dogs with connections to famous athletes, rock stars, and a British monarch have all competed there. This is the event that every dog lover wants to attend, and every exhibitor wants to win.

The individual breed competition now takes place on Monday and Tuesday at two West Side piers. But at night the show returns to the Garden for judging of the seven groups and Best in Show. Dogs and their handlers are all perfectly groomed, on their toes, and ready to perform.

There's a sudden hush, quickly followed by a burst of appreciative applause, when the day's winners gait into the big ring for the first time. The air in the arena feels electric. Clearly something special is happening.

Westminster has never forgotten its roots as a sporting event for serious dog fanciers. But it has also evolved into spectacular entertainment for a national audience. The result is pure magic for dog lovers.

"Magic," I murmured. I was staring out the car window at the passing scenery, which was currently the Bronx.

It was the Sunday before the start of the Westminster Dog Show and we were on our way to Manhattan. My husband, Sam, was driving. My Aunt Peg—also known as Margaret Turnbull, esteemed dog show judge and breeder of some of the best Standard Poodles the breed had ever known—was sitting beside him in the front of the SUV.

I'd been relegated to the rear seat, which was no surprise. Aunt Peg was clever and astute. She loved a good argument and preferred her own opinions to anyone else's. But mostly she liked to be in charge. That feat was more easily accomplished from the position with the best view.

Aunt Peg's gaze flitted to the window. We were driving past a factory that had seen better days. Probably during the previous century. "Magic?" She turned to look at me over her shoulder. "This?"

"No, I was thinking about Westminster."

"Of course you were thinking about Westminster." She settled back in her seat happily. "Who wouldn't be?"

Two years earlier, Aunt Peg had received the coveted letter inviting her to judge this year's Non-Sporting Group. She told us later that she'd shrieked out loud and danced around the room. Aunt Peg is seventy years old, nearly six feet tall, and not known for her agility. I wish I'd been there to see that.

"Your judging assignment is a huge honor," Sam said. He kept his blue eyes trained on the road but he was following the conversation. Sam and I have been married for six years and he's always been able to manage Aunt Peg better than I do.

"It is indeed," Aunt Peg agreed. "I only hope I prove worthy of the faith the Westminster board has placed in me."

"You will," I told her. "You're an excellent judge."

"I know that." Lack of confidence has never been a problem for Aunt Peg. "But Westminster is more than a dog show. It's a grand spectacle for the dog-owning masses. Not to mention a wonderful opportunity for good canine public relations. The show's television audience numbers in the millions."

"Don't tell me you're nervous about being on TV," I said.

"No, that part of it is just a distraction. My job is about the dogs—not the lights and the cameras."

"Yes, but you'll still have to get your hair and make-up done beforehand," I teased. Over Aunt Peg's objections, both appointments had already been made.

"That's just a lot of pointless fuss and bother," she grumbled. "Everybody already knows what I look like."

"Not in TV land," Sam said with a grin. "You know, the dog-owning masses?"

"You're not helping." Aunt Peg reached over and smacked his arm. "I'm already well aware that this assignment is a big deal. But what I'm feeling about it isn't nerves. It's anticipation. I can't wait to get my hands on all those wonderful dogs. But at the same time, I want to be sure that I rise to their level. My judging must be every bit as good as the champions in front of me."

Sam and I nodded. We could both understand that.

"Not only that, but when you look at the list of Poodle breeders who have judged this group before me, I am following in some very distinguished footsteps," she continued. "Heaven forbid I let the side down."

"That's not going to happen," Sam told her. "If you weren't every bit as good as those judges who've preceded you, the Paugussett Poodle Club wouldn't have asked you to conduct today's seminar on evaluating Poodles."

"Yes, well, that's another thing," Aunt Peg said with a frown. "Before I can even get to tomorrow evening's show, first I have to make it through the rest of the weekend."

From my perch in the middle of the back seat I could see that her hands were fidgeting in her lap. Whatever she was doing, Aunt Peg almost always had one of her beloved Standard Poodles at her side. Today we'd had to leave our dogs at home. Without a warm Poodle body to caress, her hands must have felt empty.

"Surely you're not worried about the symposium?" I asked.

"Heavens, no. I could lead a judging seminar

in my sleep. It's Victor Durbin who's a concern. Along with that dratted Empire Poodle Club specialty that will be running at the same time. All things considered, it's drawn quite an entry."

All things considered, indeed.

Victor Durbin was a Miniature Poodle breeder and a former member of Connecticut's Paugussett Club. He'd been asked to resign from the club several years earlier after the board discovered that Victor had been allowing Cocker Spaniel and Schnauzer owners to breed their bitches to his Mini Poodle stud dogs. The resulting mixed-breed litters of Cockapoos and Schnoodles were flooding the local pet shops.

After his expulsion from the club, Victor claimed to have changed his ways. He'd petitioned to be reinstated. His request was summarily denied. Aunt Peg had led that charge—but a majority of the other members agreed with her. Most hoped that Victor would quietly move on. Perhaps find another breed with which to become involved.

But Victor had had other ideas. Instead, he'd decided to form his own Poodle club. Though the tri-state area was already home to several other affiliate clubs, Victor was undeterred. He'd taken the other groups' membership rosters, and proceeded to search their ranks for disgruntled members who could be convinced to jump ship and join his nascent club. Once he had enough names, Victor had doggedly shepherded his Empire Poodle Club through the steps required for AKC accreditation.

EPC had received a license to hold its inaugural Poodle specialty the previous year. A date that fell on the day before Westminster had been applied for and approved. A Manhattan venue was booked. The single-breed show would take place in the ballroom of a hotel on Seventh Avenue. It happened to be the same hotel where the Paugussett Poodle Club was hosting its judging seminar at the same time.

Nobody thought that was a coincidence. Least of all Aunt Peg.

"You don't need to worry about Victor." Sam exited onto the Henry Hudson Parkway to head south. "His specialty show is in the second floor ballroom. The conference room for the symposium is on the fourth floor. There's no reason that your paths should even cross."

"Our paths have already crossed, in a manner of speaking," Aunt Peg replied tartly. I couldn't blame her for being annoyed. "It's perfectly obvious that more people would have signed up for the seminar if there weren't a competing Poodle event happening right downstairs."

"If more people had signed up, the club would have had to book a bigger room," I pointed out. Poodles' three varieties—Toy, Miniature, and Standard—meant the breed offered aspiring judges entrée into both the Toy and Non-Sporting Groups. That automatically made them a popular breed for which to apply. "Even with the specialty, there are more than a hundred people coming to learn more about Poodles from you."

"You needn't sound so surprised," Aunt Peg said drily.

Sam cast her a glance. "Actually I'm a little surprised that the Westminster show committee is allowing you to participate in both this symposium and their event tomorrow. We all know that they frown on even a hint of bias or favoritism. The group and Best in Show judges are barred from attending the show before they arrive to do their part, for that very reason."

"The committee would indeed be very unhappy if I was socializing with exhibitors who might later find themselves in my ring," Aunt Peg admitted. "But in this case, they agreed that I could hardly get up to much trouble in the company of my fellow judges."

"They must not know you nearly as well as we do," I said under my breath.

"I'm sorry." Aunt Peg turned in her seat again. "Did you say something?"

Fortunately, I was saved from having to answer by the buzzing of my phone. Our home number came up on the screen. Knowing that between the symposium and the dog show we'd be busy all day, Sam and I had left our kids at home in Connecticut.

Davey was fourteen, and halfway through his first year of high school. He was babysitting his younger brother, Kevin, who would turn five next month. Both boys shared our interest in Standard Poodles. But Kevin was too young to follow us around quietly for hours at a time. And Davey had no desire to devote a weekend day listening to Aunt Peg deliver a lecture. That sounded entirely too much like schoolwork to him.

I lifted the phone to my ear. "Hey, Davey, what's up? Is everything okay?"

"Yup." Now that he's a teenager, Davey doesn't expend extra words on his parents. "But we need carrots."

"Carrots?" My sons were asking for vegetables? That was a first.

"Kev and I are building a snowman in the backyard. The dogs are helping. Except Bud. You know."

I did. Bud, a small spotted mutt we'd adopted two summers earlier, was more trouble than our five Standard Poodles combined. I gave Davey props for the snowman idea, though. We'd had four inches of fresh, powdery snow on Friday night. Now on Sunday morning, it would be packed just right for building.

"You want a carrot for the nose?" I asked.

Davey laughed. "You would think—but no.

Kevin wants them for his ears. So they stick straight up like Bud's."

Technically only one of Bud's ears stuck up. The other flopped forward over his eye. It wasn't worth debating.

"Did you check the vegetable bin in the bottom of the refrigerator?"

"I looked there first. The only thing in there is onions."

"Ewww!" I heard Kevin say in the background.

"Yes, I can see how that wouldn't work." I looked up at Sam. "Are we out of carrots?"

He shrugged. Traffic was light on a Sunday morning. Even so he was paying attention to the route as he pulled off the highway onto a side street.

"What do we have that's long and skinny?" I mused, putting the phone on speaker.

"How about straws?" Aunt Peg offered from the front seat.

"Too small," Davey replied. "This is a big snowman. Almost a snow monster."

"It's a snow monster." Kevin giggled. "Except he needs ears."

"Wait a minute," I said. "How about a couple of hot dogs? That could work. They'd even wiggle in the wind like real ears."

"Good idea," Davey agreed. "I'm on it." He ended the connection.

"Hmmph," said Aunt Peg.

I tucked the phone back in my pocket. "Now what?"

"Am I to understand that your kitchen is lacking in vegetables but well stocked with hot dogs?"

I wanted to deny it, but really there was no point.

"Something like that," I said.

"Sometimes you feed kids what they'll eat rather than what's good for them," Sam mentioned.

Thanks, honey.

Aunt Peg wasn't appeased. "It sounds as though I feed my Poodles better food than you give your children," she huffed.

"You might," I agreed easily. I would never argue with Aunt Peg about canine care. Hers or anyone else's.

"Stop squabbling, you two." Sam turned on his blinker and turned into the entrance to a parking garage. "We've arrived."

Chapter 2

We entered the Manhattan hotel lobby loaded down with gear.

Sam was carrying the grooming table tucked beneath his arm. Aunt Peg had a briefcase filled with slides and notes she'd brought from home. I was holding a box that contained handouts for the attendees. The only thing we didn't have with us was a live Poodle.

The audience for the seminar would be made up of people who wanted to learn how to judge Poodles. With that in mind, Aunt Peg wanted to display a dog that looked exactly as it would appear before them in the show ring. Coral, the teenage Standard Poodle that she and Davey had been showing together, was too young to serve as a model. However Crawford Langley—a professional handler who was showing at the Empire specialty on the second floor—had offered to supply her with a demo dog later that afternoon.

I looked at my watch as we headed for the elevators. It was eleven a.m. Both the specialty and the seminar were scheduled to begin at noon. Once again, probably not a coincidence.

"After I deliver this stuff to the conference room, I'm going down to spend some time at the show," I told Aunt Peg. Though the judging wouldn't start for another hour, the ballroom would already be full. Poodle exhibitors always arrived early since they had plenty of pre-ring grooming to do.

Aunt Peg turned to me in mock outrage. "You're not going to attend my seminar?"

We'd been over this before. Possibly a dozen times. I'd lost count of how often this complaint had come up during the past month.

"Not all of it," I said. "First, I'm going to the specialty."

"You're passing up a wonderful learning opportunity."

"How do you figure that?" I asked. "You've been lecturing me for years. It hardly seems possible you might have more stuff to say that I haven't heard yet."

Aunt Peg looked at me down her nose. "I don't see why. I learn new things all the time."

I juggled the heavy box to one side and pushed the button for the elevator. "Then it's a good thing Sam will be listening to your entire talk. He'll be able to fill me in on anything I miss."

The elevator door slid open. We fit ourselves inside. "Thank goodness one of my relatives is here to support me," Aunt Peg sniffed.

"Yes," I said, punching the next button with more force than was strictly necessary. "Lucky you."

Sam was standing behind Aunt Peg, trying not

19

to grin. He'd always been her favorite. I was used to that by now.

"I should think you'd want a first-hand report on Victor Durbin's specialty," I mentioned. "It's the Empire Club's first attempt to stage an event—and in New York City, no less. I wonder if they've taken into account all the things that could possibly go wrong?"

Aunt Peg considered that, then nodded. "You have a point. I suppose you'll be making yourself useful, after all."

It was a small victory, but I'd take it. Especially as it meant I could now attend the specialty with a clear conscience.

The conference room was open and waiting for us. Rows of folding chairs had already been set in place. There was a slide projector in the back of the room. A dais in the front held an empty table and a podium with a microphone. Behind it, a white screen had been pulled down from the ceiling.

I put the box I'd been carrying down on the table. A hotel employee came over to make sure that Aunt Peg had everything she needed. Several Paugussett Club members had also been waiting for her arrival. They gathered around too.

Aunt Peg appeared to be in good hands. That was all I needed to know. I sketched Sam a wave and made a hasty exit before my esteemed relative could change her mind.

The Poodle show awaited downstairs. *Excellent.*

The conference room had been quiet and nearly empty. By contrast, the ballroom on the second floor hummed with activity.

Dog shows generate their own particular buzz of excitement. Some exhibitors thrive on the winning, and the thrill of competition. Others come to show off the best dogs that their breeding programs have produced. Many treat the shows as social events, since they're a wonderful opportunity to spend a day surrounded by friends.

Indeed, the first dog shows were simply gatherings of neighbors who brought their dogs together for the purpose of debating their relative merits. Though the sport has grown tremendously since then, at its core, not a lot has changed.

Breeders still strive to produce the finest dogs they can, always bearing in mind the purpose for which the breed was intended. And judges and exhibitors still argue over which dog is actually the best. It all makes for a lively exchange. As well as the occasional impassioned dispute.

A specialty is a dog show devoted to a single breed of dog. On this weekend before Westminster, a dozen different breed clubs were holding specialties in Manhattan. With the top dogs coming to New York for the big show, it made sense for the clubs to capitalize on the influx of out-of-town exhibitors. In various ballrooms around the city, spectators could enjoy watching Boston Terriers, Pekingese, and French Bulldogs all strut their stuff.

The ballroom I entered, however, held only Poodles. Just what I wanted to see.

A large rectangular ring had been set up in the center of the room. Though it was currently empty, the perimeter of the floor had already been lined with nonslip mats. The judge's table was in place. All was ready for business.

The day's exhibitors had arranged their setups around the outside of the ring. Crates were stacked. Tack boxes were open. Blow dryers were in use. Dozens of Poodles were already out on their tabletops, being groomed. Thanks to the layout of the room, exhibitors would be able to prepare their dogs and spectate at the same time.

According to the judging schedule, Standard Poodles would be shown first. They were followed by the Miniatures, then Toys. As the largest variety, Standards took the longest to prepare for the ring. It was no surprise, then, that most tables held the bigger dogs, while the Minis and Toys waited their turn in nearby crates.

I paused just inside the doorway to the room. It only took me a few seconds to locate my good friends Crawford Langley and his life partner and handling assistant, Terry Denunzio. When I spotted their setup, my eyebrows rose. Even in the crowded ballroom, Terry was hard to miss.

Which was probably the point, I thought, smothering a laugh.

Terry has a flamboyant streak a mile wide. Since the last time I'd seen him, he had changed his hair color again. Blond before, he'd now opted for a shade not often found in nature.

Perhaps he'd been inspired by the Westminster's own club colors, I realized. Either that or an eggplant. Standing out amidst the beautifully coiffed Poodles with their black, brown, and white coats, Terry's hair was a brilliant shade of purple. I wondered what Crawford thought of that.

Probably not much.

Terry and Crawford were opposites in many ways. Maybe that was why they made such a great couple. In his sixties, Crawford was staid and dignified. The consummate professional, he'd been at the top of the handling game for more years than I'd been going to dog shows. Terry was closer to my age; we were both edging toward forty. He was a blithe, free spirit who took almost nothing seriously. Except his longstanding relationship with Crawford.

I made my way quickly through the setups that clogged the area between us. Some of the exhibitors I passed were familiar to me, as we were frequent competitors at the local shows. Others had come from all over the country; they were in town now for the Westminster show. Previously I'd only seen their Poodles on the pages of the glossy canine publications. I couldn't wait to have a chance to admire them in person.

"Air kiss," Terry said as I approached. There was a white Standard Poodle lying down on the grooming table between us. He leaned over it and aimed a pair of smooches in my general direction.

I followed suit. It wouldn't do to muss his make-up. Then I walked around the table, lifted a hand, and feathered it through his locks. "Really?" I said.

He batted his eyes. "Don't you love it?"

"I don't know." I tipped my head to one side and considered the look. "I'm still deciding. What does Crawford think?"

The older handler was standing no more than four feet away. He must have heard my question. Even so, he didn't turn around. I sighed and looked at Terry. He frowned, then gave a slight shrug.

Apparently I still hadn't been forgiven.

The previous summer I'd done something that betrayed Crawford's trust. I knew he was a very private person—and that he wouldn't appreciate my delving into his past. Sam had warned me not to do it. But at the time the risk had seemed worth taking.

I'd learned what I needed to know, and Terry

had been enormously grateful for the way things had turned out. But despite his efforts to bring about a reconciliation, my relationship with Crawford had been strained ever since.

"Good morning, Melanie," the handler said now. He still didn't turn around. "Standards go in the ring in less than an hour. We're a little busy here."

Well. I guessed that meant I wouldn't be sticking around to chat.

"It's okay," Terry said quickly. He reached out and laid a hand on my arm so I wouldn't move away. "I'm a man of many talents. I can talk and brush at the same time."

Crawford harrumphed under his breath. I winced. Terry ignored him.

"So," he said brightly. "Where's McDreamy today?"

He was referring to Sam, of course. Apparently I wasn't the only one who had a crush on my husband. And no wonder. Sam had slate blue eyes, a killer smile, and charm to spare. Not to mention that body.

"You know Sam hates it when you call him that," I said.

"Yes, I know. Ask me if I care." Terry stuck out his tongue. "If he was here, I wouldn't do it. Hence the question."

"He's upstairs with Aunt Peg. You know, at PPC's judging seminar?"

Terry picked up his pin brush and went back to work while we talked. The white Standard on the table had her eyes closed. She was probably asleep.

"Of course I know about the seminar. Who doesn't? Margaret Turnbull offering a master class in evaluating a Poodle for the show ring? This weekend, that's probably the hottest ticket in town."

"Don't let Aunt Peg hear you say that." I laughed. "Her ego is big enough as it is."

"And justifiably so," Crawford muttered. Still facing the other way, he'd declined to join our conversation. But he was obviously paying attention.

"Anyway, I don't know about a hot ticket," I said. "The seminar is full, but it would have drawn a bigger crowd if Victor Durbin hadn't scheduled this show to take place opposite it."

Terry looked surprised. "You think he did that on purpose?"

"Don't you?"

Terry considered the question. "I knew there was bad blood between them. Peg was on the board when he was kicked out of the Paugussett Club, wasn't she?"

I nodded.

"But that happened years ago. Is he still holding a grudge?" Terry looked around for a misting bottle.

I plucked one off a nearby table and handed it to him. "You tell me. The date for Aunt Peg's seminar was announced more than a year ago. The Empire Club could have scheduled their specialty to take place yesterday. But they didn't. Victor's the one who created the conflict. It seems to me like he wanted to draw a line on the ground between them, then make people choose sides."

I paused to gaze around the room. "Speaking of Victor, I haven't seen him yet. I assume he must be here somewhere?"

"Oh, he's here all right." Terry smirked. "Last time I saw him, he was strutting around the ballroom like a rooster who thought he owned the barnyard."

"That figures." I sighed. "This place is crammed with Poodles. His specialty drew a terrific entry. Victor must be feeling very pleased with himself."

"Points are points, Melanie," Crawford interjected. "And Victor hired a fine Poodle judge in Louise Bixby. Some of us have to take our opportunities where we find them."

Strictly speaking, I knew that wasn't true. For a handler like Crawford there would always be judges who enjoyed seeing him in their show ring, and who were more than happy to reward the dogs he brought them. Crawford never lacked for opportunities to win.

To be fair, however, I could also understand the appeal of wanting to nab a nice win now, right before Westminster. All the top competitors were in town. For this one week, the attention of the entire dog community would be focused on New York City.

A success here would be a big feather in any handler's cap. Not only that, but a specialty win today would give a dog added impetus to do well in the breed judging at Westminster tomorrow.

"I'd like to see a topknot in that Standard," Crawford mentioned pointedly.

Terry had just finished brushing the Standard bitch. He sat her up on the table. Reaching into the tack box, he grabbed a knitting needle for making parts and a bag of tiny, colored rubber bands.

"It's coming right now," he said.

"Maybe if your fingers were moving as fast as your mouth, it would already be in place," Crawford replied.

I was pretty sure that was my cue to move along. Considering how prickly Crawford had been lately, I had no intention of overstaying my welcome. At least not any more than I already had.

"I'll see you guys later," I said. "Good luck! Louise Bixby should love your Mini special. Topper's been on a roll."

Topper was Champion Gold Dust High Top,

a sparkling apricot Miniature Poodle with whom Crawford had been tearing up the show ring for the previous three months. A finished champion—also known as a specials dog— he was entered both here and on Monday at Westminster. I knew Crawford and Terry were really hoping that the Mini would win the variety there and go on to compete in the Non-Sporting Group.

"Shush!" said Terry. "Don't jinx us." He glanced at his partner to see if he'd heard me.

I hadn't expected that. "Since when did Crawford become superstitious?"

Terry rolled his eyes as if he was surprised I even had to ask. And maybe he had a point.

"It's Westminster week," he said. "Everyone wants a win here more than anything. That means we're all on edge."

Chapter 3

The next person I ran into was Bertie Kennedy. A tall, striking redhead, Bertie was a professional handler who specialized in the herding and non-sporting breeds. She and I had originally met at a dog club meeting. We'd been friends for several years before she married my younger brother, Frank, and became my sister-in-law.

Hands down, that was the luckiest day in Frank's life.

Not that I don't love my brother, but trust me when I say that Bertie was by far the better catch of the two. I don't entirely understand what she sees in him but they are blissfully happy together. Bertie and Frank have two young children, Maggie and Josh. That, added to the fact that they are a two-career family, means that everyone is always busy.

I don't get to see Bertie nearly as often as I would like. So running into her here was a nice surprise.

I threw my arms around Bertie and gave her a hug. "I didn't know you were coming today. I thought Maggie would have an art class, or kung fu, or an ice hockey game. You know, something on the calendar that would keep you closer to home."

Okay, so I was a little hazy on the details. Sometimes it's hard enough to keep my own kids' schedules straight without having to remember everyone else's too.

"She does, but I skipped out anyway." Bertie grinned. "I told Frank that since it was Westminster week, he was on his own when it came to child care."

"Good for you." I could just picture the look on my brother's face when he'd heard that. "You're not showing today, are you?"

Bertie was casually dressed in slacks and a turtleneck sweater. Plus, she didn't have her hands on a Poodle. So I was guessing no.

"Here? At Victor Durbin's show? You must be joking. Peg would probably never forgive me." Bertie wasn't a member of the Paugussett Poodle Club, but she'd heard the stories. "Actually I've been running around the city since first thing this morning. There's dog stuff going on everywhere. I already checked out the Pug and the Shih Tzu specialties. After I spend some time here, I'll stop in on Peg's seminar. Then I'm off to watch the Havanese do their thing."

While we'd been speaking, the steward had entered the ring. She began handing out numbered armbands to the Standard Poodle handlers who were gathering at the gate. The woman was tall and wiry. Her short black hair formed a sleek cap around her head. She performed the task quickly and efficiently, and she had a smile ready for each exhibitor.

"That's Hannah Bly," I said.

"Friend of yours?" Bertie asked.

"More of an acquaintance. She used to be a member of PPC. Before."

"Before Victor, you mean?"

I nodded.

Bertie deepened her voice to a low rumble. "Before she went over to the Dark Side?"

"Precisely." We both laughed.

I realized I'd forgotten to buy a catalog and dashed away to pick one up. When I returned, Louise Bixby had arrived to begin her assignment. An attractive woman in her late forties, she looked like a judge who knew what she wanted, and who had every intention of finding it in her ring this afternoon. She was wearing a lovely designer suit, paired with minimal jewelry and sensible shoes. Aunt Peg would have approved all of her choices.

Mrs. Bixby took stock of the judging table. She rearranged her ribbons and opened her book. Bertie and I grabbed a couple of chairs and sat down to watch.

The first classes were divided by sex and open to Poodles who had yet to complete their championships. Entrants were competing for a portion of the fifteen points that were required to become "finished" champions. The specialty show had a large entry, so there were majors—awards of three to five points—available in all three varieties. With that much on the line, the competition was going to be fierce.

The first class to enter the ring was Standard Puppy Dogs. Four dog-and-handler pairs filed through the gate and lined up along the mat. At first glance, they all looked wonderful. No surprise, considering that it was Westminster week.

As soon as the Poodle puppies appeared, I put all thoughts of Victor Durbin aside. It was time to sit back and enjoy the show.

"This should be great," I said to Bertie. "I'm not even showing and I'm tingling with anticipation."

"I know what you mean," she replied. "Victor may be an idiot, but Mrs. Bixby was an excellent choice to judge his specialty. She drew a terrific entry."

The handlers set up their puppies. Louise Bixby stepped to the opposite side of the ring and ran her gaze down the line, studying the dogs as a group. After a minute she lifted her hands, indicating it was time to gait the puppies around the arena for the first time.

Although we were outside the ring, Bertie and I began to judge the class too. Other spectators around us were doing the same thing. Judging dogs was a subjective exercise and we all had opinions. Mrs. Bixby's opinions were the only ones that mattered today, but that didn't stop the rest of us from mentally reshuffling the line into an order that we liked better.

The brown puppy was plain and lacking in underjaw, I decided. The small black dog was too immature to win in this company. The bigger black puppy was very handsome. I loved his balance and the way he moved. He would be my class winner. There was a white puppy who also possessed many admirable attributes. I decided I would place him second.

I glanced over at Bertie. Her gaze was following the same black puppy I'd liked. When that Poodle gaited again after his individual examination, he drew a smattering of applause from ringside. Clearly Bertie and I weren't the only ones who were smitten.

When Mrs. Bixby rearranged her class, however, she put the white puppy on top. The smaller black dog was second. The puppy I'd chosen was third, and the brown placed fourth.

"Drat." Disappointed, I sat back in my seat, as the dog I liked left the ring with a yellow ribbon. "I thought he looked great. What did I miss?"

Bertie shrugged. "I thought he'd win too. But we couldn't see everything from here. Maybe he had a bad bite. Or a wonky topline."

That was the problem with judging from ringside. The real judge was the only one who was able to put her hands on the dogs. And the dense Poodle coat—especially in a puppy trim that covered the dog's entire body—could hide a multitude of flaws. Not to mention that the Poodles at this show had all been trimmed by experts. It was their job to make the dogs look perfect, whether they were or not.

"Don't worry," Bertie said. "You'll do better in the next class."

I did, but only because the American-Bred class had just a single entry. It was hard to go wrong there. The Bred-by-Exhibitor class that followed had three dogs in it. And once again, the dog I picked didn't win.

"I guess it's a good thing I'm not a judge," I said with a frown.

Aunt Peg could correctly sort out the merits of a dozen black Standard Poodles in mere minutes. Sam also had a discerning eye when it came to separating the great dogs from the merely good ones. I knew that my skills weren't comparable to theirs, but after all the time I'd spent attending dog shows, I thought I'd begun to learn *something*.

Apparently I'd given myself more credit than I deserved.

"Don't be so hard on yourself," Bertie said. "Take a look around. You're not the only one who appears to be baffled by Mrs. Bixby's placements."

Experienced show-goers knew to keep their voices down at ringside. So I couldn't hear what anyone else was saying. But in the same way that the presence of a truly superb dog could send a frisson of excitement coursing through a crowd of spectators, now the ringside seemed to be united in the opposite emotion. There was a palpable air of discontent in the room.

"Maybe we're doing this wrong," I said to Bertie. "I've been watching the dogs. Maybe I should have been looking at their handlers instead. Do you suppose she's playing politics?"

Bertie frowned. Then sighed. "If she is, you and I both know that it wouldn't be the first time."

Indeed.

For an owner handler or a small-time professional, politics could be the bane of their dog show experience. Good judges only cared about the quality and performance of the dogs in front of them on the day. But unfortunately, there were plenty of judges who based their decisions on other factors.

Some were more influenced by the handler on the end of the lead than by the virtues of the dog itself. For judges who were lacking in knowledge, giving the win to a top handler—who was assumed to have brought a good dog into the ring—was an easy shortcut to make themselves appear smart. Other judges rewarded their friends' dogs—and hoped their friends would return the favor in the future.

Economics could also factor into the judges' decisions. Those who drew large entries were rewarded with future assignments, since more entries meant more money for the show-giving clubs. And the big professional handlers brought multiple dogs to every show. So it was always in the judges' best interests to keep the handlers happy.

"Could be," Bertie replied. "But nearly all the Poodles here today are with a handler. I can't say I've noticed that's she's favoring one over the others."

Crawford had a gorgeous Standard Poodle in the big Open Dog class. He won handily, but his dog was then beaten by the white puppy for Winners Dog—the only award that would confer points. Crawford was a consummate professional. Though he knew he had the better Poodle, he accepted his striped ribbon for Reserve Winners graciously.

"Ouch," said Bertie.

My sentiments exactly.

I cast a glance back to the setup where Terry was waiting with Crawford's Open bitch. Terry didn't possess Crawford's poker face. Everything he was thinking was readily apparent, and he was *not* amused. I couldn't blame him.

The Standard bitches were up next. Bertie and

I continued to watch. Our opinion of what was happening in the ring didn't improve. Crawford lost with both his Open bitch and his specials dog. So far, he'd been entirely shut out. It must have been an unfamiliar feeling for him.

"I can't bear to look anymore." Bertie turned in her seat to face me as the first Mini class entered the ring. "Let's talk about something else. Terry and Crawford's wedding is next week. Terry told me he's making all the arrangements. Does he have everything under control?"

"Good question. I saw him earlier, but we started talking about Victor and I never got a chance to ask about anything else. But there's only a week to go, so I'm sure Terry must be on top of things."

I was crossing my fingers for luck when I said that. Bertie simply looked skeptical.

"You're kidding, right?" she said with a laugh. "This is Terry we're talking about. Crawford must have been crazy to let him take charge."

"They're holding the ceremony at their home in Bedford, so the venue is all set," I pointed out. "And apparently the guest list isn't huge. Terry says they're having a simple country wedding. So how hard can that be to pull together?"

"Yeah, like that's really happening." Bertie looked like she wanted to laugh again. "When have you ever known anything Terry was involved with to be simple?"

She had a point. I thought back to some of Terry's previous escapades. And abruptly realized that almost anything was possible.

"You don't suppose he's planning some sort of Greatest Show on Earth, Macy's parade, Fourth of July fireworks extravaganza, do you?" I asked.

"It could be all of that, and more." Bertie sounded pleased by the prospect. "Especially since they're getting married on Valentine's Day. That ought to give us a clue what to expect."

"Like big red hearts for the decor?" I suggested. "And little kids dressed up as cupids, running around with bows and arrows? Maybe three tiers of red velvet wedding cake?"

"Oh, I hope so." She turned around in her seat to face the ring again. "All I know is that I expect to be thoroughly entertained."

The Miniature Poodle judging proceeded in much the same way that the Standard judging had. Bertie and I continued to be baffled by the results.

Crawford lost with both his class dog and his class bitch. Now he was oh for five. He continued to present his Poodles to the judge with a smile on his face, however. The tension in the set of his shoulders was the only sign of the agitation he'd begun to feel.

Then it was time for Best of Variety. Crawford took his place at the front of the line with Topper. Including his apricot Mini, there were four champions, plus the Winners Dog and Winners Bitch in the class. It was immediately apparent that Topper was the crowd favorite. Applause followed the pair around the ring every time he and Crawford moved.

I agreed with everyone else. Even in this nice company, Topper should have been an easy winner.

It appeared that Mrs. Bixby had other ideas. She made Crawford work hard for the win. Even at the end of the class, when she took her last look down the line, I still wasn't sure what she was going to do.

When she finally pointed to Topper for Best of Variety, my shoulders sagged in relief. The spectators around the ring gave the pair a sustained round of applause. As Mrs. Bixby handed Crawford the purple and gold rosette, she permitted herself a small smile. It occurred to me that was the first time I'd seen her look happy all day.

"Thank goodness," I said. "At least she got something right."

Crawford accepted congratulations from the other handlers and quickly exited the ring. Topper would go back on his tabletop now. He would need to return later to compete against the other two Best of Variety winners for the Best of Breed.

Earlier in the day I'd thought that the BOB win

would be a given for Topper. Now I had no idea what might happen next.

"I don't understand it," I said to Bertie. "Louise Bixby is supposed to be a good judge. I know Aunt Peg thinks highly of her. But the results today have been all over the place. Do you suppose she's feeling all right?"

"If she was before," Bertie muttered, "it's a sure bet that she won't be soon. Look."

I followed the direction of her gaze and saw Victor Durbin for the first time that day. The man was crossing the ballroom with long, angry strides. He appeared to be heading toward the show ring. The expression on his face was thunderous.

I wondered what that was about.

Chapter 4

That can't be good," I said.

"No, it can't," Bertie muttered darkly.

I'd been acquainted with Victor back when he was still a member of the Paugussett Club. But our paths had seldom crossed since then. Now, however, the arrogant sneer on his face quickly reminded me of the disdain with which Victor had treated the Poodle club members whom he'd felt were less important than he was.

Not Aunt Peg, of course. But me. And others like me, who had very small breeding programs, and who competed in dog shows for fun rather than to prove that our dogs were better than anyone else's.

Victor was an attractive man who kept himself in good shape. His sleek moustache should have been ridiculous, but instead it somehow made him look dashing. He was probably in his fifties, but women still noticed when he walked by—even when he wasn't moving with an air of menace, as he surely was now.

Exhibitors around us were busy putting the finishing touches on their Toy entries. The ring was currently empty, so most spectators were chatting with their friends or looking down at their phones. Nobody else appeared to be paying attention to Victor's precipitous approach.

Bertie and I both stared as he crossed the room. The day had already been full of surprises. Once again, I couldn't wait to see what would happen next.

Personally, I was hoping for a full-out brawl. Something that would really liven up the proceedings. I was sure that Victor had chosen the date for his show with the express purpose of sabotaging Aunt Peg's seminar. So I wouldn't be at all upset if his event ended in disaster.

Plus, think of the entertainment value.

By the time Victor reached the in-gate, I was sitting on the edge of my seat. The Toy Poodle competitors had begun to gather outside the ring, but the steward had yet to call the first class. Victor inserted himself neatly into that lull in activity.

Mrs. Bixby had bent down over the judge's table to mark her book when the Mini judging ended. Now as she straightened again, she saw Victor coming. Her expression set in a hard line. It was difficult to tell with the stark fluorescent lighting, but she might have paled slightly.

What Louise Bixby didn't do, however, was dodge the confrontation. Instead, as Victor approached, she moved forward to meet him. The two of them met in the opening provided by the in-gate.

Unfortunately for us, that was all the way on the other side of the ring. I couldn't hear a word either of them was saying. All I could tell was that both Victor and Mrs. Bixby looked annoyed.

I glanced over at Bertie. She shook her head. She couldn't hear anything either. Where was Aunt Peg when we needed her? That woman had ears like a fox.

"How well do you read lips?" I asked.

"Not well enough," said Bertie. "I have no idea what's going on over there. All I know is whatever it is, it shouldn't be happening. A show chairman isn't supposed to interrupt a judge in the middle of her assignment."

"Mrs. Bixby would agree with you about that. She looks like she'd like to punch Victor. What could possibly be so important that he felt the need to talk to her right now?"

"Maybe they're continuing the argument they had earlier," Bertie said.

I turned and stared at her in surprise. "What argument?"

"I saw them together this morning when I arrived here at the hotel. As I walked through the lobby, they were standing off to one side talking. I didn't think anything about it. A minute later, when I was waiting for the elevator, Mrs. Bixby came over and joined me. Victor was nowhere to be seen at that point, and she and I got on the elevator together. That seemed like a lucky break, so I decided to introduce myself to her."

I nodded, encouraging her to continue.

"Mrs. Bixby gets plenty of assignments, and I figured a little networking couldn't hurt. Then

44

maybe the next time I walked in her ring, she might remember who I was. But then I looked over at her and changed my mind."

"Why?"

"She just looked pissed, you know? Angry, like she wanted to snap somebody's head off. And all I could think was that I sure didn't want it to be mine. Because that *really* wouldn't help my career. So instead I slunk over to the other side of the elevator and didn't say a word."

"That's odd," I mused.

"I know," Bertie agreed. "And here we are again. I had no idea Louise Bixby had such a temper."

"And I had no idea you knew how to slink. Slinking doesn't seem like your kind of thing at all."

"You're wrong," she informed me. "I'm a very good slinker. I can skulk too, if the situation calls for it. But in that moment all I wanted to do was to be invisible."

"If Victor and Louise don't get along with each other, how do you suppose she got the judging assignment?" I asked.

Bertie shrugged. "These things get decided way in advance. Maybe they used to like each other and now they don't."

"I remember something Aunt Peg told me back when Victor's misdeeds were beginning to come to light, and the Paugussett board was up in arms about what to do. She said, 'Everybody likes Victor until they actually get to know him. Then nobody likes him.' "

"That sounds about right," Bertie said.

Abruptly Victor spun around and left. His conversation with Mrs. Bixby had lasted less than a minute. As soon as the in-gate was free, the steward resumed her job. She quickly called the first Toy Poodle class into the ring.

Bertie settled in to watch the Toy judging. I ran upstairs to see how Aunt Peg's seminar was coming along. By now, it would be half over.

A few minutes earlier, I'd seen Terry slip out of the ballroom with a black Standard Poodle in tow. I figured he'd gone to deliver Aunt Peg's demo dog. That meant my timing was just right. Once she was pointing out features and flaws on a live Poodle rather than a two-dimensional picture on a slide, things were bound to be more interesting.

The door to the fourth floor conference room was open. When I walked in, I saw that the seminar was on a break. The audience members were up and milling around. Many were talking in small groups. Some were helping themselves to coffee from the urn in the back of the room.

Aunt Peg now had the grooming table set up on the dais. Terry was about to get Crawford's class dog settled on top of it. The Poodle knew the drill. As soon as his front feet were lifted and placed on the rubber-matted edge, he hopped up the rest of the way. Terry patted the tabletop and the dog lay down quietly.

I saw Sam standing off to one side with two members of the Paugussett Poodle Club. I made my way toward them. Terry went hurrying past on his way out of the room. Having made his delivery, he needed to get back downstairs to help Crawford with their Toy entry.

"Show going well?" Sam asked Terry as he went by.

Terry paused just long enough to frown and shake his head before picking up speed again. By the time I reached Sam and the others, the handler was already gone.

"Melanie, you know Mattie and Olivia," Sam said to me by way of a greeting.

"Of course," I replied. "It's nice to see you both again."

Mattie Gainer bred Miniature Poodles. She'd moved to Connecticut and joined PPC several years earlier. With her cheerful disposition and her willingness to take part in any and all club projects, Mattie had quickly endeared herself to the rest of the membership.

Olivia Wren was in her eighties. She was a tiny woman with slightly stooped shoulders and wispy white hair. Olivia had shown Toy Poodles and been a member of the Paugussett Club for decades. Now retired, she never missed a club function. The events were the highlight of her social life.

"It's lovely to see you too, Melanie." Olivia's voice was clear and strong. "Sam has been amusing us with stories of your younger son's escapades."

"That could take a while," I said with a smile. "When Kevin and Bud are on a roll, almost anything can happen. How are things going here? Is Aunt Peg doing a good job?"

"She's doing a wonderful job," Mattie enthused. "I thought four hours might be a long time for Peg to lecture. But she's had so much to say, it seems like she's barely paused to breathe. The first half of the seminar has just about flown by."

"Peg definitely knows how to work a crowd," Sam said. "She's delivered lots of valuable information, but she's also kept things light by sprinkling in plenty of entertaining anecdotes."

"Peg had us howling in our seats," Mattie told me. "I had no idea she was such a funny woman."

"Wait until you get to know her better," I said with a straight face. "She's a laugh a minute."

"Speaking of which," said Sam, "Terry looked pretty glum a minute ago. Does that mean that things aren't going Crawford's way downstairs?"

"Pretty much," I replied. "Although if I had to pick someone who is having a good day under Mrs. Bixby, I'd be hard pressed to do it. Some of her choices have been inexplicable from ringside. Crawford finally managed to snag a win a few minutes ago when he took the variety with

Topper. Right after that Victor came storming over, and he and Mrs. Bixby had words."

"In the ring?" Sam said, surprised.

"Nearly. They were standing by the in-gate. I can't imagine what Victor was thinking."

"Nor can I." Olivia's lips pursed in annoyance.

"What were they talking about? Surely it couldn't have been Topper's win. He'll be one of the favorites in tomorrow's group. Today should have been a cakewalk for him." Sam had posed the question, but the other two women were curious too. All three leaned in to hear the answer.

"You would think," I told them. "But it seems as though nothing about the judging has gone as expected so far. Unfortunately, I was too far away to hear what Victor and Mrs. Bixby were saying."

"It serves Victor Durbin right if his specialty has to take a few lumps," Mattie said stoutly. "When I heard that he'd purposely scheduled the show to conflict with Peg's seminar, all I could think was, 'Isn't that just like Victor?' I didn't know him long—he left PPC only a few months after I joined. But I remember that he liked to ride roughshod over people. He always thought that what he wanted mattered more than anyone else's wishes."

"You're quite right," Olivia agreed. "Victor Durbin is not an honorable man. Peg took much of the heat stemming from the decision to expel him from the club, but she and I were both on the board at the time. I believed just as strongly as she did that Victor had to go. Indeed, the vote was nearly unanimous."

"I was a newbie back then, so I wasn't privy to much of what was going on," said Mattie. "His expulsion had something to do with his breeding practices, didn't it?"

"It did," Sam confirmed. "As we all know, PPC is a club dedicated to the preservation and betterment of the Poodle breed. It's baffling how Victor ever thought he could remain a member in good standing while engaging in a practice our charter expressly forbids—allowing his Mini dogs to be used as studs to create mixed breed puppies for sale to pet stores."

"Victor claimed to have repented after we kicked him out," Olivia told us. "But that was a bald-faced lie. The man has always been a bit of a cad, but now I'm afraid there isn't a decent shred of moral fiber left in him. If anything, his behavior has only gotten worse."

I hadn't heard about that. Probably because Aunt Peg remained mostly mum on the subject of Victor Durbin since news of their scheduling conflict had first become known. Now I had no qualms about pumping Olivia for information.

"Are you referring to his specialty?" I asked. "Or is there something else?"

"With Victor there's *always* something else."

Olivia issued a small, ladylike snort. "My Lord, I've known that man since he was barely old enough to wear long pants. In those days, I admired his persistence. He was always busy, always on the lookout for new opportunities. I thought those traits would serve him well. And they would have, if he hadn't turned around and headed in the entirely wrong direction."

"Victor's gotten some things right," Sam mentioned. "His Victory Haven Kennel produced some nice Miniature Poodles through the years."

"Yes, it did," Olivia allowed. "But that's not enough to make me want to forgive his other transgressions. His newest venture is a puppy café in Tarrytown. Have you heard about that?"

I shook my head. "Is it one of those coffee shops that has puppies running around for customers to play with while they drink their lattes? I once read about something like that, but it was in another country."

"I believe the idea started in Japan," Mattie interjected. "But kitty and puppy cafés are getting to be all the rage here too."

"So of course Victor was interested," Olivia continued, frowning. "As I understand it, some café owners offer adoptable pets as playmates for their clientele. But Victor took a different approach. The puppies that entice dog lovers into his café are for sale. He brags that the Doodles and Schnoodles he has are better than the usual designer dogs because his are sired by champion Poodles."

"That's pretty low," I said.

Sam and Mattie nodded.

"It gets even worse," Olivia told us. "Victor doesn't bother to check out his puppy buyers to make sure they'll make good homes. He just takes their money and lets them walk out the door with a dog. Nor does he do any genetic testing on his stock, because the pet market doesn't demand it. As for the puppies' dams, anything goes as long as the breeder—and I use that term loosely—is willing to give Victor half of the resulting litter to sell in his café."

"You're very well informed about what Victor's been up to," Sam said.

"There's a reason for that." Olivia sighed. "Victor's mother is one of my dearest friends. Which makes his behavior even more disappointing. It's gotten so that Bonnie and I can barely hold a decent conversation anymore. I find myself cringing every time she brings up his name."

"I don't blame you," I said.

"Me neither," Mattie retorted.

Olivia gave us a small smile, then turned away. She was ready to change the subject. "It looks like Peg's about to get things rolling again. Let's find our seats, shall we? I can't wait to hear what other treats she has in store for us."

Chapter 5

I sat down next to Sam as Aunt Peg resumed her talk. Half an hour later, Bertie came up from downstairs and slipped in beside us.

Aunt Peg had come prepared with a plethora of good information to convey to her audience. And demo dog, Riley, kept us entertained with his Poodley antics. But I'd spent much of my recent life being lectured to by Aunt Peg. So I didn't find the experience of sitting through yet another lesson to be nearly as stimulating as the other participants did. When she finally began to wind down an hour and a half later, I was ready to move on.

Although Aunt Peg had finished her talk, she continued to field questions from the audience. Sam and I gathered our things. I prepared to stand up. Actually I was preparing to make a beeline out the door.

"Someone had better go up there and stop her," I told Sam under my breath. "You know Aunt Peg. She could talk about Poodles all day and night."

"There goes Olivia now." Sam gestured toward the older woman. "She'll take care of it. Besides, Peg has a meeting with the network people this afternoon. She wouldn't want to be late for that."

Oh, right. I'd forgotten. Seven groups plus Best in Show would be judged on Monday and Tuesday nights at Madison Square Garden. All eight prime-time judges were getting together with representatives of FOX Sports this afternoon to talk about their schedules and responsibilities.

Previous years' judges had told Aunt Peg that the network liaisons had mostly stressed the need for efficiency and dispatch in selecting the winners. Television wasn't a leisurely medium. And the time slot for the Westminster show was only so long. Anyone who fell behind left his fellow judges with the unwelcome task of making up the lost time.

I wasn't worried about Aunt Peg. She was usually two steps ahead of everyone else when it came to making decisions. Lack of speed wasn't going to be a problem for her.

Unless she decided to pause and bask in the moment, I thought with a sigh. Much as she was doing now.

Up at the front of the room, Olivia Wren was working on extricating Aunt Peg from the audience members who'd come forward and crowded around her. Olivia graciously thanked everyone for attending the symposium. She praised Aunt Peg for taking time out of her busy schedule to offer aspiring Poodle judges such a wonderful learning opportunity.

The last bit was followed by an enthusiastic

round of applause. Aunt Peg smiled and took a small bow.

"Annnd we're done," said Bertie. She stood up and stretched. "I still have another specialty or two to check out, but I'll see you guys tomorrow, right?"

Monday was the first day of the Westminster show. Everyone would be there.

"Of course," Sam and I said together.

After Bertie left, Aunt Peg appeared beside us. She'd already put on her coat. Aunt Peg almost never wore hats, but now she had a cloche pulled down low over her eyes.

"I am going to leave this room, go directly down to the lobby, then exit the hotel and walk straight to Madison Square Garden for my meeting," she said. "I intend to look at my feet the entire time. This whole area of Manhattan is chock full of dog people. Mindful of my assignment tomorrow night, I don't want to even *see* anyone who might want me to stop and socialize."

Judging the Non-Sporting Group at Westminster would be the highlight of Aunt Peg's career. I could well understand why she didn't want to do anything to jeopardize the perception of her impartiality. Even so, I hoped she didn't bump into a lamp post.

"Now I have jobs for each of you," she added.

Of course she did.

"Sam, can you retrieve the grooming table and make sure it makes its way back to the car?"

55

"Certainly." Since he'd brought the table in, I was pretty sure Sam had already figured he was taking it back out.

Aunt Peg nodded toward the dais behind her. "Melanie, I need you to return Riley to the specialty. I promised Crawford I'd have the dog back in his setup before the end of the show."

"Easy peasy," I told her.

We agreed to meet at the parking garage in an hour. Flanked by several PPC board members, Aunt Peg hurried out the door. She was still talking. It figured.

The conference room was still more than half full. None of the attendees seemed in any hurry to leave. Numerous dog fanciers had come from other parts of the country for the Westminster show. The events surrounding it were all about networking and socializing.

Sam and I made our way to the front of the room where Riley was lying on his table waiting for us. As we approached, an African American man walked toward the big Poodle from the other side. The man held out his hand. Riley lifted his head and sniffed the extended fingers. The Poodle's tail began to wag.

The man looked up and saw us coming. He had pleasant features framed by a pair of glasses with thick, black frames. "That's a nice looking dog. Friendly too. Is he yours?"

"No, but he belongs to a friend of ours," I

said. "We're about to return him to the dog show downstairs."

"You mean Victor's show." The man smiled. "The Poodle show, right? I'm Clark Donnay. I don't know a thing about dog shows, but Victor and I are partners in a café in Tarrytown. It's called the Pooch Pub. Maybe you've heard of it?"

Sam and I shared a look.

"We have," Sam told him.

Clark's eyes lit up. "That's great. Have you ever been there?"

"Not yet," I said. "We live in Connecticut."

"That's not far," Clark assured us. He stuck a hand in his pocket and pulled out a card. "Let me give you a coupon for a free coffee. Get your first visit off to a good start. Believe me, if you're a dog lover, it's worth the trip."

"Thanks." I took the coupon and tucked it away without making any promises about its future use. I figured Sam and I were about as likely to visit the Pooch Pub as we were to see the Great Wall of China. But you never knew.

"Nice meeting you both." Clark started to leave, then turned back. He gestured toward Riley. "If your friend ever wants to stud out his dog, tell him to get in touch with Victor. I'm sure he can find some mates for him."

Sam looked struck dumb by the suggestion. We both knew there was no way in hell that was going to happen.

But Clark looked so pleased with himself for making the offer that I found myself saying, "We appreciate the thought. It was nice to meet you too."

"We appreciate the thought?" Sam repeated when Clark was out of earshot. *"Really?"*

"I was trying to be polite," I said. "You heard what Clark told us. He doesn't know anything about dog shows. I'm sure he has no idea that any reputable breeder would be insulted by his offer."

"That being the case"—Sam stared after Clark thoughtfully—"what do you suppose he was doing here at a seminar for aspiring judges?"

"I don't know. Maybe he was killing time while Victor is busy downstairs."

At any rate, it wasn't my problem. I had a Standard Poodle to attend to.

I introduced myself to Riley, then opened up his tightly wrapped leash and hopped him down from the grooming table. The big black dog had no idea who I was, but in the way of all Poodles everywhere, he was delighted to make a new friend.

Having been shown earlier, Riley was still fully done up for the ring. That had suited Aunt Peg's purposes perfectly. But now that we were going to be on the move, Sam fished a couple of small rubber bands out of his pocket. I looped them quickly around the dog's copious ear fringes to keep them out of the way. Terry would finish breaking down the Poodle's hair-sprayed topknot and coat downstairs. Sam quickly folded up the grooming table and we were good to go.

Down in the ballroom, the specialty show was almost over. Best of Breed was being judged. In the ring, the three variety winners were lined up in size order. A black Standard Poodle was at the head of the line. Crawford was next with Topper, the apricot Mini. A silver Toy Poodle brought up the rear.

All three dogs looked fantastic. Each was being shown by a top professional handler. Crawford was local, but the Standard was from Texas and the Toy was a West Coast dog. All the heavy hitters were in town this week.

Sam set down the folded grooming table just inside the door. I hustled Riley over to Crawford's setup, where Terry was waiting. His eyes never left the activity in the ring as he lifted the Standard Poodle onto a table.

"Topper looks great," Sam said.

Terry nodded. "So does the Toy, Sterling. Mrs. Bixby hasn't taken her eyes off him since he walked into the ring."

That wasn't a good sign. Mrs. Bixby had judged all three variety winners earlier. So when they returned to compete for the top award, presumably she should already know which one she favored.

From my vantage point at the setup, I studied

the three Poodles in the ring. I had disagreed with some of Mrs. Bixby's previous choices. But now, looking at her three finalists, I couldn't find fault with any of them. They were all deserving winners.

The judge gaited the trio together one last time. They were still in size order. The Standard Poodle commanded attention at the head of line. His long stride ate up the length of the ring. Behind him, Crawford and Topper were flying along. The Mini was ahead of his handler, moving all on his own at the end of a fully extended lead.

Sterling's handler wisely made no attempt to keep up with the other two. Instead he let his much smaller Toy dog find his own best speed. Head cocked to one side, his attention focused on the judge, Sterling trotted around the ring as if he owned it.

The entire crowd at ringside seemed to be holding its breath as we waited for Mrs. Bixby to make her choice. Finally she did, motioning the silver Toy over to the Best of Breed marker. The spectators erupted in applause. Sam and I joined in.

Terry did not. I heard him sigh, then he turned away from the ring. "Oh well. At least Topper was beaten by a good one."

Sam nodded in agreement. "If Sterling shows like that tomorrow, he'll be a threat in the group."

"The Toy Group." Terry brightened at the thought.

Standard and Mini Poodles both competed in the Non-Sporting Group. So Sterling and Topper wouldn't cross paths again except in the unlikely eventuality that both Poodles won their respective groups and met in the Best in Show ring.

Sam and I had to leave, but we waited for Crawford to return to the setup so Sam could congratulate him on his earlier BOV win. Crawford was philosophical about Topper's loss for Best of Breed.

"Tomorrow will go better," I told him. Tomorrow Aunt Peg would be judging. I didn't add that.

Crawford slanted me a sharp look. "There's no need to placate me, Melanie. Today was plenty good enough."

I snapped my mouth shut. I probably shouldn't have opened it in the first place. I'd had no idea that my friendship with Crawford was built upon such a fragile foundation. Now I desperately wanted things between us to go back to the way they'd been. The problem was, I had no idea how to make that happen.

"It's time for us to go." Sam grabbed my hand and turned me around. We headed for the door.

"Don't you dare say I told you so," I muttered.

Sam shook his head. "I'm not that dumb."

When we reached the parking garage, Aunt Peg had Sam's SUV waiting in the entrance with the motor running and the heat turned on full blast. I briefly wondered how she'd managed that since Sam still had the claim ticket in his pocket. Then I dismissed the thought. It was Aunt Peg. She'd simply made it happen.

It wasn't just cold on the city street, it was blustery too. The sun had disappeared behind the tall buildings to our west and wind gusts were whipping down the cross streets. I slid gratefully into the warm back seat as Sam stowed the grooming table in the rear.

"I hope you thanked Crawford for the use of his Standard," Aunt Peg said once we were on our way.

Oops, I'd forgotten. "I'll do it tomorrow," I told her.

Aunt Peg frowned. She wasn't impressed by that promise. She pulled out her phone and sent the handler a text. If she was going to do that, why had she even asked?

"Is Crawford still mad at you?" she inquired when she was finished.

Now it was my turn to frown. She knew the answer to that. Sometimes it seemed like *everybody* knew the answer to that.

"Maybe," I said.

"You never did tell me what you did to get on his wrong side," she prodded.

That was because it was a secret. Crawford's secret, not mine. I hadn't told anyone but Sam. And he knew how to keep his mouth shut.

When I didn't reply, she added, "Whatever it was, I'm sure you deserved his censure."

"She did," Sam agreed.

"Hey," I piped up from the back seat. "That's a matter of opinion."

"Except that everybody's opinion is that you were wrong," Sam replied.

"Not Terry's," I defended myself.

"Is that so?" Aunt Peg spun around in her seat. "The plot thickens. Perhaps you should tell Terry to intercede for you."

"He already tried that," I said unhappily. "It didn't work. Do you mind if we change the subject?"

"I don't mind," said Sam. "Here's something else we can talk about. From the sound of it, Victor's specialty turned out to be interesting, to say the least. Why don't you fill Peg in?"

"No names! Not even one!" Aunt Peg bellowed before I could say a word. "Until I've done my part tomorrow night, I refuse to hear any specific details. Don't tell me who won or lost. Just give me your general impressions."

She paused for a wicked grin. "Tell me Victor fell flat on his face. That would make my day."

"Consider it made," I said. "Because he came close."

"Oh?" Now she was intrigued. "I take back what I said a minute ago. Maybe I could hear just a few details. What went wrong?"

"Mrs. Bixby, for one thing. I didn't see Toys, but she judged Standards and Minis like a woman who was feeling her way through her first Poodle assignment with great difficulty."

"That doesn't make sense. Louise has been judging Poodles for years."

"You certainly couldn't tell that from today's results. Plus, she and Victor had a disagreement about something inside the show ring."

"While she was judging?" Aunt Peg was horrified by the thought.

"In the break between Minis and Toys."

"Even so, that's not right," she muttered. "I've known Louise for a long time. Of course, I can't say anything to her now. But perhaps after Westminster she and I will have a little chat."

"She's the one who accepted the judging assignment from Victor," Sam pointed out. "Remind her that if you lie down with dogs, you get up with fleas."

"I just might be tempted to do that," Aunt Peg said darkly.

Chapter 6

S am and I live in Stamford, a coastal city in lower Fairfield County, Connecticut. Traffic was light on Sunday afternoon, so the drive from Manhattan took less than an hour. We stopped along the way to drop off Aunt Peg at her home in Greenwich.

Much of Stamford is a thriving metropolis, but our house is located well north of downtown. Our residential neighborhood sometimes feels like a throwback to earlier times. It's quiet enough that kids can ride their bikes in the streets and play outside without supervision. Neighbors all know each other, and we look out for one another. So I hadn't been worried about leaving Davey and Kevin on their own while we were gone.

The boys were in the living room when we arrived home. Sam and I had been away for more than half the day, so I thought Kev and Davey would be delighted to see us. When we walked in the door, however, neither glanced away from the video game that was playing on the TV.

Instead, the most effusive greeting we received came from our five Standard Poodles. Sam's and my blended canine crew consisted of my mother and daughter duo, Faith and Eve; Sam's older bitch, Raven; and his Best in Show winner and occasional stud dog, Tar. Davey's Standard dog, Augie, had been a more recent addition to the group.

All our Standards were black, and all were retired show champions. We kept them in the easy-to-care-for sporting trim. Their faces, their feet, and the bases of their tails were clipped. A short blanket of dense curls covered the remainder of their bodies.

With some breeds it might be hard to live with that many dogs in one house. But these were Poodles. The breed is smart, entertaining, and charismatic. They also have a sense of humor, so they do best with an owner who knows how to take a joke. Poodles fit into any kind of lifestyle and they make the perfect canine companions. Most days our house didn't feel crowded at all.

Our dogs might have looked similar in their matching trims, but each had a different personality. Faith was just a puppy when she'd been a gift to me from Aunt Peg. We'd immediately formed a tight bond that had only grown closer through the years. Faith could read my thoughts and emotions, just as I'd always been able to understand hers. She was almost nine now, and I hoped she would live forever.

Faith's daughter, Eve, was a free spirit. She took life as it came and was always happy. Sam's bitch, Raven, was the oldest of our group. Her mind was still sharp, but these days she was more likely to watch rather than join in when the other dogs ran and played.

The two males, Tar and Augie, were a boisterous pair. Tar was wonderfully sweet. He was also the only dumb Standard Poodle I'd ever met. His antics were as amusing to us as they were confusing to him. Augie was the youngster of the pack. Davey had handled the big Poodle to his championship almost entirely by himself, and the two of them made a solid team.

Bud was the honorary member of our Poodle pack. Davey and I had brought the small mutt home with us after he'd been dumped by the side of the road. Once here, he was ours forever. Bud was the Artful Dodger of dogs: clever, sneaky, and the worst sort of influence on the Poodles. We all adored him anyway.

Sam and I maneuvered around the Poodles as we took off our coats and gloves. The dogs milled around our legs, each one vying for attention. I patted as many heads as I could reach. We greeted all of them by name.

When the initial furor subsided, I crouched down and wrapped my arms around Faith's neck. Her tongue slipped out and licked my ear. "I know," I whispered, pulling her close. "I missed you too."

Then I blinked and took another look around the hallway. "Where's Bud?" With all the commotion, I hadn't noticed that the little dog was missing.

"Upstairs," Kevin said from the depths of the couch. He had his father's blond hair and blue eyes. And just like Sam, he was a charmer.

"By himself?" I asked.

Kev nodded.

That was unexpected. "How come?"

"Dunno."

"Maybe someone would like to find out?" I suggested, looking pointedly at my two sons.

"I'm on it." Davey set down his joystick and hopped up from the couch.

He was my son from my first marriage. Eight years old when Sam and I got married, Davey counted himself lucky to have two dads. He adored Kevin and took his role as older brother very seriously.

Davey had shot up four inches in height over the past six months. Now he sounded like an elephant going up the stairs. "Nothing too bad going on up here," he called down after a minute.

"Define not too bad," said Sam.

"Bud's asleep."

"Maybe we got lucky," I said.

Sam was more skeptical. "Where?"

Davey came clattering back down the steps. Bud was following him. "You know that basket of clean laundry Mom didn't get around to putting away? Bud made himself a nest in there."

All eyes turned to look at me.

"I was in a hurry this morning," I mentioned. "How come no one else helped out and put the laundry away?"

"That's your job," Kevin told me. Once Davey left, he'd given up on the game.

"Be careful there." Sam grinned. "You're skating on thin ice."

"I like skating." Kev missed the point entirely. "Can we go skating tomorrow?"

"Three of us have school tomorrow," I told him. "Then we're all going back to the dog show."

Kevin's eyes opened wide. "In New York City?"

"It's Westminster." Davey perched on the arm of the couch. "Aunt Peg is judging tomorrow night. We're all going to watch. And it's going to be on television."

Kev's mouth dropped open. "I'm going to be on TV?"

"Sorry." I reached down and ruffled his hair. "Not us, just Aunt Peg. But it will be exciting to see the dog show in person, won't it?"

Kev nodded. He was easy.

I turned toward the kitchen. "I'm going to start cooking. Who's ready for dinner?"

I'd expected a chorus of assent. Instead there was only silence.

"Kevin and I got hungry earlier," Davey said after a moment. "So I cooked us a couple of hot dogs."

Sam chuckled. "Hopefully not the same hot dogs you used on the snowman?"

That comment was greeted with more silence. I guessed that meant we had our answer.

"There was peanut butter and jelly in the pantry," I said. "Along with soup and tuna fish. Not to mention a bowl of hard-boiled eggs in the refrigerator. You didn't notice any of those things?"

"Nope." Davey shrugged. Kevin followed suit. And that settled that.

Monday morning was chaotic. That was nothing new. Every morning is a whirlwind at my house.

First person up—usually me—put the dogs out in the fenced backyard, then fed them when they were ready to come in. By the time I had the kids' breakfast mostly made, Sam was dressed and downstairs. He took over in the kitchen while I ran up and checked on the kids. With luck, Kevin would be putting on the outfit I'd laid out for him the night before—and not something completely different and totally inappropriate.

Then I ran to take a shower and get dressed. If all went according to plan, the four of us ended up in the kitchen at approximately the same time. There we would sit down together to share a delicious and nutritious breakfast, before heading out to start our days.

What a pipe dream. If that actually happened even once a week, it felt like a miracle.

Just after eight o'clock, Davey's bus picked him up at the end of the driveway and took him to his North Stamford high school. Kevin was in preschool five mornings a week at Graceland Nursery School. My younger son and I shared virtually the same schedule. Weekdays, I worked from eight-thirty to one p.m. as a special needs tutor at a private school in Greenwich.

Howard Academy had been founded early in the previous century by robber baron Joshua Howard, who'd sought atonement for his sins by devoting some of his ill-gotten gains to the cause of education. The school was housed in his former mansion, situated high on a hill overlooking the town of Greenwich. Despite Howard Academy's ritzy location and history, Headmaster Russell Hanover II was determined that its current principles be in tune with the times. The school's student body now comprised equal parts children of privilege and scholarship students, all afforded a top-notch education meant to mold them into the leaders of the future.

I loved my job at Howard Academy. I especially loved that I could take Faith to school with me. The big black Poodle was a warm and comforting presence in my classroom. She was particularly adept at providing emotional support for students who were struggling with the curriculum. To my delight, Faith was now regarded as the unofficial school mascot.

This particular Monday, however, I couldn't wait for the school day to end. While I'd been sitting in my classroom, the breeds in the Westminster Hound, Toy, Non-Sporting, and Herding Groups were being judged on two West Side piers in Manhattan.

In previous years, Aunt Peg, Sam, and I had sat ringside for each day's judging. This year, I had to be content with sneaking peeks at the classes that were live streaming on the Westminster Web site. It was a paltry substitute for being there in person and watching it all happen live.

By one o'clock, Faith and I were out the door. We stopped to pick up Kevin at preschool, then drove straight home.

Aunt Peg had the remainder of my afternoon organized to the minute. Indeed, Hannibal had marched elephants across the Alps with less advance planning than Aunt Peg had devoted to mapping out her Westminster campaign. I'd already been warned that no tardiness would be tolerated.

The four Westminster group judges performing that night had to be at Madison Square Garden no later than six-thirty. Between now and then, Aunt Peg and I would be driving into the city and checking into the hotel where she'd booked a room for the night. This afternoon she had appointments to have her hair styled and her make-up professionally applied. Then there might be time to grab a small bite to eat before she changed into her gown. After that she and I would make our way to the Garden together.

Once at the Garden, Aunt Peg and the other judges would have a chance to freshen up, before each was scheduled to do a taped preinterview. After that, they'd be shown to their seats. The telecast would start promptly at eight p.m. Judging would begin shortly thereafter with the Hound Group. Aunt Peg's Non-Sporting Group was third in the lineup.

Sam, meanwhile, would be holding down the fort at home. He and the boys would be driving into the city this evening. Sam had secured the four of us near-floor-level seats from which to view the proceedings. At the end of the night, he and the boys and I would drive home together. Aunt Peg would be staying over in New York. Having concluded her part in the event, she would be free to attend the rest of the show on Tuesday.

It was a plan with a lot of moving parts, but with any luck, it would all proceed like clockwork. One could only hope.

I met Aunt Peg at her house. She and I loaded up her minivan in the driveway. We handled the long hanging bag containing her evening gown with extra care. She kissed each of her Standard

Poodles on the nose, while I bid good-bye to the pet sitter. Minutes later, we were speeding down the Merritt Parkway toward the city.

Aunt Peg drove like a woman whose tailpipe was on fire. I'd checked the clasp on my seat belt twice before we even crossed the state line into New York. Aunt Peg pretended not to notice. Which wasn't to say that she kept her eyes glued to the road. Instead she kept fiddling with the radio.

That was new. Perhaps she wasn't as complacent about the evening's events as she'd led us to believe.

"Tell me about yesterday's meeting with the network liaisons," I said. Maybe that was the source of her anxiety. "Did they have lots of tips for you and your fellow judges?"

"Tips?" Aunt Peg stared at me across the front of the minivan. "More like commandments. Those people put the fear of God into us. Clearly they aren't dog people. They weren't interested in the quality of the dogs we'll be judging, nor in the amount of time it might take to adequately assess them. On the contrary, they made it abundantly clear that the only thing that matters to them is their broadcast. They want it to be lively, interesting, and above all *on time*."

"You can manage that," I said.

"That's what I thought," she grumbled. "Until they started talking about attaching buzzers to our clothing so they could let us know when we were moving too slowly."

I bubbled out a laugh. "You mean like a shock collar?"

"I suppose. I didn't delve into the particulars. Apparently it's difficult to find a place to hide the device on a woman's dress, so only the male judges will be subjected to that indignity."

"Lucky you." I was still laughing.

"I'm also meant to keep my eye on a pair of flashing lights," she added. "Silly me. I thought my eyes were meant to be on the dogs in the ring during the limited time that's been allotted to me. A green light means keep going. When the light turns red, the broadcast is taking a break for commercials. I must quickly stop what I'm doing and go sit down."

Considering that I would merely be watching from the sidelines, I was finding all this rather amusing. "Is that all?"

"One would hope, but not quite," Aunt Peg replied. "We were also told that there will be cameras everywhere, even where we might not expect them. We are to ignore them and go about our business as if they aren't there."

"Try telling that to the dogs," I said. "Every year some of them get spooked by the cameras and lights. Not to mention the magnitude of the setting."

Aunt Peg nodded. "I may share that feeling

myself, depending on how the night progresses. We will be wearing microphones when we're judging, so we must be aware of everything we say—or don't say. And when we talk, we must speak clearly. And concisely."

She paused, and issued an audible sigh. "Before I went to that meeting, I was mostly concerned about not tripping over the hem of my long dress. Now I have a whole new host of potential problems to consider."

Aunt Peg's sartorial style was devoted mainly to casual clothes. I couldn't remember the last time I'd seen her in formal attire. I was lucky. Since I was only a spectator, I had on a wool turtleneck dress and leather knee-high boots, topped by a warm, camel hair coat. I could run around the city in the outfit all day and still be comfortable in it tonight.

"You'll be fine," I said.

"Of course I'll be fine," Aunt Peg snapped. "Once this is all over, everything will be just dandy."

"Don't forget to breathe."

She harrumphed under her breath.

"And to enjoy yourself. This assignment isn't just an honor. It's the opportunity of a lifetime."

She slanted me another look. "Are you implying that I'm so old I may be in my doddering retirement before the Westminster club gets around to inviting me again?"

"You most certainly will be if you ignore a red light, or knock over a camera, or trip over your dress."

Aunt Peg straightened in her seat. Her shoulders stiffened with resolve. "None of that is going to happen. Not on my watch."

I smiled and folded my hands demurely in my lap. That was just the response I'd hoped to hear. Things were back to normal now.

Not on her watch indeed.

Chapter 7

Aunt Peg left her minivan with the valet in front of the hotel. As we crossed the sidewalk to the entrance, I could see Madison Square Garden. It was only a block away. She'd chosen this hotel for its location. We wouldn't have to travel far to get to the show this evening.

Aunt Peg barely had time to unpack her small suitcase before it was time to head out for her first appointment. She'd gotten recommendations from friends who'd previously judged Westminster, so the professionals at the salon where she was booked knew exactly what she needed.

"Don't you dare cut my hair," Aunt Peg told the stylist. She was perched on the edge of a plush salon chair.

"No, of course not." His name was Ricardo and his hands fluttered in the air as he settled a pale pink cape over her clothing. "Not unless you want me to. But first you must sit back and relax. Would you like a cup of tea?"

By the time Aunt Peg and Ricardo had shared a pot of Earl Grey, they were good buddies. Aunt Peg's gray hair was shoulder length. She usually wore it in a low bun or a ponytail. But Ricardo swept her locks up into a sleek chignon that would be just right for tonight's formal occasion.

When he was finished, he handed her a small mirror and slowly spun the chair around so Aunt Peg could see the effect from the back. "It looks wonderful, yes?"

Reflexively, Aunt Peg lifted a hand toward her head. Ricardo quickly batted it away. "No touching now! Your hair has to stay perfect until midnight. That means you must coddle it."

"Think of yourself as a Poodle that's ready for the show ring," I told her. I couldn't count the number of times we'd had to restrain spectators from touching our perfectly coiffed entries.

Aunt Peg smiled at that. "It looks perfect, Ricardo. Thank you."

He clasped his hands in front of his chest and gave her a small bow. "It is my pleasure. Now Elise will take over and see to the next step in your transformation. When she is finished, you will look like a princess who is ready to go to the ball."

"A dowager queen, perhaps," Aunt Peg muttered, but she looked pleased nonetheless.

Ricardo's every move had possessed theatrical flair. Elise, the make-up artist, was calmly professional. The tools of her trade were lined up along a counter beneath a lighted three-way mirror. She studied Aunt Peg's face briefly in the strong light, then showed her to a straight-backed chair

"Don't make me look like a clown," Aunt Peg instructed.

"Certainly not," Elise agreed. "That wouldn't

do either of our reputations any good. Now don't frown. Think happy thoughts."

Right away, I liked this woman. "Think Poodles," I said. It had worked earlier, and it worked again now.

Aunt Peg's face relaxed. Elise winked at me over Aunt Peg's shoulder and went to work. Her craft was fascinating to watch.

Half an hour later, Elise laid down her brushes. She stepped back out of the way so Aunt Peg could admire herself in the mirror. Aunt Peg stared at her reflection. Then she blinked and looked again.

"I think she likes what you've done," I said in a stage whisper.

Elise beamed with satisfaction. "It's not too much," she told Aunt Peg. "I've just enhanced your natural beauty, then taken things up a notch so you won't look washed out on TV. And don't forget that in an arena that size you will mostly be seen from a distance. For the purposes of making an impression, you should think of the show ring as your stage."

"I like that idea," Aunt Peg replied. "I like it quite a lot. I must say you've done a masterful job with your cosmetics. I can hardly believe that a little make-up could make such a difference."

"You see?" Ricardo appeared. He clapped his hands in a quick staccato beat. "Just as I said, you look like a princess!"

Aunt Peg thanked them both profusely and added a sizeable tip to her bill. She and I took a cab back to the hotel. It grew dark early in February. The buildings and streets of Manhattan were already lit up around us. If I gazed out the window through half-closed eyes, it looked like a magical wonderland.

We got back to Aunt Peg's hotel room with an hour to spare before she needed to be at the Garden. I sent downstairs for some food. I had missed lunch, so when it came, I was ready to dig in. Aunt Peg, usually a hearty eater, only nibbled at her meal.

"Butterflies?" I lifted a brow.

"Now it's beginning to seem real," she said, pushing her plate away. Then she smiled happily. "*Finally.* I can't wait."

When we'd arrived, I'd removed the long gown from its protective wrapping and hung it up in the closet. Now Aunt Peg took it out. Before putting the gown on, she stood before the full-length mirror and held it up in front of herself.

The dress was a shimmering shade of midnight blue. It had a beaded lace bodice with a boat neck and three-quarter-length sleeves. The skirt fell to the floor and was loose enough so Aunt Peg would be able to move freely. When she walked, it would ripple around her legs in soft pleats.

"That will do," I said.

"I should hope so," Aunt Peg retorted. "Helen

Mirren wore a dress just like it recently. It looked fabulous on her."

"It will look fabulous on you too. The non-sporting dogs will be lucky if anyone even notices them."

"Oh pish," said Aunt Peg. "Now you're just being silly."

A few minutes after six o'clock, we were on our way. When we exited the hotel, the doorman started to wave a cab forward, but Aunt Peg shook her head.

"You're sure?" I said. "Even in that dress?"

"I'll be fine," she told me firmly. "It's barely more than a block. A nice walk will be just what I need to settle my nerves. Let's be on our way, shall we?"

In Stamford, the streets near my house would have been quiet at this hour. Here, in the city that never sleeps, there were still plenty of people strolling along Seventh Avenue. Aunt Peg had topped her evening gown with a three-quarter-length faux fur to keep out the cold. No one gave her a second glance as she marched along the sidewalk with such a determined stride that I virtually had to trot to keep up.

Briefly I stopped to stare up at a giant billboard. When I looked around again, Aunt Peg was suddenly twenty feet in front of me. If not for her height, and that silver-tipped fur, I might have lost her in the crowd. I assumed she would still be moving, so I was surprised at how easy it was to close the distance between us. When I drew near, however, I realized it was because Aunt Peg had come to an abrupt halt.

And she wasn't alone.

A man, his face shadowed by the brim of his hat, had grasped her upper arm in his hand. I saw her try to shrug him off. The man held firm, refusing to release his hold.

I didn't like the looks of that at all.

Three quick strides later, I was close enough to hear what they were saying. Aunt Peg noticed my approach, and shook her head slightly. She seemed to be indicating that she had the situation well in hand. I stopped and hung back. I hoped that was what she'd meant.

"Just one drink," Victor Durbin was saying. "A quickie. A celebratory cocktail before you go inside to join the exalted ranks of Westminster group judges."

"Unhand me, Victor." Aunt Peg's voice was firm. It was the same tone she might have used to chastise a misbehaving puppy. "Even if I wanted to have a drink with you—which I do not—I don't have time. I'm due inside the Garden shortly."

"The show doesn't start for another hour and a half. They'll wait for you," Victor wheedled. "Everybody always dances to your tune. Come with me. Let me apologize for ruining your seminar."

Aunt Peg reared back. When Victor still didn't let go, that caused him to step toward her. The two of them looked as though they were engaged in an odd dance. A steady stream of pedestrians eddied around them. Nobody paid any attention to the pair but me.

"Your specialty didn't ruin my seminar," Aunt Peg corrected him. "We had a sellout crowd. Listen to me, Victor. I have neither the time nor the inclination to accompany you anywhere, much less to a bar."

He gave her arm a small yank. Aunt Peg held her ground. I wasn't about to let Victor continue to manhandle her. Despite Aunt Peg's wishes, I stepped closer anyway.

"Get hold of yourself, Victor," she snapped. "If you persist in this unbecoming behavior, you will force me to do something you will regret."

"Like what?" he sneered. "Scream? I wouldn't have figured you for a woman who liked to make a scene."

Aunt Peg was less likely to scream than she was to punch Victor in the nose, I thought. Or perhaps to raise her knee and apply it to the portion of his anatomy where it would do the most good.

I decided to make my presence known before she could opt to exercise either option. "Hello, Victor," I said. "What a surprise running into you here. Aunt Peg and I need to be moving along. I'm sure you understand."

Victor squinted at me in the half-light. Then recognition dawned. "Melanie." He smirked. "Peg's little sidekick. I should have known you'd be around here somewhere."

Little sidekick. Ouch.

Victor's hand was still wrapped around Aunt Peg's faux fur–covered arm. Like he thought it had a right to be there. *Like hell.* I reached up and grabbed his pinkie finger. He was too startled to protest when I lifted it and bent it backward over the knuckle.

The move immediately produced the desired effect. Victor not only released his grip, he yanked his hand away and jumped back several steps. Cradling his finger in the opposite hand, he began to swear vociferously.

"Perhaps I should have warned you," Aunt Peg said mildly. "I'm a woman of moderate disposition myself, but you wouldn't want to cross my little sidekick. She's been known to have a temper."

Victor whipped around. I was sure he'd have a scathing retort ready. But the sudden move caused something to fly out of the pocket of his topcoat. A small, clear packet went fluttering toward the pavement.

I went to catch it, but Victor moved faster. He swooped down and snatched the little bag before I could see what it contained. Quickly he shoved it out of sight. Without another word, Victor spun away and took off. Within seconds he'd disappeared into the crowd.

"Well, that was unexpected." Aunt Peg stared after him thoughtfully. "What do you make of it? Do you suppose Victor actually wanted to make amends?"

"I doubt it," I replied. "More likely he wanted to cause trouble. Maybe he intended to make you late for your judging assignment. What do you suppose was in that little packet he was carrying?"

"What packet?" she asked. My mention of the time made us both start walking again. We'd almost reached the Seventh Avenue entrance.

"It fell out of his pocket when he was hopping around. You didn't see it?"

"No." Aunt Peg frowned. "Not a thing." She stopped on the sidewalk and looked down at me. "I could have handled him by myself, you know."

"Of course you could have," I agreed.

"But I enjoyed watching you do what you did."

"Thank you," I replied. "I enjoyed doing it."

"You don't suppose you broke his finger, do you?"

"I don't think so. I didn't feel anything snap."

"More's the pity," she said.

Once inside the big building, Aunt Peg and I rode the escalators to the exhibition floor together before going our separate ways. She was meeting the other judges in the coat room, where they would get ready to join up with the network liaison. I was heading to the Expo Center, where Monday's breed and variety winners would be at their benches.

Westminster is one of very few benched dog shows remaining in the United States. At one time they were the norm. Now they are a rarity.

The benches—where the dogs were kept when they weren't being shown—looked like small, raised stalls that were open in the front. Canine entrants were required to be on-site and available for viewing for as long as the show was in progress. At Westminster, both benching and grooming were in the same place. I knew that was where I would find Crawford and Terry.

Aunt Peg had been required to isolate herself, remaining unaware of the breed results until she saw the winners in her ring this evening. I'd faced no such restrictions. Earlier, I'd watched online as Crawford's apricot Mini, Topper, had won the Miniature Best of Variety. He'd also picked up a breed win with his Havanese, who would be competing in the Toy Group. Both dogs would be here at the Garden now, being prepped for their performances.

Those wins gave Crawford and Terry two reasons to celebrate. I hoped that meant I would find the handler in a good mood.

It was still early—the judging wouldn't begin for another hour. So the backstage area was thronged with spectators who'd come to see and enjoy the canine spectacle. TV cameras and commentators were everywhere too. I knew where I wanted to go. Even so, it took me a while just to make my way through the heavy crowds.

The first thing I noticed as I approached Crawford's two side-by-side benches was that Terry's hair was still purple. At least the neon shade made him easy to find among the sea of dogs and handlers. I decided that the color was growing on me.

The Toy Group would be judged second. Crawford's Havanese was out on a grooming table, while Topper was still resting in his crate. With time to spare, Terry was thumbing through the thick, glossy Westminster catalog. Crawford stood nearby looking very dapper in a crisp white shirt, black pants, and patent leather shoes. His jacket and a blue Hermes tie were inside a garment bag that was hanging from the side of their bench.

"Congratulations on both your wins," I said. "Well done! I knew Topper would make it into the group."

Crawford looked up. He lifted a bushy brow. Even with all his accomplishments—including triumphing in six previous Westminster groups over the years—he never took a single win for granted. "Then you must have known something I didn't."

"I knew he would be a very deserving winner,"

I told him honestly. "And I hoped the variety judge would think as highly of Topper as I do."

"How about this for a nice surprise?" Terry gestured toward the cream-colored Havanese. "He's Crawford's class dog. He had to beat five specials to get here."

"And he finished his championship in the process," Crawford added with a small smile.

"I hope you do well tonight with both of them." It was nice to see the handler looking happy. "What do you think, Crawford? Maybe Terry's hair color brought you luck?"

I heard a loud snort from behind me. Of course it came from Terry.

"What?" I turned and asked innocently. "He doesn't like purple?"

Crawford was very conservative in his views. So I could guess the answer to that. But right now, I was just grateful that he was talking to me.

"It's his head," Crawford said gruffly. "He can do whatever he wants with it."

"We love it," a woman called over from the next setup. She and her husband were grooming a Silky Terrier. "Way to rock the Westminster vibe, Terry. But if you want to get it perfect, you need to add some blond highlights."

They had a point. The Westminster Club colors were purple and gold.

"A pair of gold earrings would do the trick," I said.

Crawford rolled his eyes, but he looked amused. "Stop it, all of you. Don't encourage him."

"I don't need encouragement to be fabulous," Terry said with a sniff. He twirled in a small circle for our approval. "I was born that way."

"Yes, you were," Crawford agreed fondly. "Now if only I could get you to rein it in occasionally."

"Who, *moi*?"

We all laughed together. Competitors at the surrounding setups joined in. Westminster was important. A win here really mattered. There'd been plenty of tension in the air as exhibitors readied their dogs for the ring. But now, just for a moment, the mood lightened.

Then everyone took a deep breath and got back to work. It was almost showtime.

Chapter 8

Crawford took his garment bag and went to the men's room to finish getting dressed. I remained at the setup, watching Terry put the finishing touches on the Havanese. While he did that, Terry brought me up to date on the gossip he'd picked up at the piers.

"Rumor has it that yesterday's specialty will be Victor Durbin's last hurrah," he said.

I stared at him in surprise. "Why? What happened? Aside from some questionable judging—which, let's face it, isn't entirely unusual—the show looked like a success. Certainly it drew a big entry."

Terry leaned closer. He dropped his voice. Numerous TV cameras were filming in the large hall. Clearly he didn't want to be overheard. "I heard Victor is going to be stepping down as president of the Empire Poodle Club."

"No!"

"Yes."

"He can't," I protested. "It's *his* club. He built it from scratch. He practically handpicked the members."

Terry smirked. "By which you mean he personally plundered every other Poodle club in the region until he'd dredged up enough unhappy people who could be enticed away to join his start-up."

"Yes, something like that. I can't imagine who would want to belong to a club made up of a bunch of malcontents. There's already enough politics and infighting to deal with in these clubs without adding that to the mix."

Terry had a hand beneath the Havanese's chin and a comb clutched between his lips. He settled for nodding in agreement.

"Did I ever tell you that Aunt Peg thinks Victor chose the name for his club to declare his own aspirations?"

Terry nearly spat out the comb when he laughed. "That's funny. And maybe slightly unfair. After all, the Empire Poodle Club is based in New York, whose nickname is the Empire State."

"Or it could refer to Victor's delusions of grandeur," I pointed out. "He's a man who's always wanted to be in charge. Now that he's finally there, I can't imagine him choosing to give that up. Empire isn't a very big club, is it? It would probably fall apart without him at the helm."

"Even so," Terry said, "I heard it's happening."

"But why?"

"I don't know." He glanced up at me and waggled his eyebrows. "Yet."

"There's actually something you don't know?" I teased. "I had no idea. You must be losing your touch."

Gossip was Terry's stock in trade. He always had the juiciest tidbits of information to share. And sometimes to barter. Terry was vastly entertaining, but nobody's secrets were safe when he was around.

"I said *yet,* didn't I?" He lowered his voice again. "All I know is whatever happened, it was bad. It had to be, didn't it?"

One would think.

"Now I want to hear the rest of the story," I told him. "So you'll have to find out what it is. Aunt Peg will want to know too." Abruptly I stopped speaking. Mention of Peg's name reminded me of what had happened earlier.

Terry's gaze swung my way. "What?"

"Aunt Peg just had the strangest encounter with Victor outside the Garden."

"How is that possible?" he asked. "Isn't she avoiding everyone until after she does her thing later tonight?"

"Absolutely. She's been a total fanatic about it. Aunt Peg hadn't said a word to anyone until Victor accosted her on Seventh Avenue."

Terry looked shocked by my choice of words. "He *accosted* her?"

"I'd say so. Victor grabbed her arm and refused to let go." There was a second grooming table behind me. The Mini Poodle wasn't using it, so I hopped up and had a seat.

"What did he want?"

"Supposedly he wanted to buy Aunt Peg a drink. Like, right then. When she was needed inside to meet up with important people."

"The network?" Terry guessed.

I nodded.

"Victor's an idiot," he muttered. "I assume Peg put him in his place?"

"Actually I did," I told him. Okay, maybe I was a little proud of myself. "I nearly broke his finger."

"You tiger, you." Terry grinned. "I never would have guessed. Nicely done."

"Guessed what?" Crawford asked, coming up behind us. He looked sharp in his dark suit and tie. "That Melanie needs to get around to the front of the house and find her seat? Haven't you two been listening to the announcements? The Hound Group has already been called."

I looked down at my watch. It was ten minutes to eight. Sam and the boys would have already arrived. No doubt they were waiting in our seats for me to join them.

"Yikes," I said. "I'm on my way."

I slid down off the tabletop. "We never had a chance to talk about the wedding," I told Terry. "I wanted to hear all the details."

"Not now," Crawford said firmly.

"Of course not." I leaned in close and brushed a quick kiss across the handler's cheek. The gesture took him by surprise. Crawford didn't have time to pull away. "You look wonderful. Good luck tonight! Have fun out there."

"I don't care about fun," he told me. "We came to win."

The seats Sam had gotten for us were on the side of the arena, only a dozen rows above the ring. I had no idea how he'd managed that, and I was quite sure I didn't want to know what they'd cost. But I was grateful he'd sprung for the purchase. From there, we would have a wonderful view of everything that happened.

"Where have you been?" Davey asked when I slid in between Sam and Kevin. They'd been using the empty seat to hold their winter coats. I had to redistribute them before I could sit down. "We've been here for at least half an hour."

"Half an hour!" Kev echoed. There was a smear of something yellow on his sleeve. The boys had been eating hot dogs again. Or maybe nachos. "And we haven't seen any judging at all."

"That's coming right up," I told him. "Starting with the Hound Group in just a few minutes." I turned to Sam. "I was back at the benches visiting with Crawford and Terry. Crawford has his Mini and a Havanese to show tonight."

"We know all that," Davey informed me loftily. He was sure teenagers knew everything.

Sam nodded. "We watched replays of the judging when Davey got home from school.

Topper looked terrific. And Kaz won in Standards. It should be a great group."

"There's Aunt Peg!" Kevin stood up and pointed.

The judge's table was on the opposite side of the arena. Aunt Peg was taking a seat nearby, beside the Toy and Herding Group judges. Her shoulders were ramrod stiff. She was staring straight ahead into the nearly empty ring. Kevin lifted his hand over his head and waved.

No surprise, Aunt Peg didn't wave back.

"She looks different," Sam commented.

I gave him a look. *"Different?"*

"Awesome," he quickly amended. "That's what I meant to say. She looks awesome. Whatever you two got up to this afternoon was well worth it."

It didn't sound like he wanted to hear details, so I gave him a brief summary. "Aunt Peg was resistant to the process at first. But I think she ended up enjoying it. She informed the stylist that the Westminster broadcast might be the only exposure that millions of people would ever have to a dog show. So it was important for her to make an effort to look like it mattered."

"She succeeded," he replied. "That's no surprise."

The audience fell silent as a color guard marched into the arena. We all stood for the singing of the national anthem. When that was finished, the sonorous voice of the Westminster announcer called the dogs from the Hound Group into the ring.

The sight of thirty-five beautiful hounds—each a superb representative of its breed—gaiting across the bright green carpet was electrifying. Their entrance gave me chills.

Kev was staring at the parade of breeds with his mouth gaping open. I'd worried about keeping him up past his bedtime. I'd also been concerned that he might get bored having to sit in a seat for so long. But judging by the rapt expression on my son's face, keeping him interested wasn't going to be a problem.

"What is *that?*" he asked, pointing at an Irish Wolfhound. "I want one!"

Of course that particular dog had caught his eye. The Irish Wolfhound was the biggest breed in the Hound Group. Massive and shaggy, they weighed well over a hundred pounds.

"You have Bud," I told him brightly. "Bud is better than an Irish Wolfhound any day."

Kev screwed up his face. He didn't look convinced. But his gaze was already moving on. There were so many fun dogs in the ring, he couldn't decide where to look first.

Before the hounds were finished being judged, my younger son had also fallen in love with a Borzoi, a Beagle, and a Petit Basset Griffon Vendeen. He wanted one of each. Meanwhile I was having a great time watching him discover the wonder of the Westminster Dog Show.

The Saluki won the Hound Group. Sam thought that was a good decision. Davey declined to offer an opinion. Kevin pouted for a few minutes—he'd wanted one of his favorites to win—but then the Toy Group came strutting into the ring and he forgot all about the hound breeds.

"There's Crawford." Davey motioned excitedly as the handler appeared with his Havanese. Now that he had a rooting interest in the outcome of the judging, he sat up to pay attention.

Two rows of square, yellow boxes ran the length of each side of the arena. Each bore the name of a breed, listed in alphabetical order. Exhibitors set up their dogs in front of the low boxes when they were being judged and allowed their dogs to relax behind them when they were not.

Crawford and his Havanese were toward the end of the first line. The two of them looked great—but then so did every other toy dog and handler in the ring. These dogs were the best their breed had to offer. Each had earned its place in this spotlight. They all deserved the adulation that the spectators had come to bestow on them.

Crawford walked the Havanese into a perfect stack. Then he stood in front of the dog, holding a piece of bait in his hand. Crawford kept one eye on his small dog and the other on the judge.

Don't ask me how he made that work. It's a gift that all the best handlers possess, and one that I have yet to master.

As the judge began her individual examinations, Sam leaned over and said, "Crawford's dog is outclassed in this company."

I sighed. "Yes, I know. I'm sure he does too."

The other toy dogs the Havanese was competing against all had more experience than he did. Most were accomplished specials—with previous group and Best in Show wins gracing their lofty resumes. Many were grand champions. The Pomeranian was the current top-winning toy dog in the United States. The Pekingese was the number one toy in England. He had already won Crufts—a show even bigger than Westminster— and his handler was hoping for similar success here.

By contrast, Crawford's Havanese had fought his way to Best of Breed from the classes. That accomplishment was quite a coup by itself, and I suspected it was all he would get. My guess was confirmed when the judge's eye slid right past the Havanese when she prepared to make her cut.

The judge pulled eight toy dogs out into the middle of the ring. Crawford's wasn't among them. Minutes later, she'd placed the Pomeranian first and the Peke second. The audience cheered their approval.

"That's too bad," said Davey.

"Don't worry," I told him. "He'll do better with Topper."

Kev was frowning. He crossed his arms over his slender chest. "I wanted Crawford to win. Crawford *always* wins."

"It might seem that way at the dog shows we go to," Sam allowed. "But Westminster is different. This is a whole new ball game."

"There's a ball game?" Kevin's eyes opened wide. He looked from one end of the arena to the other. "Where?"

"Not a real ball game," I said. "It's a figure of speech. But keep your eye on the ring. Because Aunt Peg's turn is coming up next."

"Yay!" Kev got excited all over again. "I hope she wins."

"She can't win, silly." Davey ruffled his brother's hair. "She's the judge."

"Cool." Kevin was impressed. "I hope she wins the judging."

Davey shot me a look. "You explain it to him."

"Aunt Peg will win the judging," I said to Kevin. "She's going to do a terrific job."

Davey grinned. "You know that's gonna come back to bite you someday."

Since there was no way to "win" at judging, Davey was probably right. On the other hand, Kevin believed in Santa Claus and the Tooth Fairy. And his grasp of abstract concepts was still evolving. Not to mention that on a normal night he'd have been asleep an hour ago. With luck, Kevin would forget all about this conversation by tomorrow morning. As long as Davey didn't remind him.

"There's Peg now." Sam drew our attention back to the ring as she stepped out onto the green carpet.

Aunt Peg looked resplendent under the lights. She was statuesque and imposing. Her posture was impeccable. Her beaded dress glittered. Best of all, she had a huge smile on her face.

As the non-sporting dogs came flying into the arena, I saw Aunt Peg's fingers clasp at her sides. She was impatient to begin. The sight of so many gorgeous dogs in her ring had to be an incomparable treat. I knew she couldn't wait to get her hands on them.

The moment we'd been waiting nearly two years for had finally arrived. And then it seemed to go by in a flash. Aunt Peg had twenty-one dogs to judge and only a limited time in which to decide how she was going to place them. I watched her make every second count. From the moment she took her first walk around the arena, Aunt Peg never took her eyes off the group of dogs.

Even during commercial breaks, when the two previous judges had sat down to catch their breath, Aunt Peg never stopped staring at—and evaluating—her group. Obviously she wanted to do a superior job. But I knew it was even more important to her that every exhibitor felt their entry had been judged fairly, and given an equal chance to win.

Non-sporting was the most diverse of the seven groups. It consisted of breeds with different sizes, shapes, coat textures. Aunt Peg appeared to be judging the dogs against each other. But what she was really doing was comparing each one to its own breed standard, and assessing how near it came to achieving that level of perfection.

Of course she was immediately drawn to the two Poodles in her group. But anyone in the audience who expected her to favor her own breed didn't know Aunt Peg. More than anyone else, she was aware what a truly great Poodle should be. If anything, that would make her more critical of the Standard and Mini in front of her, rather than less.

Even so, I knew early on that Topper had caught her eye. She also liked the French Bulldog and the Tibetan Spaniel. And her gaze returned more than once to the snowy white Coton de Tulear.

As the dogs were brought forward for their individual examinations, Aunt Peg confirmed with her hands the attributes she'd gleaned from her first look. She weighed each dog's merits against those who had come before. That meant she was also constantly reevaluating the make-up of her first cut. There were many top-quality dogs in the ring, and many deserving winners. It would have been almost impossible to make a mistake.

Aunt Peg wasn't worried about doing a job that was just good enough, however. She wanted her choices to be perfect.

"She likes the Xolo," Sam said. Last to be examined, the hairless dog was being gaited down and back by his handler. The breed, originating in Mexico, was formally called Xoloitzcuintli. But Xolo (pronounced show-low) was enough of a mouthful for most people.

I nodded. "She likes Topper too."

"I like the Dalmatian," Kevin said loudly. Of course he did. Like Bud, it had spots. But I was pretty sure that dog wouldn't be in Aunt Peg's final line up.

"Topper may get a piece," Sam whispered back. "But not the whole thing. It's not his time yet. I'm betting on the Frenchie. He's been virtually unbeatable all year."

"It's Westminster. Crawford would be delighted with a placement," I said. "I know I would be." Who was I kidding? I would be over the moon just to have a chance to walk in the ring.

Aunt Peg took one last look at her entire group. Then she walked down the two rows and pulled out the dogs who'd made her cut. The Bichon and the Coton were first to form a new line. They were followed by the Frenchie, the Keeshond, and the Miniature Poodle. After that came the Tibetan Spaniel, the Tibetan Terrier, and the Xolo.

Just that quickly, we went from twenty-one contenders to eight.

Aunt Peg paused for thirty seconds to let the tension build. I knew I wasn't the only spectator who was sitting on the edge of my seat.

New York audiences weren't shy about making their preferences known. When Aunt Peg put the Frenchie on top, the arena exploded with applause. Handler and dog danced happily over to the first place marker. Aunt Peg placed the Coton second, followed by Crawford's Mini. The Xolo was fourth.

Sam and I stood up and clapped for a job well done. Aunt Peg congratulated her winners and handed out her ribbons. Then she gazed around the ring and out over the crowd. Despite how hard she'd been working for the past half hour, Aunt Peg didn't appear tired. Instead she looked exhilarated.

This night had been a dream come true. She intended to savor every single minute.

Chapter 9

Tuesday morning it was time to go back to real life. After the previous night's excitement, that felt like a letdown to me.

Faith didn't agree. We don't make a habit of leaving our dogs home alone for any length of time, and especially not late at night. Now the big Poodle was happy to have her family back and her routine restored.

"It was worth it," I told her, as I made the bed before going downstairs. Faith was sitting in the bedroom doorway, supervising. "Westminster was fantastic. And so was Aunt Peg."

Faith woofed at that. Aunt Peg was one of her favorite people. She recognized the name. And she was probably agreeing that Aunt Peg was fantastic.

Davey came walking down the hall. He paused in the open doorway. "Are you talking to yourself?"

"Of course not. I'm talking to Faith."

"It figures."

Davey shook his head like he thought I was crazy. I had no idea why. He talked to the dogs too. It was a family trait.

"I just wanted to let you know that after Kevin told you he was going to get dressed, he went back to bed instead," he told me.

"Did you get him up again?"

"No. Why would I do that?"

"Because you know he has school." I glanced at the clock. "He and I have to leave in twenty minutes, or we'll be late."

"Maybe you should have thought about that before you took him into New York last night."

"Maybe the next time I'll leave both of you home," I shot back.

"I don't think so." Davey grinned.

"Try me," I invited.

With a heavy sigh, he shifted his backpack off his shoulder and let it drop to the floor. Then he turned and disappeared. Davey was heading back in the direction of Kevin's room. I hoped that meant he'd gotten the point.

"Teenagers," I grumbled.

Faith came over and pressed her body against my legs in a gesture of solidarity. Dogs can always be counted on to take your side. Even when you're wrong. Which I wasn't. But still.

Downstairs, Sam had the coffee made. There were blueberry muffins, containers of yogurt, and a bowl of apples on the kitchen table. He'd obviously decided it was going to be a grab-and-go kind of morning.

I poured myself a generous mug of coffee and listened for sounds of progress from upstairs. I couldn't hear a thing. I tried to console myself with the thought that the bedrooms were pretty far from the kitchen. It didn't entirely work.

"Where are the boys?" Sam asked.

"Coming soon." The coffee was hot. Nevertheless, my first therapeutic sip was a large one. "I hope."

"Want me to check on them?"

"Not yet." I still had fifteen minutes. Enough time for Davey to decide to do the right thing. As long as he got a move on.

Instead, Sam opened the back door. The other Poodles, plus Bud, came flying in from outside. Eve's and Raven's legs were covered with snow. Bud, Augie, and Tar looked as though they'd been tunneling through the stuff. Bud even had crystals on his eyelashes.

I'd been sharing a blueberry muffin with Faith. Now I had to stop slipping her pieces, or else everyone would want some. Tar strolled over to my chair, looking for a handout. I gave him a pat on the head instead. The big dog responded by suddenly realizing that he was wet and giving his body a massive shake.

"Hey!" I jumped up. "That was rude."

Tar wagged his pom-ponned tail happily. It was a good thing he meant well, because corrections were mostly lost on him. Instead of acknowledging he'd been wrong, Tar continued to stare at the remainder of my muffin with a goofy grin on his face.

"No," I told him sternly.

"Good luck with that," Davey said.

He and Kevin came walking into the kitchen. Both boys were dressed for school. Their faces and hands were clean, and their hair was combed. One could only marvel at the sight.

Davey snagged an apple from the bowl. "Tar and Bud never listen when it comes to food."

Bud had flopped down on a bed in the corner. Now he jumped up again. The spotted mutt had heard his name and the word *food,* both in the same sentence. Even though he'd just had breakfast, Bud figured it must be time for another meal.

"No to you too," I told him.

Sam just stared at the ceiling. He knew it was a lost cause.

"I don't want to go to school," Kevin announced. "I want to go back to the dog show."

"Me too," I said.

Today at Westminster, the competition in the sporting, working, and terrier breeds would be held at the piers. Tonight the winners of those groups would be decided at Madison Square Garden. It was all followed by the ultimate prize, Best in Show.

"You know Westminster streams the judging live," Sam pointed out. "You can follow it while you're at school."

"I'm supposed to be working while I'm at school," I said with a sigh.

"I'm supposed to be working while I'm at home." Sam worked freelance as a designer of computer software. He ran his business from a home office that was just down the hall. "But I'm pretty sure I can still manage to find time to check in every so often."

"I want to check in too," Kev announced.

"You can't," Davey told him. "You don't have a phone."

My younger son arranged his face in a scowl. "I want a phone."

"Now look what you've done," I said to Davey.

He held up his hands, a protest of innocence. Then he cocked his head toward the front of the house. "Hey, I think I hear my bus coming." He grabbed his parka off the back of a chair and snatched his backpack up from the floor. "Gotta go."

Davey could move quickly when he wanted to. Within seconds he was gone. We all felt a sudden blast of cold air. Then the back door slammed behind him.

"Have a good day," I said in the general direction that he'd disappeared.

"Davey can't hear you." Kevin giggled. "He already left."

"It's time for us to go too," I told him. "Where are your jacket and your rubber boots?"

Sam was already on his way to the closet in the front hall. I gathered up my stuff and made

109

sure that Faith was ready. She was easy. She was always available to do whatever I wanted.

It was a good thing Westminster happened only once a year, I decided. The event was exciting, but it was also exhausting. Like Faith, I was glad it was time to get back to my regular routine.

Howard Academy offered an education to children from kindergarten through eighth grade. Its mission was to provide students with a solid academic foundation, then send them on to other distinguished institutions of learning for their high school and college years.

I was fortunate in that most of the pupils who attended HA were bright, cultured, and highly motivated. Many students had parents who were overachievers themselves. So the bar for acceptable performance had already been set quite high at home before the children even graced our hallowed halls.

Parents trusted Howard Academy with their children because the school's standards were high and its curriculum was rigorous. Even the brightest students had to apply themselves to keep up. Which meant that sometimes kids fell behind. Those who did ended up in my classroom. It was my job to figure out what had gone wrong, then deliver whatever kind of scholastic nudge was needed to get the pupils back on track.

It was early in the semester, so my schedule was

pretty light. Currently I had only four students whom I was tutoring regularly. On Tuesday, that allowed me a little free time to watch the dog show.

I devoted the rest of my school day to making sure that my classroom looked impeccable. Howard Academy's semi-annual Parents' Night was going to be held the following evening and Headmaster Russell Hanover expected the occasion to proceed flawlessly. Just as it always did. I had no intention of being the teacher who let him down.

When Kevin, Faith, and I arrived home at one-thirty, Sam was closeted in his office, working. I grabbed the other dogs, then Kev and I took everyone for a run.

The Poodles behaved beautifully. Keeping both Kevin and Bud heading in the same direction for more than a few steps at a time, however, was like trying to herd cats. I had a leash on Bud. I probably should have had one on Kevin too. Just kidding. Sort of.

Sam met us at the door when we finally got back. He took one look at me and offered me a beer from the fridge. I opted for a bottle of green tea instead.

His laptop was open on the counter. Of course it was showing Westminster. Gordon Setters were being judged. I squinted at the screen for a minute but didn't see anyone I knew.

"I just got off the phone with Crawford," Sam said as he turned on the cold water to refill the dogs' water bowl. "I called to congratulate him on last night."

"Was he happy about how things went?" I hoped the handler was pleased with Topper's group placement. But he'd told me he was there to win so I wasn't sure.

"He was delighted. The Havanese showed well, which was really all he wanted, or expected. And Crawford thought the Non-Sporting Group was particularly strong this year. He'd told Topper's owner that he was hoping they would make the cut. So that third place ribbon was a thrill. Especially under a judge of Peg's caliber. The Mini's owner was so happy that he renewed Crawford's contract for the entire year. He wants to take Topper back to Westminster next February to see if they can do better."

"That's terrific," I said. "And well deserved. What about the wedding?"

Sam turned to look at me. "What about it?"

"I never got a chance to ask Terry about it yesterday. Is everything proceeding according to plan?"

He set the bowl on the floor. The Poodles immediately clustered around it. I could hear the sound of multiple tongues lapping at once. Sam would have to fill the bowl again when they were finished.

"How would I know that?"

"Because you were on the phone with Crawford," I said.

"Here's a news flash. Men don't talk about wedding plans. Especially since there are about a million other things that we'd rather discuss. Or basically pretty much anything else."

"I get that," I agreed. "But the wedding's only a week away."

"So?"

"So, Terry is in charge. And you know he's like a magpie. Brilliant when he wants to pay attention, but also easily distracted by any shiny object that happens to catch his eye. Am I the only one who thinks that someone ought to check and make sure that he's on top of things?"

Sam laughed. "And you seriously think that's a job for me?"

Okay, he had a point. Maybe not.

That night after dinner, we all got comfortable in front of the television in the living room to watch the second night of Westminster. Sam and I were on the couch. Kevin had wedged himself in between us.

The Standard Poodles scattered on the floor around us. Faith was lying across my feet. Bud and Augie were under the coffee table, chewing on either end of a braided rope toy.

Davey chose a club chair on the side of the

room. Since he'd also kept his phone close at hand, I figured he wanted his privacy so he could keep tabs on what his friends were doing while he was here with us.

The thought made me a little sad. Davey wasn't my little boy anymore. I knew the increasing separation between us was inevitable. And even necessary. But that didn't make it any easier.

I curled my arm around Kevin's shoulder and drew him against my side. Instead of pulling away, Kev snuggled closer. I rested my head on top of his and breathed in deeply. Thank goodness he was in no hurry to grow up.

An Irish Water Spaniel won the Sporting Group. Kevin was rooting for the Pointer because it had spots. He would have been disappointed by its loss if he'd still been watching. But after his big day on Monday, Kev was already asleep by the time the group ended.

Sam carried Kevin upstairs and put him to bed. He got back in time to watch the second half of the Working Group, where the Boxer triumphed over its competitors. A Soft-Coated Wheaten was the surprise winner in Terriers. That set the stage for a contentious battle for Best in Show.

One by one the group winners were announced and brought into the ring. Each dog was treated to enthusiastic applause when it appeared. Already the audience members were cheering for their favorites.

The BIS judge, like all dog show judges, was supposed to be impervious to spectator opinion. Nevertheless, when the camera briefly flashed her way I saw that she was smiling. She had to be enjoying the exuberant approval with which the crowd was greeting her seven contenders.

The dogs formed a line in size order. The Saluki from the Hound Group was in front. The Pomeranian from the Toy Group brought up the rear. Sam and I stared at the TV screen, studying each dog intently as if there was going to be a quiz later.

Davey took a more relaxed approach. "I'm rooting for the Old English Sheepdog," he announced. We'd watched that dog win the Herding Group on Monday night after Aunt Peg was finished.

"Why?" I asked him.

Davey shrugged. "I think he looks like a big ball of hair."

"But—" I began.

"That's as good a reason as any," Sam interrupted me.

It was *not*. I let the comment stand anyway. I was just happy Davey was watching the dog show rather than looking at his phone.

"I think the judge likes the Pomeranian," I decided.

"I think the *spectators* like the Pom," Sam said. "And that's making the cameras spend a lot of time on him. That little dog certainly knows how to play to the crowd."

Sam had that right. The toy dog wasn't currently being judged, but he was hamming it up on the sidelines. First he extended his front legs to take a long, leisurely stretch. Then he bounced up in the air to catch a furry toy his handler tossed to him.

"That's because they're New Yorkers," said Davey. "They like little dogs because they all live in apartments."

The judge took a last look at the seven-dog line up. She accorded each group winner an equal amount of attention, but I was betting she'd already made up her mind. Then she turned and walked over to the table to mark and sign her book. Westminster club officers gathered up armloads of trophies and ribbons for the presentation.

Reserve Best in Show was announced first. It went to the beautifully balanced Saluki. After that, the judge awarded the enormous purple and gold rosette for Best in Show to the French Bulldog, who'd become a finalist by winning Aunt Peg's Non-Sporting Group.

"Peg will be pleased about that," Sam said. We watched the Frenchie's handler pump his fist in the air in celebration. The other handlers gathered around to congratulate him. "She's there, isn't she?"

"Of course she's there. She wouldn't miss it. Especially since she had to forego watching yesterday's judging. Aunt Peg stayed over in the city last night and spent all day today at the piers. She had a lot of catching up to do."

It was late and we were all tired, but the day had ended on a high note. While Sam let the dogs out, I hustled Davey off to bed. Sam and I followed shortly thereafter.

At six-thirty the next morning the phone rang. I opened one eye, looked at the clock on the bedside night table, then groaned. I'd still had another half hour of sleep left.

Sam woke up more quickly than I did. He picked up the phone and held it to his ear.

"Who's calling at this hour?" I mumbled.

He gave me that look. The one that told me I should have known. That answered my question. It was Aunt Peg.

Sam listened for a minute. His expression turned grave. At the end, he said, "I see. We'll wait to hear from you."

By that time I was sitting up in bed. Faith knew something was wrong. She'd jumped up to join us. I pulled her into my lap. The big Poodle and I were both wide awake now.

I didn't even wait until Sam had put down the phone before blurting out, "What happened?"

"It's bad news."

I'd already guessed that. I loved my husband

dearly, but right at that moment, I wanted to shake him.

"Who?"

"Victor Durbin," said Sam. "He's dead."

Chapter 10

Immediately I had a million questions. Unfortunately Sam didn't have many answers.

"When?" I asked. "Where? How?"

"Sometime last night at Madison Square Garden," he told me. "As for how, Peg was a little short on details."

"She's getting more, isn't she?" I pushed back the covers and hopped out of bed. "That's why we're waiting to hear from her, right?"

Sam stared at me. I was already halfway across the bedroom, on my way to grab a quick shower. "Has anyone ever told you that you have a ghoulish fascination with violent crime?"

I stopped and looked back. "I don't know. Maybe."

"That was a rhetorical question," my husband muttered.

"Oh." I frowned. "Then no."

Sam got out of bed too. The other Poodles in the room were beginning to stir. Bud slept on Kevin's bed and Augie was in with Davey, but I was sure we'd be hearing from both of them shortly.

"I don't know where you think you're hurrying off to," Sam said. "It's Wednesday. Before you can do anything else, you have to go to school this morning."

My job at Howard Academy. For a moment, I'd forgotten all about it.

"I know that," I said.

"Right." Sam wasn't convinced. "I'm going to start the coffee and let the dogs out. I'll see you downstairs." He paused in the doorway, the Poodle pack eddying around his legs. "Don't bother calling Peg back as soon as I leave."

"I wasn't going to."

"Yes, you were."

Okay, I was.

"She doesn't know any more than I already told you."

"Maybe you didn't ask the right questions," I said. "In fact, I didn't hear you ask any questions at all."

"That's because Peg had already told me everything she knew."

"Maybe, maybe not. Aunt Peg is sneaky that way."

Sam might have rolled his eyes. I couldn't really tell because he was already turning away to take the dogs downstairs. All right, so I wouldn't call Aunt Peg back. *Yet.*

I had a half day of school to get through first. Dammit.

At one o'clock, Faith and I were on our way to Aunt Peg's house. Actually, it might have been closer to twelve forty-five. Thankfully we didn't run into Mr. Hanover as we were making our getaway.

Nothing that happened at Howard Academy escaped our esteemed headmaster's notice. Sometimes I wondered how he did that. But mostly—especially when I was the one skirting around the edge of the rules—I tried not to think about it.

Sam had volunteered to pick up Kev at preschool, so Faith and I didn't have to make any stops on the way to Aunt Peg's home in back country Greenwich. A straight shot up North Street got us there in record time.

I hadn't bothered to call ahead. I knew Aunt Peg would be waiting for me. Actually I wouldn't have been surprised if she'd interrupted my morning tutoring sessions with one of her surprise visits to Howard Academy. To tell the truth, I was kind of disappointed that hadn't happened.

Aunt Peg lived in a converted farmhouse on five acres of land that had once been the hub of a working farm. She and her late husband, Max, had purchased the property decades earlier. They'd founded their Cedar Crest Kennel shortly thereafter. Together, they had bred some of the best black Standard Poodles in the country there.

Now Max was gone. More recently, the kennel building that had housed so many illustrious dogs had been lost too. It had burned to the ground eighteen months earlier. Aunt Peg lived in the house with her five remaining Standard Poodles, whose bloodlines were intertwined with those of Sam's and my dogs.

Twelve-year-old Beau was the elder statesman of the group. Next in line was Faith's litter sister, Hope. Zeke, who'd been bred by me, was Eve's brother. Willow was Tar's sister. Coral, the newest member of the group, had just turned a year old in the fall. The previous summer Davey had been showing her in the puppy classes for Aunt Peg. Now Coral was taking time off to grow into her adult continental trim.

Faith loved to ride shotgun but I'd banished her to the back seat of the Volvo for her own safety. That didn't stop her from having opinions about my driving. As soon as I turned onto Aunt Peg's quiet lane, Faith jumped to her feet. She began to whine softly. Her tail flagged from side to side. She knew where we were going and she couldn't wait to get there.

"Give me a minute," I told her. "We're almost there."

I'd just hopped Faith out of the car when Aunt Peg's front door opened. Her gang of Standard Poodles came streaming down the steps like a canine landslide. Zeke and Coral led the charge.

Faith's tail snapped up over her back. She danced over to meet the oncoming horde. Noses were quickly touched. Then the polite greetings turned into a raucous game of tag in the home's front yard.

Aunt Peg observed the proceedings from her doorway. Her arms were crossed over her chest. "I don't have cake," she announced.

No cake? It was almost inconceivable. Aunt Peg *always* had cake. Or at least something similarly sweet. It was one of the best reasons for coming to visit. Not that I would ever tell her that, of course.

I climbed the stairs to the wide front porch. "Don't tell me you're dieting again."

"Goodness no, that was no fun at all." Aunt Peg was six feet tall and as strong as a horse. Eventually her doctor had been forced to concede that the few extra pounds she'd gained satisfying her sweet tooth weren't doing any real harm.

"It was the police," she said.

"Police?" I stopped and stared.

Aunt Peg didn't notice. She was still watching the Poodles. Their game had devolved into a free-for-all and she was making sure that no dog committed the cardinal sin of pulling on Coral's growing show coat.

"The police?" I repeated.

Aunt Peg's gaze cut my way. "Two New York City detectives. They looked like they'd come from a casting call for *Law & Order*. As you might imagine, I was quite surprised to find

123

the pair of them standing on my doorstep this morning. It's a shame you took so long to get here. Otherwise, you might have had the pleasure of meeting them yourself."

"I had to work." The impulse to defend myself was automatic. I had no idea why. It never made any difference.

Aunt Peg wasn't impressed by my excuse. She turned away and snapped her fingers. All Poodle play in the yard promptly ceased. It was real life magic, Aunt Peg style. The six dogs immediately spun around and raced toward the steps. I barely got out of their way in time.

When everyone was inside, I shut the door behind us. It took me only a few seconds to pull off my coat and scarf and hang them on a nearby coatrack, but Aunt Peg was already on her way to the kitchen. I followed along behind. The only people Aunt Peg didn't entertain in her kitchen were those she didn't like. I wondered where she'd hosted the two detectives.

Five minutes later we were both seated at her butcher block table. Compared to the February chill outside, the room was warm and cozy. The Poodles had claimed a section of floor that was warmed by the sunlight streaming in through a wide bay window.

Aunt Peg had a mug of her favorite Earl Grey tea. I'd boiled some water and made instant coffee. It tasted stale. The jar of crystals I'd used had probably been in her cabinet for months. At least the drink was hot.

I wrapped my fingers around my coffee mug and said, "Tell me everything."

"I wish I *knew* everything," she replied with a windy sigh.

"Fine, then tell me what you know."

"Victor Durbin is dead."

I stared at her across the table. I'd known that since six-thirty this morning. There had to have been further developments since then. Surely she'd learned something from the visiting policemen.

"I didn't kill him," said Aunt Peg.

I'd just lifted the mug to my lips to take a cautious sip. I ended up with a gulp of hot coffee instead. It scalded all the way down.

When I'd gotten my voice back, I said, "Does someone think you did?"

"Apparently so." Aunt Peg didn't look concerned. If anything, she sounded pleased.

"The New York detectives?"

She nodded.

"I don't understand," I said. "What were they doing here? How did they even get your name?"

"A member of the Empire Poodle Club gave it to them. The detectives declined to tell me who it was."

"That's not fair." I frowned. "Isn't there a law that says you have a right to face your accuser?"

"Very good," Aunt Peg replied. "You've cited the Sixth Amendment to the Constitution. I knew your expensive education wasn't entirely a waste of time."

I was pretty sure I'd just been insulted. But if I derailed the conversation to defend myself again, I'd never get any answers. So I ignored that and said, "And?"

"That privilege applies in a courtroom, not an investigation. But there's something else. Whoever gave the detectives my name also told them that Victor Durbin and I were mortal enemies."

I nearly choked on my coffee again. "Mortal enemies, *seriously?* Who even says something like that? It sounds like a line from a Stan Lee movie."

"I enjoy a bit of hyperbole myself," Aunt Peg said. "But under the circumstances, I quite agree with you. That comment was definitely uncalled for. Of course, it was the 'mortal' part of it that got the detectives' attention. That, and the fact that I was present at Madison Square Garden last night when Victor was killed."

"I don't know anything about that," I said, sitting back in my chair. "Start at the beginning."

"Last night I was one of thousands of people in attendance at the Westminster Dog Show," she told me.

I hadn't needed her to go that far back. But I

didn't dare interrupt. It was easier to just let Aunt Peg tell the story her own way.

"The Frenchie won," she said. "It was wonderful. Francine came over afterward and shook my hand. She said the Frenchie was sublime."

Was it just me or were we really off track now?

"Francine?" I asked.

"The Best in Show judge," Aunt Peg replied, as if I should have known.

Francine indeed. I was just a lowly exhibitor. I'd thought of that venerable judge as Mrs. Donaldson. But whatever.

"Does this have anything to do with Victor Durbin?" I asked.

"Not that I'm aware of." Aunt Peg blinked. "I was just starting at the beginning. Until Victor turned up dead it was a marvelous night."

For everyone except Victor presumably.

"How did he die?"

"He was stabbed." Aunt Peg shuddered slightly. "Probably at some point during the competition. He subsequently bled to death. It happened in a men's room at the facility."

Finally things were beginning to get interesting.

"Do the police think he was the victim of a robbery?" I asked.

"They said no. Victor's wallet was still in his pocket. It didn't appear to have been touched. And I gather he was wearing a very expensive watch."

"A gold Rolex," I said. I'd seen it the other night.

Aunt Peg nodded. "Obviously that's the first thing a thief would have grabbed. So the detectives are exploring other possible motives for his death."

"And people like you," I said flatly. "Victor's mortal enemy."

"Quite so."

"Victor was murdered," I said.

She peered at me across the table. "I just told you that, didn't I?"

She had. "I'm just summing up," I said. That, and trying to process the information. "The deed took place in a men's room. Doesn't that let you off the hook?"

"Hardly," Aunt Peg sniffed. "If I followed someone with the intention of killing them, I wouldn't change my plans at the last minute because I was squeamish about the locale."

"Don't tell me you said that to the detectives."

"It might have slipped out," she admitted. "Perhaps when I was telling them that Victor Durbin would have been horrified to know he'd come to such a sordid end. Dead in a public bathroom, indeed."

"Victor is beyond caring," I told her. "And you put yourself right back on the hook again."

"I was trying to be helpful," Aunt Peg said primly. "It isn't a good idea to lie to the police, you know."

"It also isn't a good idea to volunteer information that they might find incriminating."

"I was doing my civic duty. And there's something else."

"Wonderful." I sighed. I probably don't need to mention that where Aunt Peg is concerned, there is always something else.

"Think about it, Melanie. Unless someone is quite skilled, or exceedingly lucky, it takes strength to kill a person with a knife. You can't just stick it anywhere and hope for the best."

"So that's good news," I said. "Once again, it sounds as though the person who attacked Victor must have been a man."

"Or a large woman."

"Not you," I snapped. "You're seventy."

"I'm in very good shape for my age."

Honestly, I didn't know whether to laugh or scream. "I can't believe we're even having this conversation. Are you trying to convince me that you did murder Victor Durbin?"

"I'm just trying to point out that it's a possibility."

"No, it's *not*," I said firmly. "And we both know it."

"You used to be more fun," Aunt Peg said.

Was this fun we were having? I couldn't tell.

"How did you hear about what happened to Victor?" I asked. "You knew early this morning. When I checked the news reports, all I saw was a vague reference to a possible death at the Garden."

"Victor's body was found as the place was emptying out last night. The police were called immediately. The president of the Westminster Kennel Club was notified at the same time. He informed the board members. After that, the news spread like wildfire."

The dog show grapevine was a model of efficient communication. By now, the entire dog community would know what had happened. The version of the story that was circulating might be the truth. Or it might just be a reasonable facsimile. That didn't matter. If the gossip was hot enough, either one would do.

"The killer took quite a risk," I realized abruptly. "Dispatching Victor like that in such a public place. And at a time when there were so many people around. Why wasn't he afraid of being seen?"

"Good question," Aunt Peg agreed. "Was the perpetrator fearless, or was he foolhardy?"

"Maybe he was neither," I said. "Maybe he was desperate."

Chapter 11

The lights were blazing on Joshua Howard's former mansion as I drove the Volvo up Howard Academy's sloping driveway that evening. The large stone house—built in opulent times by a man for whom money was no object—had been designed to impress visitors, and perhaps to inspire their envy. Now, more than a century later, it still accomplished both goals handily.

Though the mansion's salons and galleries had been converted into administrative offices and classrooms, much care had been devoted to maintaining the home's character and charm. The soaring front hall had a burnished hardwood floor, a dramatic split staircase, and an ornate crystal chandelier. Those elegant features had purposely remained untouched through the years.

The graceful entrance was the first thing parents saw when they visited the school. Its composition quietly conveyed an image of dignity and refinement. Those were traits embodied by Russell Hanover himself, and ones he felt were an integral part of the Howard Academy experience.

For school functions, Mr. Hanover would begin the evening by taking a position just inside the mansion's oak double doors. There, he would welcome parents into the softly lit entryway, praise their children, and thank them for their generous patronage. Harriet, Mr. Hanover's longtime secretary, was equally busy behind the scenes, directing family members to the appropriate classrooms and making sure that the refreshment tables were constantly replenished.

Compared to that, my job was easy. Since I didn't teach a specific grade, my only assignment was to stand in my classroom and converse with any parents who happened to drop by. My room was located in the new wing at the rear of the mansion, so I was able to bypass the busy front hall and slip in through a back entrance. As I hurried down the hallway, I saw the door was open and the lights had already been turned on.

Once inside, I hung up my coat in the closet, then quickly checked to make sure that everything was in order. Within minutes, Mr. Hanover would be opening the festivities with an address to the parents in the auditorium. Shortly after that, a crush of family members would descend upon us.

Honestly, I had no idea who found these occasions to be more of a chore, the parents or the teachers. What I did know was that regardless of our feelings on the subject, we all felt obliged to show up, plaster a smile on our faces, and attempt to look as though we were having a wonderful time.

Fortunately, the students I was tutoring were all making good progress in their studies. My conversations with their families were not only positive, they also left us feeling as though we were working together to achieve a worthwhile result. That seemed like a good night's work to me.

When my classroom was finally empty, I glanced up at the clock on the wall. Just half an hour of the two-hour event remained. I decided it was a good time to head over to the dining room in the main part of the mansion. Harriet had set out the refreshments there. So that was where everyone ended up gathering as an event drew to a close. It wouldn't hurt for Mr. Hanover to see me mingling with the remaining parents.

Like the rest of the mansion, the dining room was a showpiece. It had a high ceiling, dark wainscoting, and mullioned windows that sparkled when the sun shone through them. A light buffet supper had been set up on two long trestle tables pushed against the near wall.

I knew better than to drink coffee at that time of night, but I poured a cup from the silver urn anyway. I added a generous dollop of real cream from a nearby pitcher, then helped myself to a bright pink petit four. Harriet had made all the arrangements so I knew the food would be delicious.

Fortified with food and drink, I turned away

from the table and gazed around the half-full room. There were plenty of chairs available, but most people had remained standing. Parents and teachers were chatting in small groups. Mr. Hanover was busy making the rounds. I knew he would count tonight's event as a success.

I was about to grab another petit four when, to my surprise, I saw Louise Bixby conversing with two other women on the opposite side of the room. I hadn't realized that the Empire specialty judge had a Howard Academy connection. When I stopped to consider, I recalled there was a seventh grader named Marla Bixby. The girl was cute, vivacious, and a serious student—which meant that she'd never had need of my tutoring services.

Mrs. Bixby must have felt the weight of my stare because she glanced in my direction. A minute later she excused herself from the conversation and came striding across the room. Aunt Peg was acquainted with the Poodle judge, but Mrs. Bixby and I had not previously met. Apparently that was about to be remedied.

"Hello." She stopped in front of me and extended a hand. "I'm Louise Bixby. You look familiar but I'm afraid I don't remember your name. Are you one of Marla's teachers?"

The dog show world was a relatively small community. Once you'd been involved long enough, everybody began to look like someone you knew. Or maybe Mrs. Bixby had noticed me sitting ringside at the specialty.

"My name is Melanie Travis. I'm the special needs tutor here," I said. "Marla is a great student so I've never had an opportunity to work with her. I probably look familiar because I show Standard Poodles. I watched you judge the specialty in New York last Sunday."

"Oh, right." She gave a small laugh. "That's entirely different then."

"My aunt is Peg Turnbull," I added. "I believe you two know each other?"

Mrs. Bixby nodded. "Everybody knows Peg. She's a force of nature in the Poodle world."

And just about everywhere else, I thought.

"I would like to have gone to her seminar," she said. "I was sorry to see it scheduled at the same time as the show."

"That actually happened the other way around," I told her. "Victor Durbin chose that show date to conflict with the symposium. As you probably know, he doesn't have a good reputation in the Poodle world. What made you decide to accept the assignment to judge his club's specialty?"

Mrs. Bixby's eyes narrowed slightly. She hadn't liked the question.

"Of course I was aware of Victor's previous transgressions. But I was also well aware that a show Westminster weekend would be bound to draw a stellar entry—one that any judge would want to get her hands on. After due consideration, I decided to accept Victor's invitation. It was time to let bygones be bygones."

Wow. I paused to drink my coffee, because I couldn't come up with an answer for that statement. Had Mrs. Bixby really just admitted that she'd put aside ethical concerns in favor of self-interest? If so, she didn't seem to have a problem with it.

Abruptly I noticed that Mr. Hanover was watching us from the other side of the room. Had he somehow picked up on the undercurrent of friction in our conversation? I certainly hoped not. The headmaster didn't expect his teachers to be obsequious, but we were meant to conduct ourselves with deference toward school parents and alumna.

Deliberately I relaxed my shoulders and gave Mrs. Bixby a friendly smile. "The specialty did draw a wonderful entry. Did Victor ask you to judge because you and he were friends?"

She looked at me sharply, as if trying to discern whether the question implied something else entirely. When she replied, she appeared to be choosing her words with care. "Victor and I were acquainted, of course. But I wouldn't have characterized our relationship as friendship. When he started the Empire Club, he asked me to join. But that didn't mean anything. I think he asked just about anyone who'd ever seen a

Poodle to join that club. He was desperate to add more local members."

I set down my cup and saucer on a nearby tray. "Did you become a member of EPC?"

"No. I attended a couple of meetings and knew right away that it wasn't for me. Victor was an autocrat. He wanted to do everything his own way. That club works better for people who want to follow rather than lead. I'm not surprised there's been quite a turnover in membership through the years."

"Victor did seem to have a hard time getting along with people." I paused in case Mrs. Bixby wanted to elaborate about her own problems with the man. When she didn't take the bait, I added, "I suppose that's not surprising, considering what happened."

Mrs. Bixby frowned. Her eyes narrowed. "Now I know who you are," she said abruptly. "You're that girl who goes around solving mysteries."

My cheeks grew pink. She'd made that sound like it was a bad thing.

"Everybody's heard about what happened to Victor. Has his death become your new puzzle to solve?"

"No, I—"

"Because in your shoes, it should be."

That caught me by surprise. I had no idea what she was talking about. "Why?"

Mrs. Bixby leaned in closer. She said with relish, "Rumor has it that Peg was involved."

"No," I said quickly. "She wasn't."

"I can certainly understand why you would deny that."

"I'm denying it because it isn't true."

Her smile had a malicious edge. "That's not what the gossip says."

"The gossip is wrong," I told her firmly.

"Is it?" Mrs. Bixby shrugged as if it didn't matter to her either way. "I heard that Peg and Victor were engaged in some kind of ongoing feud. I'm sure the police will look into that. Of course, if it isn't true, Peg has nothing to worry about."

Okay, now this woman was really beginning to get on my nerves.

"I imagine they'll look into anyone who was seen arguing with Victor recently," I said. "Like you, perhaps—who had a very public disagreement with him in the middle of judging on Sunday. What was that about?"

"It was nothing," she snapped. "Just a small misunderstanding. I wasn't feeling well. I'd grabbed a sandwich in Penn Station and it must have disagreed with me. I didn't feel right all afternoon."

"Were you feeling well earlier in the day?" I asked. "Because you were seen arguing with Victor then too."

Mrs. Bixby reared back. "I don't know what you're talking about," she said haughtily.

"Whoever told you that is a liar. As for the rest, I have no idea why Victor came barreling into my ring. I presume he wanted to draw attention to himself, just like he always does. Did you know Victor?"

"I did."

"Then you know the kind of man he was. Victor thought of himself first, last, and always. He was trouble with a capital *T*. You never knew what he might do next."

"I'm sure the police will be looking into all of that," I said, purposely tossing her own words back at her. "Of course, if what you're saying is true, you won't have anything to worry about."

Out of the corner of my eye, I saw Mr. Hanover heading our way. He didn't look happy. That was never a good thing. Harriet was signaling to me frantically from behind the headmaster's back. I was pretty sure she was telling me to shut up.

I could do that.

I was standing like a mummy when Mr. Hanover drew up beside us. The man was tall and trim. As always, he was impeccably turned out. His suit came from Savile Row. His tie and silk pocket square matched. His brown hair was thinning on top and a pair of wire-framed glasses—a relatively new addition—rested on the bridge of his patrician nose. Mr. Hanover appeared to be staring down that nose at me now.

Before he could speak, Mrs. Bixby treated him to a blinding smile. "Good evening, Russell. What a delightful soiree you've arranged for us tonight. I was lucky to run into Melanie here. She and I have been catching up on the activities of some mutual friends. I hope you don't mind that I'm monopolizing one of your teachers?"

A moment earlier, I'd been silent. Now I was speechless. Mrs. Bixby had morphed into an entirely different person right before my eyes. That was quite a trick.

"Not at all," the headmaster replied smoothly. "I just came by to pay my respects. But since you ladies are enjoying your conversation, I will leave you to it."

"Thank you," I said when he was gone. "I think you just saved my bacon. And maybe my job."

"I didn't do it for you," Mrs. Bixby said.

Why wasn't I surprised?

"Perhaps you were right to point out that the police might also see me as a person of interest," she continued. "That's the term they use, isn't it?"

I nodded.

"What happened to Victor had nothing to do with me. And I want nothing to do with it. I have a reputation to maintain. I'm a single mother. I have a very good PR job that—among other things—allows me to pay my daughter's tuition at this school. Whatever kind of muck is going to be raked up by the investigation into Victor's demise, I don't want any of it to stick to me."

I nodded again. I could understand that.

"Aunt Peg feels the same way," I told her.

Mrs. Bixby's short, clipped nod indicated that she'd gotten the message. Her earlier comments about Aunt Peg had been out of line.

"Maybe it's a good thing we ran into each other tonight," she mused. "It seems you'd be doing both Peg and me a favor if you helped the police conclude their investigation into Victor's death as quickly as possible."

Before I could speak, she added meaningfully, "You should know that I always repay my debts. In my position, it's easy for one favor to be returned with another."

I stared at her in surprise. Was Mrs. Bixby actually offering to help me out in the show ring—perhaps by awarding a Poodle of mine undeserved points? Aunt Peg would have a fit when I told her. She'd probably also strike Louise Bixby from her Christmas card list.

"I could ask a few questions," I told her. I didn't give two hoots about this woman's stake in the matter. I did, however, care about Aunt Peg's.

"Good," she replied coolly, as if she'd never expected any other answer. "I'm glad we understand each other."

I sincerely doubted that. But at least for now, I was willing to play along. "You knew Victor better than I did. Can you think of anyone who might have wanted to harm him?"

This time Mrs. Bixby didn't hesitate before replying. "Larry Bowling."

"Who's he?"

"The most vocal malcontent in the Empire Club. He and Victor were engaged in a bitter quarrel over stud fees that were owed. Or possibly not owed. Depending on who you chose to believe."

That sounded promising. "Where does Larry live?" I asked.

"North Salem or South Salem, I don't remember which one. Blackbriar Kennel. I'm sure he has a Web page. You'll find it."

She was right about that. I most certainly would.

Chapter 12

I was seated at my desk the next morning when my cell phone vibrated. If it had been tucked away in my purse like it was supposed to be, I would never have known. But I had a free period between tutoring sessions and the device had somehow found its way into my pocket.

I checked the caller ID and sighed.

"I heard what you did last night," Aunt Peg barked into the phone. She knew personal calls at work were allowed only in case of emergency. But Aunt Peg figured everything she had to say qualified.

"I did several things last night," I replied mildly. "Which one are you talking about?"

"At Howard Academy Parents' Night. You cornered Louise Bixby."

Now that was unfair.

"I didn't corner her. She was the one who sought me out." Then a sudden thought hit me. "Wait . . . who did you hear that from?"

Lord, I hoped it wasn't Russell Hanover. Aunt Peg was a loyal and generous HA alum who counted the headmaster among her wide circle of friends. Sometimes it felt as though her tentacles extended into every aspect of my life. But surely my conversation with Mrs. Bixby hadn't made that big an impression on him?

"Louise called me this morning," she said.

I exhaled a relieved breath. Okay. That I could handle.

"Did she ask you if you killed Victor Durbin?"

It sounded as though Aunt Peg might have snorted out some tea. "No. Why would she do that?"

"She was happy to inform me last night that the rumor mill says you were involved."

"Phfft, gossip. Who listens to that?"

"You do," I pointed out. *All the time,* I wanted to add. I managed to refrain.

"Louise said you interrogated her." Aunt Peg sounded pleased. "Did you ask *her* if she was involved?"

"Not exactly." I frowned, thinking back. "Though now I wish I'd been more direct."

"Why is that?"

"First, because I watched her lie to Mr. Hanover flawlessly."

"That's impressive," Aunt Peg agreed.

"And second, because she offered me *future favors*—I'm sure you get my drift—if I looked into Victor's death. She framed the offer as an opportunity for me to help both of you."

"I don't need your help," Aunt Peg said brusquely.

"Of course not. You never do."

We both considered that for a minute.

"Future favors, *really?*" I knew she would circle back around to that. She was probably frowning as she said it.

"I could finish Coral for you," I pointed out.

Aunt Peg wasn't amused. "That will not be necessary. But the offer does raise an interesting question."

"What's that?"

"Obviously Victor's death is being investigated by the New York City police. So what is Louise afraid they might find out?"

"I have no idea," I told her. "She recommended that I talk to a man named Larry Bowling."

"Who's he?"

"A member of the Empire Poodle Club. One who didn't get along with Victor."

"*Nobody* got along with Victor," Aunt Peg said. "Your list of suspects is going to be huge."

"Who says I'm making a list of suspects?"

"Aren't you?" she inquired.

"You just told me that you didn't need my help."

Aunt Peg huffed out a breath. "Since when did you start listening to everything I say?"

Since forever, I thought. But who was counting?

"Time is passing," she informed me. "If you don't already have a list, you'd better get moving."

I guessed that meant we had that settled.

She disconnected the call just as there was a brisk knock on my classroom door. Almost immediately, the door opened. I barely had time to shove the phone back into my pocket before Mr. Hanover came striding into the room.

Quickly I jumped to my feet. Faith followed suit. A fleeting look of amusement crossed the headmaster's face. The big Poodle wagged her tail in a friendly greeting. *Good girl.*

"Please," he said. "Sit."

Faith and I both complied. Mr. Hanover looked amused again. Faith and I made a good team. We could have been a comedy act.

Mr. Hanover rarely made an appearance in my classroom, however. And when he did appear, his visits seldom augured good news. So I was pretty sure the felicitous mood wouldn't last long.

"Tell me about last night," he said.

The headmaster had remained standing. That meant he was now towering over me. I knew that wasn't an accident.

"Parents' Night was a big success," I said brightly. "The turnout was huge. And Harriet did a wonderful job of pulling everything together."

Mr. Hanover quirked a brow. "Is that what you think I'm here to discuss?"

"No?" I made the answer sound like a question. We both knew it wasn't.

"Let's start again then, shall we? Tell me about

your conversation with Marla Bixby's mother. I assume you were not catching up on old friends. Even from across the room I could tell that."

"You're right," I admitted. "We weren't. Not exactly."

He crossed his arms over his chest and waited in silence for me to continue. Mr. Hanover had that technique down cold. Plus, his mere presence was intimidating. Idly I wondered if he'd ever worked for the CIA.

"A man Mrs. Bixby and I knew was murdered Tuesday night," I said unhappily.

The headmaster's shoulders stiffened. He probably hadn't expected that. "Where?" he demanded. "Not here."

By "here" I knew he meant the school. *His school*. The institution that Mr. Hanover would do anything in his power to protect. Unfortunately, during the time I'd been a teacher at HA, the school had found itself on the periphery of several similar crimes.

"No, of course not," I told him quickly. "It happened in New York City."

"Well, then." He relaxed fractionally. "What business is it of yours?"

"We were merely discussing the crime. That's all."

"*All?* You're sure about that?"

I nodded uncomfortably. I'm not nearly as good a liar as Louise Bixby is.

"Because I would be very disappointed, Ms. Travis, if your exploits were to once again expose Howard Academy to publicity of any kind. Do we understand one another?"

I might have tried arguing that the previous problems hadn't been entirely my fault. Or not my fault at all. But really, what was the point?

"Yes, Mr. Hanover, we do," I said.

"Excellent." He walked over to the corner of the room where Faith was sitting on her cedar bed. He'd been frowning at me. Now he actually smiled as he reached down to pat her head. Faith had that effect on people.

Mr. Hanover turned back to me before leaving. "You will give my regards to your aunt," he said. "The next time you speak with her."

Was it my imagination or was there a subtext to that request? Dammit, don't tell me he knew I'd been talking on my phone too.

"Of course," I replied. "I know she'll be happy to hear from you."

As soon as he was gone, Faith rose from her bed and came padding over. She pressed her warm body against my legs and laid her head on my lap. I slipped a hand down and caressed beneath her ears. I couldn't help but smile. She had that effect on me too.

It turned out that Larry Bowling didn't live in either North or South Salem. Instead, his

Blackbriar Kennel was located in Cross River, a semirural hamlet in eastern Westchester County. According to Larry's Web site, he bred "outstanding Toy and Miniature Poodle puppies for discriminating owners who only want the very best."

Funny thing about that, I'd never heard of him before. Nor had I ever seen the Blackbriar prefix on a Toy or Mini Poodle at a dog show. And there was no mention anywhere of his dogs' health, or temperament, or of any genetic testing he was doing on his stock. Aunt Peg would have wasted no time in telling Larry Bowling that his assessment of his dogs' quality was nowhere near the truth. So it was a good thing she wasn't with me when I drove to Cross River that afternoon, after dropping Kevin and Faith at home.

I had called Larry earlier, introduced myself as an acquaintance of Victor's, and asked if he had time to talk to me. I'd expected to have to come up with a ruse to get my foot in the door—but Larry had surprised me. He'd merely inquired if I also bred Poodles, and what size they were. After I answered both questions, he'd told me he would be at home after one o'clock that afternoon.

I wondered what I should make of that. Was Larry just a friendly guy? I hoped that was the case, but somehow it didn't seem likely. Maybe I wasn't the only one with a game plan.

On the Web site Blackbriar Kennel appeared

to be a cute bungalow home with a wide porch and dormer windows, surrounded by mature trees, and nestled in a pastoral setting. The reality looked quite different. For one thing, the driveway had yet to see a snowplow this winter. For another, a large tree limb had fallen down across thc yard at some point. It was still leaning against the side of the house. And then there was the noise.

As soon as I got out of my car I heard it, the harsh cacophony of multiple dogs barking. Loudly. Incessantly. Poodles, presumably. The easiest dogs in the world to train. So . . . two things. Why were the Poodles outside in this cold weather, and why hadn't they been taught to be quiet?

I was standing there listening to the noise when the front door opened. Larry Bowling looked like the kind of man who would have blended into any crowd. He was of average build and had a face that was remarkable only for its everyman features. Larry was in his forties, an age when most men would have been at work on a weekday. Once again, I wondered why he'd been so readily available to meet with me.

"You must be Melanie," he said. "No need to stand out there in the cold. Come on in."

"That's a lot of barking," I said without thinking, but Larry didn't take offense.

"You know Poodles. They have strong lungs.

150

And plenty to say." He beckoned me closer and I climbed two steps to the porch.

"Don't your neighbors mind?"

"One or two." Larry shrugged. "But hey, it's my property. I can do whatever I want here."

Unless your town has a noise ordinance, I thought.

Most places I visited, I was greeted by enthusiastic canines. Not at Larry's house. Once inside, I didn't see a single Poodle. Or even a picture of a Poodle. And when he closed the front door behind me, the noise level dropped too. Now his dogs' existence was almost imperceptible. Apparently his idea of living with Poodles and mine were very different.

I followed him down a narrow hallway to a cramped living room with a lovely brick fireplace. Unfortunately, it wasn't lit. Larry must have been saving money on his heating bills because when I exhaled I could see my breath condense in the air. I opted to keep my coat on.

"Have a seat," he said, sinking into an upholstered chair that looked older than I was. Gingerly I perched on the edge of a couch cushion. "You said you wanted to talk about Victor. Am I correct in assuming that he was annoying the crap out of you too?"

I looked up, surprised. "I'm sorry . . . what?"

"Victor. The corpse of the hour. May he rest in peace. Not." Larry blinked at the horrified expression on my face. "I'm sorry. Do I have that wrong? Were you and Victor friends?"

"No, we weren't," I replied firmly. "At one point he and I both belonged to the Paugussett Poodle Club but other than that I barely knew him."

"So you didn't have any business dealings with him?"

"No."

"Then you're lucky." Larry reached over to a side table and picked up a pack of cigarettes. "Mind if I smoke?"

Actually I did. But it was his house, so I shook my head.

"I thought perhaps you wanted to join my lawsuit," Larry continued after he'd tapped a cigarette out of the pack, lit the tip, and inhaled what looked like a satisfying drag.

"Your lawsuit," I repeated. Would everything this man said come as a surprise?

"Yeah, I figured that was why you wanted to talk to me. I'm putting together a lawsuit against Victor Durbin." He frowned. "Now I suppose I'll have to sue his estate instead."

"I heard that the two of you had had a dispute over stud fees?"

"Stud fees." Larry snorted smoke out through his nose. "That's rich."

I leaned back in my seat. It was beginning to look as though I was going to be here a while. "It wasn't about stud fees?"

"I guess it started that way. But that was a while ago. Victor needed a steady supply of puppies for his café. You know, the Pooch Pub?"

"I've heard of the place," I said. "But I've never been there."

"You should visit sometime. It's a fun spot. Great selection of coffees, decent food. But of course, the puppies are the real draw. Who doesn't love puppies?"

Nobody I knew. But that wasn't the point.

"So you were supplying puppies for Victor's café?" I prompted.

"Some of them. Probably most of them." Larry sounded proud of himself. "It's a great setup he has there. You wouldn't believe how many puppies the pub can move in a month. People come in for a cup of coffee, sit down for a few minutes, and an adorable floppy-eared puppy climbs into their lap. Next thing they know, they've fallen in love. Women are the softest touch, but it works with men too. And kids? Don't even get started about how easy they are."

He grinned. "I've seen a mother buy a puppy just so her little darling would stop screaming. It blows my mind. Props to Victor for coming up with a crazy good idea. Even if he was an ass."

My hands clenched into fists in my lap. Other than that, I remained very still. I hoped my face didn't betray what I was thinking. Because if it did, Larry would probably leap to his feet and show me to the door.

The whole idea of puppies being marketed as an impulse purchase made my blood boil. What happened when people who'd bought a dog on a whim got home and realized that their new purchase needed care and training? Not to mention vaccinations and exercise. What if dog ownership was incompatible with their lifestyles?

There were so many objectionable things about the scenario Larry had described that I didn't even know where to begin. People like him and Victor were the reason why pounds and rescues were always full. I couldn't afford to lose my temper just yet, however. First I needed to find out more about Larry's lawsuit.

"So your problem with Victor began with a dispute over stud fees," I said evenly. "Then what happened?"

"See? Here's the thing." Larry leaned forward eagerly. He wanted me on his side. Little did he know that it was already much too late for that. "Victor and I had a deal. Before we even met, I was already breeding Poodles anyway. The market for them is great, especially the little ones. And at Christmastime? Man, they just about fly out the door."

I growled under my breath. Larry stopped talking. He tipped his head inquiringly.

"Sorry," I said. "Go on. I'm listening."

"Victor had this idea that the puppies in the pub would be more in demand if they were sired by his champion Poodles. Kind of a special selling point, you know? I didn't think it mattered, but since we were both making money who was I to quibble? The deal was, he would supply the stud dogs and I supplied the bitches. Then we'd split the litters between us." Larry paused to make sure I was paying attention. "In lieu of stud fees, you see?"

A nod was the best I could manage. I didn't trust myself to speak.

"But then Victor decided that my business here was cutting into his potential profits. Rather than selling puppies from two locations, he wanted us to consolidate in one place."

"The Pooch Pub," I gritted out.

"Right." Larry leaned over and tapped the long ash at the end of his cigarette into the fireplace. "So Victor came to me with a proposal. All the puppies we produced would go to him. In exchange for the use of my bitches and all the time and effort I was putting into raising the litters until they were old enough to sell, he was supposed to give me an eight percent share in the Pooch Pub's profits."

"You said he was supposed to do that," I pointed out. "Did it happen?"

"What do you think?" Larry snapped.

"I'm guessing no. Is that what your lawsuit is about?"

155

"You'd better believe it." Larry stood up. For a moment I thought he was indicating that our conversation was over, but Larry didn't even look at me. Instead, he began to pace back and forth across the small room.

"Victor was a snake," he said. "Everyone knows that. The only reason he started that Poodle club of his was because he got kicked out of his old club."

"Yes," I replied. "I'm aware of that."

"Oh." He glanced my way. "I guess so, since you're a member and all. But it just goes to show what kind of man Victor was."

"A snake," I said to help him along.

"You know it." He raked his hands through his sparse hair. "A man like Victor, he deserved what happened to him. It doesn't surprise me that somebody killed him. He deserved to die."

Chapter 13

W here were you on Tuesday night?" I asked. Larry stopped and spun around. "What do you mean?"

"Did you go to New York for the Westminster Dog Show?"

"What? A canine beauty pageant? You must be kidding. All those pricey pooches prancing around a ring—why would I want to watch something like that?"

Apparently it hadn't occurred to him that I was inquiring whether he'd been in the vicinity when Victor died. Or maybe Larry was brighter than I thought, and his answer was a clever dodge.

"So you were here at home then?"

"I didn't say that." Larry frowned. "It's none of your business where I was Tuesday night."

"Except that a man you feel deserved to die, did so that night."

"I don't need an alibi," Larry snapped. "I wasn't anywhere near that place."

"Someone who hated Victor clearly was," I pointed out. "But don't worry, you aren't the only person he treated badly. Tell me more about your lawsuit."

Larry sank back into his chair. He lit up another cigarette. The air in the room already reeked.

My clothes were going to smell like smoke. And probably my hair too.

"When you said you had Poodles, I thought that was why you called me. I figured Victor must have stiffed you the same way he stiffed me."

"How was your deal with Victor put together?" I asked. "You said it was Victor's idea. Did the two of you write up a contract?"

Larry looked chagrinned. He reached up and scrubbed his hand over his eyes. So I was guessing no.

"What you have to understand is that Victor and I were already doing business together. We had been for several years. So a certain level of trust had already been established."

He sounded as though he was rehearsing the words he planned to say in front of a jury. *Go ahead,* I thought. *Try to convince me that you're not an idiot.* I was happy to keep listening. I certainly wasn't about to point out that, by his own admission, the man he'd trusted was a snake.

"Victor said the paperwork was coming," Larry continued. "He told me his lawyer was swamped with work, but eventually there would be a contract for us both to sign. In the meantime, we shook hands on the arrangement."

Again—he'd agreed to do a handshake deal *with a snake.* Actually, I found that imagery rather amusing.

"How long have you been waiting for a contract?" I asked. "When did your new agreement with Victor begin?"

"At least eighteen months ago. Maybe longer. Could have been two years." Larry blew a stream of smoke in my direction. I tried not to flinch.

"So there should have been profits for you to share by now."

"Damn straight." Larry popped up again. The man was like a human jack-in-the-box. "That's what I told Victor."

"And what did he say?"

"He told me I didn't understand how business worked. That start-ups, especially restaurants, take a long time to begin turning a profit. He said the Pooch Pub was still deep in the hole. Even with how well the puppy sales were doing, everything else was still in the red."

Larry was near the fireplace. He banged his fist on the mantelpiece. I jumped slightly in my seat.

"I let him know that wasn't the deal I signed up for. We'd agreed I was supposed to get a piece of the gross proceeds, not the net. Do you know what Victor did then?"

I could guess, but I shook my head anyway.

"He just laughed. He told me to prove it."

"Which you couldn't do because there'd never been any paperwork."

Larry nodded glumly. "That's when I realized that Victor had duped me. That the whole thing was probably a scam from the start. I had given him thousands of dollars' worth of puppies to sell in his café, and in return I'd gotten . . . absolutely nothing."

"Your pride must have been dented by that," I said softly.

"Pride, hell," Larry snarled. "It was my wallet that took the hit. Those puppies are my livelihood. I have a Web site and a great reputation. I'd built up a good business over the years. The only reason I let Victor get in on it was because he promised he'd make me rich."

Larry wasn't the first person to fall for that promise. It was the oldest scam in the book.

My thoughts must have shown on my face because he waggled a finger in my direction. "Don't look at me like that. In my place, you'd have believed Victor too. Why not? He lived in a nice house, he drove a fancy car. You can't tell me the man didn't have plenty of money."

Larry stubbed out his second cigarette on the bricks beside him. He tossed the used butt into the fireplace. It landed on top of a half-burned log beside several others.

Now that I'd gotten Larry talking, he didn't want to stop. "Every time I was in the Pooch Pub the place was doing a booming business. Victor was making a profit, all right. He just didn't want to share. Big, important man that he was, he figured he didn't have to. Victor was sure I wouldn't be able to make him live up to his word. Well, I showed him!"

The vehement declaration made me stiffen in my seat. Suddenly it seemed like a prudent time to stand up. And maybe to head toward the door.

Abruptly Larry seemed to realize what he'd said. "I was talking about the lawsuit," he added.

"I know that." Hopefully, my prevaricating skills were improving.

"No, really."

I'd reached the hallway. Three quick steps brought Larry to my side. Then he went right past. He strode to the front door and opened it. A gust of fresh air blew inside. After the tight, smoky quarters in the house, it smelled heavenly. I couldn't wait to be outside.

"I believe you," I said.

"You don't have to believe me. Talk to Manny Garza. He'll tell you."

I paused on the doorstep. Once again, I could hear Larry's dogs yapping. The noise made me want to cover my ears. Instead I said, "Who's Manny Garza?"

"Another dog breeder. He has Schnauzers and Cockers. You know, for Schnoodles and Cockapoos?"

Unfortunately, I did know.

"Manny had the same deal with Victor that I did. And he got screwed too. He's not any happier about it than I am. He's in Katonah. Hang on a second, I'll give you his phone number."

Larry found a piece of paper and scribbled down the contact information. When he handed it over, he said, "It wasn't just me. Victor made trouble for a lot of people. Talk to the members of the Empire Poodle Club. Any one of them will tell you the same thing."

I was itching to leave, but I couldn't go just yet. "Who should I start with?"

"A woman named Hannah Bly. She always has plenty to say. Maybe you already know her. I think she used to belong to that other Poodle club."

Not only was Hannah once a member of the Paugussett Club, she'd also been the steward at the Poodle specialty the previous Sunday. I wondered what her beef with Victor had been.

"Good luck with your lawsuit," I said.

"I don't need luck," Larry told me. "I'm the one who's right."

I suspected his Poodles would have disagreed with him about that.

"You're going back out again *now?*" Sam said when I got home. Earlier I'd stopped by briefly to drop off Faith and Kevin. Now I was picking Faith up—and leaving once more.

Hannah Bly lived in New Canaan. I'd called her from the car, and she'd told me she was on her way to Waveny Park to take her daily two-mile hike. When she'd invited me to join her, I'd said I could be there in twenty minutes.

"Sorry about that." I tried to sound sincere. We both knew I wasn't really.

While I was busy running around, Sam was pulling double duty on the parent front. I would definitely owe him for that. But I was also sure that he'd find a way to collect.

Sam went into the closet and pulled out my warm parka. As I exchanged it for the wool peacoat I was wearing, he plopped a knitted cap on my head. Then I kicked off my sneakers and yanked on a pair of warm, waterproof boots. I stuffed a pair of gloves in my pocket and I was good to go.

"It'll be dark in two hours," Sam pointed out.

"I know. And I'm sure Hannah does too. There'll be plenty of time to walk two miles before sunset." At least I hoped there would.

The walking trails at Waveny Park were wide and plentiful. But the woods they crisscrossed were heavily treed, and dark with shadows. The trails were much more inviting on a sunny summer day than a wintry afternoon. On the other hand, we would probably be the only people out there. That meant I'd be able to let Faith run loose, and that Hannah and I would have plenty of privacy to talk.

Sam glanced down at the big Poodle. "You'll take care of her, right?"

She wagged her tail in reply. Faith always took care of me, and we all knew it.

"Don't leave your cell phone in the car," Sam told me. He knew I was likely to do exactly that.

"Seriously?" I peered at him from beneath the brim of the cap he'd pulled low over my forehead. "I won't need to call for help. I'm going to New Canaan, not Siberia."

"You might fall into a snowdrift."

I smirked. "They clear those paths, you know."

"When in your life have you ever stayed on the narrow path?"

Good point.

I stood up on my toes and brushed a quick kiss across his lips. "I'll be home in a couple of hours. Don't worry."

"Right," he said. "Like that's going to happen."

Faith was delighted to get back in the car with me. She was even more delighted when we pulled into the small parking lot near the Waveny Carriage House and I saw that Hannah had brought along a Standard Poodle of her own.

"That's Izzy," Hannah told me as Faith hopped out of the Volvo and she and the white Standard checked each other out.

"Mine's Faith," I replied. "She loves everybody."

Hannah laughed. "So does Izzy. I'm sure they'll get along fine." She was holding a leash in her hand but it wasn't attached to Izzy's collar.

I grabbed Faith's lead and my phone and shoved them both in my pocket.

"I'm glad to see you came prepared to move along." Hannah glanced down at my sturdy boots as we walked toward the trailhead. The two big Poodles were already running on ahead of us. "I've had friends who want to come out here and walk with me—and then it turns out their idea of walking is barely more than a stroll. I hike for exercise, so I like to get my blood pumping. You okay with that?"

"More than okay," I said. "I'll love it. Lead on."

Hannah was in her early forties, probably a couple of years older than me, but she was in great shape. She had on well-worn hiking boots, a lightweight parka, and no cap. It looked like she was serious about working up a sweat. I hoped I wouldn't have trouble keeping up.

We spent the first few minutes finding a rhythm that suited both our strides, and watching the Poodles to make sure they were staying out of trouble. Aside from our two cars, the parking lot had been empty. The wide path was deserted too. Faith and Izzy were able to race around and romp freely. They were having a great time exploring the woods.

The air was crisp and cold, and the packed snow crunched beneath our feet. Connecticut winters are long, and I've been known to let myself get lazy. Now it felt great to be outdoors doing something energetic. I wondered why I didn't make the effort more often.

I was enjoying myself so much that I almost forgot there was another reason why I'd come. Then Hannah turned to me and said, "Your call came as a surprise. How long has it been since we last spoke? Two years maybe?"

"Probably about that."

That was when Hannah had left PPC and joined the Empire Poodle Club. In the intervening time, she and I had crossed paths at various dog shows. Our relationship was cordial, but definitely more distant than it had been before she'd made the switch. Victor had had that effect on people—he made them choose sides.

"I saw you at the specialty on Sunday," I said.

Her gaze tipped my way. "But you didn't come over and say hello."

"You were busy." That excuse sounded pretty lame. "And besides, it was Victor's show."

"I figured that had to be what your call was about. You want to talk about Victor, right?"

I nodded. "Were you at Westminster on Tuesday night?"

"Sure, I was there." Hannah grinned. "Along with ten thousand other people. Everybody who's anybody in dogs was there. You know that."

Except me. I spared myself a moment for self-pity, then moved on. "Did you see Victor that evening?"

"Nope. Like I said, it was a full house. There were people everywhere. And it's not as though I was looking for him. Or even giving him a second thought."

I pushed aside a low-hanging branch and ducked beneath it. "I heard that you and Victor hadn't been getting along recently."

"Like what?" She grimaced. "That's public news?"

"I might have asked a few questions."

"About me?" Hannah didn't sound happy.

"No, about Victor. But your name came up."

"And now you want to know what Victor and I were fighting about."

"Well . . . yes," I said. "Although I was going to try to be more subtle than that."

"You, subtle? That's a laugh. Everybody knows what you do, Melanie. You're always poking your nose into everybody's business." She stopped abruptly and turned to face me. "Mind you, I'm not entirely opposed to that. I can be a nosy person myself—but having you come all the way out here to interrogate me? That was unexpected."

I hadn't thought of it as an interrogation, but whatever. "Do you mind?"

"I don't know," Hannah replied. "Maybe I do, maybe I don't. I have to think about it. Let's walk."

Chapter 14

We'd covered nearly a mile before Hannah spoke again. It was a beautiful afternoon to be walking in the woods. Even if she didn't answer any of my questions, I wouldn't regret having come. Faith and Izzy were dodging in and out of trees, chasing squirrels, and bounding through the snow. The two Poodles were having fun too.

"Do you want to know why I left the Paugussett Poodle Club?" Hannah asked.

"Sure." I'd take any information I could get.

"There were too many rules. It seemed like somebody was always telling you how you were supposed to do things."

"Somebody like Aunt Peg maybe?"

A smile twitched around the edges of Hannah's lips. "Your aunt can be pretty overbearing. Plus, she always thinks she's right about everything."

Tell me about it, I thought.

"I get that she's a VIP in the dog show world and all, but sometimes people just want to live their own lives, in their own way. You know?"

Did I ever. I blew out a puff of air and watched it disperse into tendrils. Not that I was winded or anything. But Hannah was setting a pretty good pace. And I had no intention of asking her to slow down.

"When that thing with Victor came up—you know, that he was breeding his Mini stud dogs to other breeds? Sure, I thought he was wrong. But I also thought it was wrong of PPC to turn against him. First, because Victor had a right to make his own choices, whether or not the rest of us agreed with him. And second, because by giving him an ultimatum—cut it out or be thrown out—the PPC board lost a chance to educate him about a better way to do things."

"I agree with you in theory," I said. "But as I recall, the quarrel between Victor and the PPC board went on for months. And Aunt Peg spent much of that time trying to convince him of the error of his ways. Victor is probably the only person who's ever stood up to her like that."

Hannah looked at me and grinned. "Maybe Peg killed him then. You know, just for being contrary."

I shook my head. "Aunt Peg's more impatient than that. If she was going to kill Victor, she'd have done it three years ago."

As we laughed together, the two Standard Poodles circled back to us. One black and one white, the two bitches looked like mirror images of each other. Faith was clearly enjoying herself. She was also covered in snow. Izzy probably was too, but the flakes were harder to see on her white coat. I barely had time to give Faith a pat before she heard a noise in the woods and went racing away again.

"They're having a terrific time," I said. "I ought to bring Faith over here more often."

"I come every day," Hannah told me. "It's wonderful exercise. Feel free to join me any time you like."

I just might take her up on that.

"Back to Victor," I said. "You still haven't told me what you and he were fighting about."

"It wasn't a big deal," Hannah began. Then she stopped and started over. "Well, actually it *was* a big deal. But not the kind of thing someone would kill a person over."

"Go on."

"It's probably no secret that when Victor started the Empire Poodle Club he was scrambling to find members. New York, New Jersey, and Connecticut all had affiliate clubs already. So Poodle people around here who wanted to join a club, already belonged somewhere."

I nodded.

"The AKC has rules about things you need to do if you want to get your club accredited. Which obviously everybody does, because otherwise you can't hold events. The AKC wants to know how the club is organized and how its records are kept. They also ask who the members are, where they live, and what's their involvement in dogs. The AKC is serious about that stuff. You can't just go around making things up."

"Oh," I said suddenly. I could guess what was coming next.

"Oh, indeed." Hannah frowned. "Last year I got voted in as club treasurer. Don't think that's some kind of honor, because it isn't. All it really meant was that no one else was willing to do the job and I drew the short straw. One of my duties was collecting dues from the members. *All* the members. Even those I'd never met because they never seemed to show up for meetings."

"Don't tell me," I said. "You discovered that some of them didn't actually exist."

"Not right away. Because the people had names and addresses that looked real enough. Although two of them lived on the same road that Victor did, which struck me as odd because I thought he was the only Poodle breeder in Peekskill. When I asked him about it, he just told me not to worry. That he'd be taking care of any dues I couldn't collect. That was when I began to get suspicious."

"You found out that Victor had falsified EPC records in order to get the club accredited, didn't you?"

Hannah sighed. "Yes."

"Did you ask him about it?"

"Of course I did. I didn't have a choice. Eventually some AKC official was bound to figure out what he'd done and then we'd all be in trouble. It wouldn't just be Victor's problem. The fact that fraudulent documents had been filed would cause repercussions for all the officers of the club. As treasurer, I'd be held responsible too."

"What did Victor say when you confronted him?"

"He totally blew me off. He told me I was making a mountain out of a molehill. But I wasn't."

"No, you weren't," I agreed. "That's serious stuff."

"Victor was totally cavalier about what he'd done. And his attitude really pissed me off. I'd already left one Poodle club. And this one was supposed to be better." Hannah glanced my way. "No offense."

"None taken." Every affiliate club had its issues, even my own.

"How was this club going to be any better," Hannah asked, "if Victor was in charge and hell-bent on screwing things up?"

"You could have resigned in protest," I said.

Hannah looked at me like I was daft. "And then what? Hope that the Paugussett club would welcome me back with open arms? I don't *think* so. What I wanted to do was slap some sense into Victor. And until a few days ago when he went and got himself killed, I was trying to figure out how."

Aunt Peg hadn't been able to make Victor see reason, I thought. I doubted that Hannah would have been successful either. But now we'd never know.

"What will happen to your club now that Victor's gone?" I asked.

"I have no idea." Hannah grimaced. "It hadn't even occurred to me to worry about that yet. Victor was such a driving force at EPC. I don't know if the rest of us will want to sort out those problems and continue without him."

The sun was dropping low behind the trees that surrounded us. It wasn't dark yet, but it soon would be. Fortunately, the path we'd taken was circling back around to the carriage house. I could see our two cars in the distance.

Faith and Izzy rejoined us on the path. The two Poodles were tired too. Faith's tongue was hanging out of the side of her mouth, but her step was jaunty and her tail was still high in the air. She'd enjoyed our walk. So had I.

"One last question?" I said to Hannah.

"Sure, why not?" She looked resigned now.

"At the show last Sunday, Victor came over to the ring after the Mini judging. He and Louise Bixby got into what looked like a heated discussion. What was that about?"

"Hell if I know," Hannah retorted. "I was as surprised as everyone else when it happened. The judge and the show chairman? Why would either one of them want to cause a scene at their own show? They were both out of line, if you ask me."

I nodded in agreement.

"All I could do was stand there and continue doing my job like everything was proceeding normally," she continued. "I probably looked like an idiot, handing out armbands and pretending nothing was wrong."

I remembered that Hannah had turned her back and moved away. In her place, I'd have done the same.

"So you didn't hear what they were talking about?"

"No way. I didn't *want* to hear. The last thing I wanted was to have to get involved. I distanced myself as much as I could, considering that they were almost in the ring. All I know is that Louise sent Victor a note and then he came over. That's how the whole thing started."

"Louise Bixby sent him a note?" I repeated. That wasn't what she had told me. She'd claimed not to know why Victor had accosted her. "Are you sure about that?"

"Absolutely." Hannah nodded. "I was there when she did it."

We'd reached the parking lot. She opened her car door and hopped Izzy inside. I did the same with Faith. Hannah pulled out of the lot first but I was right behind her. It was dusk now. The

Waveny Park driveway was dark enough that I immediately turned my headlights on.

I gave Sam a quick call to tell him that I was on my way home. Despite his misgivings, I was glad I'd come. Faith and I enjoyed our hike. And Hannah had given me plenty to think about.

I never got a chance to call Manny Garza because he contacted me first. Apparently I wasn't the only one to whom Larry Bowling had given a phone number. Manny called that night after dinner.

I was watching a movie with Sam and Kevin. Davey was up in his room doing his homework—or, more likely, checking out his friends' social media. When my phone rang, I picked it up and carried it into the kitchen.

Bud jumped off the couch and trailed along behind me. The Poodles knew better than to look for handouts but that little mutt was ever hopeful. He figured any time he was in the kitchen, he was that much closer to having something edible fall into his mouth.

"This is Manny Garza," the man said when I held the phone to my ear. "I hear you've been looking for me."

Not yet, I thought. But I'd been about to.

"You want to talk about Victor Durbin, is that right?"

"Yes. Thank you for contacting me."

"It wasn't my idea. Larry Bowling put me up to it. He says I'm supposed to confirm a bunch of stuff he told you."

"Only if it's true," I said quickly.

"Oh, it's true all right. Leastways, most of it is. Here's what we're gonna do. Tomorrow I have a delivery to make at the Pooch Pub. I'll be there after lunch. You find your way there—I guess I might have a few minutes to spare, so you can buy me a cup of coffee. Otherwise you're out of luck. I'm a busy man, you understand?"

"Of course. What are you delivering to the Pooch Pub?" I probably knew the answer but I felt compelled to ask anyway.

Manny snorted into the phone. He didn't address my suspicions. "Tomorrow afternoon," he told me. "That's your chance. Take it or leave it."

Sam raised a brow when I rejoined him and Kevin on the couch. Tar had moved into my spot while I was gone. Faith glared at him until he shifted over to make room.

Kev was curled up underneath Sam's arm. Although the movie was *Aladdin*, one of his favorites, he was already half asleep. In this scene, Aladdin and Jasmine were riding on a magic carpet. I wished I had one of those.

"That was Manny Garza," I answered Sam's unspoken question.

"Friend of yours?" He didn't recognize the name.

"We haven't met yet but I doubt it." I wedged myself in between Kevin and Tar. "Manny breeds Schnoodles."

"Schnoodles." Kev gave a drowsy giggle. "There's no such thing."

I reached over and smoothed back the bangs that had fallen down over his brow. "Actually there is," I told him. "It's a kind of dog. A cross between a Schnauzer and a Poodle."

That made my son's eyes pop open. "Really?"

"Well, it's not a real breed. It's a mixed breed. You know, a mutt. Like Bud."

"Bud's a *Schnoodle?*"

The expression of astonishment on Kev's face made Sam and me laugh. "No, Bud's a different kind of mutt."

"What kind?" Kevin demanded. He was wide awake now. Aladdin was zipping around the television screen with a monkey, but he was long forgotten.

"We don't know exactly," Sam admitted. "Bud looks like he has some Beagle and Boxer in him. And maybe a smidge of Whippet."

Kevin sat up. He shook his head. "Nope, that's not it. Schnoodle sounds better."

"Better than what?" Davey walked into the living room carrying a bowl of ice cream. I couldn't believe he'd gotten ice cream for himself and hadn't offered any to us.

"Bud's a Schnoodle," Kevin informed him.

"Since when?"

"He was born that way. With spots and everything."

Davey considered that. He'd spent enough time at dog shows to be conversant with most breeds. "I'm pretty sure a Schnoodle wouldn't have spots," he decided.

"Would too!" Kevin tried to stamp his foot. He was sitting on the couch so much of the effect was lost. Instead, he accidentally kicked Tar, who jumped up, bounced off the coffee table, and knocked into Davey. The bowl of ice cream went flying.

Luckily the bowl was made of plastic so it didn't shatter when it hit the floor. Three dogs went scrambling to grab dessert. No surprise, Bud got there first. He snatched up the big scoop of ice cream and dove beneath the couch with his prize. Tar and Augie had to make do with licking the floor and the bowl respectively.

"Who's going to clean that up?" asked Davey. He knelt down and peered under the couch.

"Whose ice cream was it?" I inquired.

"That's not fair," said Davey.

"Good luck winning that argument," Sam told him.

Chapter 15

In the middle of the day, I could get to Tarrytown in twenty minutes if I drove there straight from Howard Academy. Manny hadn't specified a time. He'd only said that he would be at the Pooch Pub after lunch—and I didn't want to miss him. I headed out as soon as my school day ended.

Planning ahead, I'd left Faith at home that morning. She wasn't happy about that, but there was no way I was going to take her anywhere near the Pooch Pub. Faith would have been as horrified by the owners' careless disregard for puppy welfare as I was.

Tarrytown was situated beside the Hudson River, just south of Sleepy Hollow, home to Washington Irving's headless horseman. Within easy driving distance to midtown Manhattan, the village was a popular residence for New York City commuters. Its downtown area featured quaint buildings and abundant reminders that Tarrytown had been in existence since before the Revolutionary War. Most days, the village bustled with activity.

I had to give Victor credit for that at least. He'd chosen a great place in which to launch his business.

The Pooch Pub was located on the outskirts of town, housed in a freestanding brick building on a corner lot. A cheery sign announced the pub's presence and a parking lot wrapped around two sides of the building. Large bay windows on either side of the front door let in plenty of light. At one-thirty in the afternoon, the parking lot was mostly full.

I slid the Volvo into a narrow spot, got out, and paused for a look around. A white panel van was parked toward the rear of the building. Nearby, a back door to the pub was standing open. As I watched, a man unloaded a crate from the van and carried it inside. It looked as though I'd located Manny Garza.

I walked around the building and waited until he reappeared. Manny was no taller than me. He had broad shoulders and a thick body. He moved like a man who was accustomed to physical labor. When I said his name, he swiveled around. His eyes, framed by a single bushy eyebrow, were dark and intense.

"Who wants to know?" he asked.

"I'm Melanie Travis. We spoke on the phone?"

I held out a hand. Manny made no attempt to take it. I wasn't sure if he even noticed it. Instead he peered at my face so intently that I wondered if he was nearsighted. Or if my mascara was smudged. Finally, I let my hand drop.

"Oh yeah," he said. "I wasn't sure if you'd

show up. Looks like you got here just in time. I have one more crate to unload. Ten minutes later and you'd have missed me."

"This must be my lucky day," I replied. The sarcasm was lost on Manny. For some reason, he was still staring.

"Look," he said. "I'm only talking to you because Larry asked me to. Otherwise, I'm just here to deliver some dogs. That's business. You? I don't know what that's about. If you want to go inside and order me an espresso, I'll be there in five minutes. That's the deal, okay?"

"Fine by me," I told him.

I had no idea what to expect when I walked inside the Pooch Pub. I knew puppy and kitten cafés were becoming a thing, but I'd never seen one in person before. Why would I visit a puppy café when I could get all the canine kisses I wanted right in my own home?

At first glance, the airy room looked much like every other coffee bar I'd ever frequented. There was a long counter in the back. A chalkboard menu hung on the brick wall behind it. The space between me and the counter was crowded with small, round tables. Most were occupied. Many held an open laptop or the remains of a meal.

After that, however, the similarities ended. Here, only a few of the tables' occupants were conversing with each other or staring at their computer screens. The remainder had their eyes cast downward. They were playing with the puppies they held cradled in their laps.

More than a dozen puppies were loose in the room. All of them were adorable, of course, with their curly hair and floppy ears. I didn't even bother trying to sort out their breeds. Nearly all the puppies were small to medium in size. Most likely because that would make them easier to pick up and cuddle—and conveniently portable if a patron decided to carry one home on a whim.

While I waited for my order to be filled, I continued to look around. Though puppies this young couldn't all be housebroken, the pub's floor was spotless. Idly I wondered whose job it was to clean up after them.

There was a dog bed heaped with blankets in one corner, but the puppies never seemed to have an opportunity to use it. As soon as they grew tired, the drowsy babies were rotated out of the room by employees. Then new puppies were brought in to replace them.

I was guessing that the intent was for the puppies to be alert, and lively, and ready to engage with the customers at all times. Most looked happy to comply. They appeared to love the attention.

By the time I paid for my order and found a table, it had occurred to me to wonder how many additional puppies were awaiting their turns in the pub's back rooms. Just the thought alone was depressing. What happened to those puppies who outgrew their cute baby stage before anyone bought them? What kind of backup plan did Victor have in place for them?

Manny's promised five minutes had stretched closer to twenty before he appeared. I'd spent the last ten minutes staring out the window, watching the road. Considering Manny's attitude, I was half afraid that I would see a white panel van drive by.

While I was waiting, a black and white puppy had come wandering over to sniff my leg. Probably a Shih Tzu or some derivative of that breed, I decided. The puppy's interest in me didn't come as a surprise. I was sure I was covered with a host of enticing dog smells.

I reached down to scratch behind his ears, and when I looked up again, Manny was coming through the pub's front door. He scanned the room, then made his way in my direction. He skirted between the closely packed tables between us, shedding his heavy coat at the same time.

Manny's chair scraped the floor as he yanked it back and sat down. He reached immediately for the espresso. His short, blunt fingers wrapped around the small cup. He lifted it to his mouth and took a giant gulp. A shot of espresso that large would have made my eyes pop out of my head. Manny didn't react at all.

"So?" he said.

"I got us some scones." I gestured to the plate I'd placed on the table between us. "Blueberry and butterscotch. Take your pick."

He glanced down at the pastries as if he thought I might be trying to poison him. "Don't like scones," he told me. "Clock is ticking."

I guessed that meant I'd be eating both of them. I started with the butterscotch. "Larry Bowling told me that you and he had both been supplying puppies for Victor to sell here at the Pooch Pub."

Manny nodded, but didn't comment. If I was lucky, his second gulp of espresso might make him more talkative.

"He also told me that he'd made a deal with Victor. Rather than being paid for the product he was supplying"—yes, I managed to say that without wincing—"Larry was to receive eight percent of the pub's profits."

"Eight?" Manny's bushy brow rose. "I was supposed to get five."

The Shih Tzu puppy was lying on my foot. I was pretty sure he was chewing on my shoelaces. "Maybe Larry was a better negotiator than you are," I said.

"Nah, that's not it." Manny sounded smug. "It sounds like Larry's the one who didn't know how to drive a hard bargain. I don't just get a share in the Pooch Pub profits. My five percent makes me part owner of this place."

He was right, I realized. He did have the better deal. In theory, anyway.

"Do you have paperwork to support that claim?" I asked.

"Who needs paperwork?" Manny said. "Victor and me had an arrangement. It was solid."

"It might have been solid when he was alive," I told him. And if he believed that, I had a bridge I wanted to sell him. "But what about now?"

Manny stared past me for a minute. He was thinking hard. Either that or he was reading the menu on the back wall. It was hard to tell.

"Could be things are gonna get more complicated," he allowed finally.

"Have you spoken to Victor's partner about the arrangement you had with Victor?" I asked.

"You mean Clark?"

I nodded.

"Not yet. I'm working up to that. It's only been a couple days. I figure I'll give the dust a chance to settle. In the meantime, the most important thing is that business continues as usual around here. I gotta protect my stake, you know?"

Manny tipped up his cup and finished his espresso. He started to push back his chair, like he thought we were done.

Not yet. Not if I could help it.

"How long had your arrangement with Victor been in effect?" I asked.

"I don't know." He pulled his coat off the back of his chair. "Could be a year. Maybe longer."

"Larry Bowling told me that Victor never paid him any of the money that was due to him. Did he pay you?"

"Look, lady." Manny frowned. "There are things you don't understand. Like extenuating circumstances. It's business one-oh-one."

The words didn't sound entirely natural coming out of Manny's mouth. I wondered if he was repeating something Victor had told him.

"Meaning what?" I asked.

"A business is something you gotta grow. Like a puppy. If it's going to succeed, it needs to be nurtured. So even though you're making money, the smart thing to do is turn around and put that money right back in. You're building some reserves . . . you know, like a cushion for when you need it later."

Right. Manny wasn't nearly as smart as he thought. It sounded as though he'd been snookered too.

"Larry didn't care about building reserves," I told him. "He just wanted his money. And Victor wouldn't give it to him. Despite all your fancy talk, I'm guessing he never gave you anything either."

Manny started to scowl. Then he quickly wiped his expression clean. "Maybe not, but there's a difference between me and Larry. I'm part owner

186

and he isn't. Which means when I help to build up this company, I'm building my own future too."

"Too bad you don't have a contract to prove that," I mentioned. "Especially after you spent the last year working without pay."

Manny didn't reply. Instead, he stood up and shoved his arm into the sleeve of his coat. His answers to my questions conveyed a very different attitude than his demeanor did. Manny didn't like the direction my probing had taken us—and apparently that last barb had really hit home.

Either that or the jolt of espresso was making him jumpy.

"Did Larry tell you about his lawsuit?" I asked.

Manny glanced at me. "Yeah, I heard about it."

"Are you part of it?"

He leaned down. When he spoke again, our faces were only inches apart. "Lady, I don't know where you get off asking me questions like that. How I handle my affairs is none of your damn business."

He'd already straightened and started to turn away when I posed one last question. "Have you ever been to the Westminster Dog Show, Manny?"

"What do you think?" he asked.

He didn't wait to hear my answer. It was just as well. Because although Manny seemed sure he'd kept his secrets safe from me, what I'd discovered was that he was the kind of man who was easily provoked to anger. Also that he wasn't someone I would want to confront in a dark alley. Or an empty men's room.

Manny slammed the door when he left the pub. A minute later I saw the white panel van peel out of the parking lot. I watched as he ran the stop sign on the corner and sped through the intersection.

It was a good thing Manny had already made his delivery. At least I didn't have to worry about the puppies' safety with him behind the wheel in his current mood.

Chapter 16

I finished the butterscotch scone. I probably should have wrapped the blueberry one in a napkin and taken it home with me, but instead I ate that one too. Since I'd skipped lunch I figured I wasn't doing too much damage to the day's calorie count.

But honestly? I don't even lie well to myself.

Once I was alone at the table, a barista approached and asked if I wanted to hold a puppy in my lap. Maybe a cute Chihuahua mix with big eyes and a curly tail? I declined politely. I wasn't even tempted.

She'd only gone a few steps away, however, when I called her back. "Change your mind?" she asked with a smile. She held the puppy out to me. "Button loves to snuggle. It's her favorite thing in the world."

I'll bet, I thought cynically.

"Is Clark Donnay here today?" I asked her.

The question seemed to surprise her, but she nodded. "Sure, he's in his office in the back."

"Good." I rose from my seat. "Clark's a friend of mine. I think I'll stop in and say hello."

Okay, so we weren't exactly friends. More like marginally acquainted. Clark and I had briefly met for the first time the previous weekend. But the barista didn't know that. She was happy to show me to the door marked "Employees Only" that led to the pub's back offices.

The rear part of the building consisted of a short hallway that led to just three rooms. The first one had an open door. Inside the room were several rows of stacked crates and two large, newspaper-lined ex pens. Each contained several puppies of various shapes and colors.

Most of the puppies were sleeping. Several were playing tug-of-war with a braided rag. Seeing me, they dropped the toy and raced to the side of the pen. The puppies jumped up on the wire barrier between us and began to bounce up and down on their hind legs, whining to be let out.

"Sorry, guys," I said softly. "I'm not here for you."

I didn't stop for a closer look. I *couldn't* stop for a closer look. We already had six dogs. I couldn't afford to bring home more puppies just because I felt sorry for them.

The door to the second room was slightly ajar. I knocked and stuck my head inside. "Hello?"

The office was small but meticulously neat. I saw a metal desk, a matching file cabinet, two upright chairs, and a coatrack holding a puffy down jacket and a colorful knitted scarf. A window in the far wall offered a view of the back parking lot.

Clark was sitting behind the desk. He was hunched over, staring at the computer screen in front of him. A tall mound of papers had been pushed to one side of the desktop. Beside the papers was an empty cardboard coffee cup that had been knocked askew at some point. Spilled coffee dribbled down its side and there was a ring of dried liquid around its base.

Clark looked up, then sat up. He slowly straightened his back and neck, then gave his shoulders a stretch. It looked as though he'd been bent over the computer screen for some time. "Can I help you?" he asked.

I stepped into the room. "I'm Melanie Travis. We met last weekend at the Poodle seminar in New York?"

"Yes, of course." Clark stood up and walked around his desk. He held out his hand for me to shake. "I invited you and your husband to stop by for a cup of coffee. I'm glad you took me up on it."

"I am too," I told him. "This place is great. I've been out front for the last half hour. I wondered if you had a few minutes to talk?"

"Sure, I suppose I can spare a little time. I'm swamped at the moment, but I could definitely use a break." Clark removed his glasses and carefully cleaned them before setting them back on his nose. At the seminar he'd been wearing a sport coat and khakis. Now he had on pressed jeans and a flannel shirt. The casual look suited him.

"I'm sorry for your loss," I said.

Clark looked faintly surprised. "You mean Victor?"

I nodded. I hoped he hadn't lost anyone else.

"Thank you. I appreciate that." He motioned me toward the chair in front of the desk, then stepped around and resumed his seat. "Victor and I were business associates. But that was pretty much the extent of our relationship."

I draped my coat over the back of the chair and sat down. "Even so, his death must have come as a shock to you. I wasn't sure I would find you here today."

Clark paused to consider his words before answering. "An unexpected death always comes as a shock. Especially so, in this case, when you consider the manner in which it took place. But with Victor gone, it's more important than ever that I make the effort to be here. Payroll, orders and requisitions, managing the pub itself— those were Victor's jobs. Now I have no choice but to bring myself up to speed as quickly as I can."

"It sounds as though you were more of a silent partner," I commented.

"You might say that. My contribution to the business was more financial than practical. Prior to this, I had no previous restaurant experience.

And to tell the truth, I'm not much of a dog person."

Even if he hadn't said that, I'd have already known. In his place, I'd have had puppies crawling all over the office. But unlike the room next door, Clark's space was quiet and pristine. And puppy free.

"Was that a problem for you?" I asked. "Considering the nature of the business?"

"Not at all. The puppies were Victor's thing, so he took care of that. And his instincts were spot on in that regard. Right away—as soon as the pub opened—we started drawing customers away from the local Starbucks. Sure, we sell good coffee. But it was clear from the beginning that the puppies were the real reason for our popularity."

"How did you and Victor happen to become partners?"

"He and I were acquaintances when he got the idea to open this place," Clark said. "Victor's enthusiasm was contagious. He could be quite the salesman, and it was a gift that stood him in good stead. He was looking for someone to partner with him on this venture and I decided to come on board. I thought the Pooch Pub looked like a good investment, and indeed it has proven to be one."

"So the Pooch Pub is turning a profit?" I asked.

He nodded. "Not for the first couple of years, of course. But right now I would say we're operating pretty solidly in the black. That's why it's important to ensure that Victor's loss doesn't cause any disruption to the business."

I hadn't expected Clark's reaction to his partner's death to be so cut-and-dried. Or maybe cold-blooded was a better word. He'd admitted that he and Victor weren't close. Now I wondered how solid their partnership had truly been.

Abruptly Clark noticed the empty coffee cup sitting on the side of his desk. He grimaced as he picked it up. After crumpling the cup in his large hand, he tossed it over his shoulder without looking. It landed in a trash can behind him.

"Nice shot," I said.

"These last couple of days I've had plenty of practice." Clark frowned at the ring of dried coffee that remained. "Lots of stuff to do around here."

"Was Victor a good partner?"

He glanced up. "You mean did he take good care of the business? Yes, good enough to make it thrive, which is what mattered to me. Victor wasn't above letting some stuff slide. Let's just say he was better at keeping on top of the jobs he liked than the ones he didn't."

"You've just described me too," I told him with a smile.

"And me," Clark returned. "I guess that's human nature, isn't it? Victor wasn't always the easiest partner, but he and I worked together well enough on most things. . . ."

"And the others?" I prompted when he let his voice trail away.

"Victor tended to fall in love with his own ideas. Like I said, he was a salesman. He hated to hear the word *no*. If there was something he wanted and couldn't have, he'd get annoyed pretty quickly. Sometimes I gave in just because it was easier than arguing. Other times, I had to hold firm—and remind him that a fifty-fifty partnership is a negotiation, not a dictatorship."

"It sounds as though you knew how to handle him."

"I guess you could say that."

"Do you think something like that could have led to Victor's death?" I asked. "Maybe he got into a disagreement with someone who refused to back down."

Clark went still. He sat and stared at me across the desk. After a long pause, he said, "What do you do for a living, Melanie Travis?"

"I'm a school teacher. A special needs tutor actually."

"So you're not a policewoman?"

"No."

"Nor a private investigator?"

I shook my head.

"I really hope you're not a member of the press."

"Certainly not," I told him.

"In that case, I'm wondering where all these

questions of yours are coming from. Last time we met, I don't recall you submitting me to a cross-examination."

"On Sunday, Victor was still alive," I pointed out.

"And that makes a difference to you?"

"It makes a difference to my Aunt Peg. The New York City police consider her to be a suspect in his death."

Clark pondered that briefly. "That's the Poodle lady you're talking about? The woman who was running the seminar?"

"That's right."

"And she and Victor had a problem with each other?"

"They did at one time," I told him. "But it was mostly over and done with long ago."

"Mostly?" he inquired.

Suddenly I was the one answering questions, rather than asking them. I preferred things the other way around. But I also wanted to keep Clark talking, so a little quid pro quo seemed more than fair.

"It appeared that Victor purposely scheduled his specialty show to conflict with Aunt Peg's seminar," I said. "He knew the show would be a big draw right before Westminster. And he wanted the attendance at the symposium to suffer because of it."

"The room looked pretty full to me," Clark commented.

"It was. I know Aunt Peg was pleased with the turnout."

"So then she had no reason to want to harm Victor."

"Of course not," I agreed. "That's the whole point. She didn't do it."

"And that's why you're here talking to me."

I started to nod, then quickly thought better of it. Clark had neatly laid a trap for me. And I'd almost fallen into it.

"You're trying to discover whether or not *I* might have wanted to kill my business partner." His expression was grim. "Is that it?"

"Victor Durbin wasn't a nice person," I said. "Most people who had any kind of dealings with him ended up wishing that they'd never gotten involved. It occurred to me you might feel the same way."

Victor pushed back his chair and stood. "I think it's time for you to leave my office."

I stood up too. It wasn't as if I had a choice. But I did have another question. One I really hoped I'd get an answer to.

"Are you aware that Victor was handing out shares in the Pooch Pub to people who were supplying him with puppies?"

Clark had started around the desk as if he meant to escort me to the door. Now he abruptly stopped walking. I took that as a no.

"Shares?" he repeated.

"Part ownerships, percentages of the profits," I clarified. "Five percent here, eight percent there. That kind of thing."

Clark frowned. It looked like that was news to him—news he wasn't happy to hear. I watched him make an effort to compose himself.

"What Victor chose to do with his half of our mutual enterprise wasn't my concern," he said stiffly.

"Until his business affairs begin to affect you," I pointed out. "Are you aware that one of your new 'partners' is initiating a lawsuit?"

"No, I wasn't." Clark's tone was clipped. "But he can hardly sue Victor now."

"He can probably sue Victor's estate, however. It would be a shame if the Pooch Pub was tied up in litigation for years, over an issue that you knew nothing about."

"That's not going to happen." Clark was walking again. In two steps we'd be at the door.

"How can you be so sure? Did you and Victor have a partnership contract?"

"Of course. I wouldn't have done business without one. We had an ironclad agreement. My lawyer wrote it, Victor's approved it, and he and I both signed it."

Which meant Clark was smarter than both Larry Bowling and Manny Garza. No surprise there.

"We also amended our wills," he continued.

"This eventuality was thoroughly addressed. In the case of either of our deaths, the partnership was terminated and full ownership of the Pooch Pub passed directly to the surviving partner."

Now it was my turn to stop in my tracks. "So now all this belongs to you?"

"That's right." Clark positioned a hand between my shoulder blades and gently pushed me through the doorway.

When his hand dropped away, I spun around. "So Victor Durbin's death made you a rich man."

I wasn't fast enough to see Clark's expression. The door was already swinging shut in my face. If I hadn't jumped back it would have hit me in the nose. I heard a small click as the lock turned.

Our conversation was over. *Dammit.* Just when things were really starting to get interesting. I hate it when that happens.

Chapter 17

I had no choice but to show myself out. When I emerged from the back of the pub, the barista who'd pointed me in the right direction gave me a smile. "Did you find him?"

"I did. Thanks. We had a nice chat."

She gave me a thumbs-up and turned to her next customer.

Puppies were tumbling around on the floor, so I was looking where I placed my feet as I made my way to the door. I didn't want to step on a puppy. Or trip over one. The place was still half filled with customers, so I threaded my way between the tables with care.

"Psst!"

I heard the sound but didn't immediately look up. Or look up at all, actually. A fluffy white puppy with a black button nose had just come galloping out from beneath a table and barreled into my foot. He seemed to think that was reason enough to grab the toe of my shoe in his mouth. Man, that puppy was cute. He wouldn't last here long.

"Pssst!" The sound was more insistent this time.

I gently disengaged the puppy's sharp baby teeth, then stood up and had a look around. A woman with a baseball cap pulled low over her face was seated at a small table near the window. Between the cap and the glare from the sun behind her, I couldn't see her face. But when I glanced in her direction, she lifted a hand and gave me a surreptitious wave.

Was she motioning to me? I couldn't imagine why. I turned and checked behind me. Maybe the woman was trying to get someone else's attention?

Nope. That wasn't it. No one else was even looking in our direction.

"Melanie!" The mystery waver hissed. "Over here!"

Okay, this was definitely odd. The woman obviously knew me. But who was she and what was she hissing about?

I walked over and slid into the empty seat opposite her. With the sun no longer in my eyes, I could finally see the woman's face. It was Mattie Gainer.

Though it was warm in the pub, Mattie was still wearing her coat. The collar was pulled up around her ears. Now that I'd sat down, she tipped her face downward again. I realized she was cuddling not one, but two, puppies in her lap.

"Mattie—" I began.

"Shhh!" She lifted a finger and held it to her lips.

"What are you doing?" I whispered.

"I'm undercover."

I must have heard wrong. "You're *what?*"

"Shhh! Not so loud. I don't want anyone to hear us."

"Who?" I glanced around the room.

Nobody was paying any attention to us. Much less listening in. Why would they? If I wasn't part of this conversation, I wouldn't have been interested in it either.

"I'm undercover," Mattie repeated. "Nobody's supposed to know who I am."

Okay, I'd bite. "Who are you?"

I was really hoping she'd say Spiderwoman. That would have been cool—and no more strange than the rest of this encounter.

That made Mattie look up. And roll her eyes. "Don't be ridiculous. You know who I am."

"What are you doing here?"

"Performing my civic duty."

So many questions. And still not a single sensible answer.

"What does that mean?" I asked.

Mattie leaned down and gently placed both puppies on the floor. Together, the pair scampered away. "This place is a puppy welfare travesty. I'm going to get it shut down."

"How?"

"Look around," she told me.

So I did. I didn't agree with the Pooch Pub's business model either. But I didn't see grounds for closing the place down. The puppies looked healthy and mostly well cared for. And assuming Clark had the proper licensing in place, the pub functioned in much the same way that a pet store did.

"Dogs and food are a terrible combination," Mattie whispered.

Tell that to the French, I thought.

"There must be a health code violation here somewhere," she grumbled. "If I have to sit here the rest of the afternoon, I'm going to find *something* to report."

"Good luck with that," I said.

She stared at me across the tabletop. "That's all you have to say? *Good luck?* I thought you might want to help."

"There's a health code inspection sticker posted near the front door," I pointed out. "I noticed it when I came in. The Pooch Pub got a good score."

"So what? Victor probably lied to the inspector. That's just the kind of thing he would do. Did you know that when this place first opened he told everyone that all the puppies came from a local rescue? He said he was giving them needed exposure so they could find good homes. There was even a feel-good story in the newspaper about what a humanitarian he was. What a total crock!"

At least we agreed about that.

Mattie frowned ferociously. "Later on, I confronted him about that crap, and do you know what he told me? That breeding puppies to sell here was a simple matter of supply and demand. He said he was just giving the market what it wanted."

"Victor was an awful person," I said.

"Tell me about it," Mattie snapped.

"But he's dead now. So I'm not sure what you hope to accomplish."

"I'm going to shut him down."

There didn't seem to be much point in mentioning that someone had already shut Victor down. Permanently.

"I'm sure you mean well—"

"Mean well?" Mattie interrupted me. "*Mean well?* Is that what you think this is about?"

"Isn't it?"

Her eyes narrowed. "Why are you defending Victor? How well did you actually know him?"

"I'm not defending Victor," I replied evenly. Usually Mattie's enthusiasm seemed like a good thing. But this conversation was beginning to wear me out. "I didn't like the man any more than you did. I'm simply pointing out the improbability of what you're trying to do."

"Don't be such a pessimist." She slumped back in her seat. "When it comes to getting what I want, I have my ways. Who said, 'Never underestimate the power of a woman with an idea?' Was it Eleanor Roosevelt?"

I hadn't heard that before. "I think it was you," I told her. "Right now. Nice sentiment. Well done."

"Please don't patronize me."

"I wouldn't dream of it." I started to rise. It was time for me to go.

"I asked you a minute ago how well you knew Victor." Mattie looked up at me. "You didn't answer. Were you one of his women?"

I sat back down in a hurry. "What does that mean?"

"You know."

"No. I really don't."

"Victor was a flirt," she muttered. Then she paused and drew herself up. Her shoulders squared. "No," Mattie said in a firmer voice. "He was more than a flirt. He was a pushy SOB."

"I didn't know that." I thought back to the encounters I'd had with Victor when he was still a member of PPC. They'd all taken place in a group setting, either at a dog show or a club meeting. "You mean he came on to you?"

"I wish that's all it was."

I swallowed heavily. And hoped she'd keep talking. "I'm listening," I said softly.

There was a long pause. I waited her out.

"I was so happy to join PPC," Mattie said after a minute. "But it wasn't long before I started to dread going to meetings. Victor would always find a way to corner me somewhere. And then he'd

. . . you know . . . put his hands where they didn't belong. When I protested, he'd just laugh and say it was an accident—even though we knew it wasn't. Victor knew exactly what he was doing."

"That's terrible." I exhaled a long breath. "I'm so sorry. Why didn't you say something?"

She sighed. "If the 'me too' movement had been around then, I probably would have. But at the time, I was a newcomer to the area and the club. Victor was a longtime member in good standing. No one would have believed me."

Not entirely good standing at that point, I thought. Victor was already feuding with the board. Though Mattie probably hadn't known that then. Thinking back, I could see how she might have been intimidated by him.

Mattie was right, though. The "me too" movement had changed a lot of things. Women now had a voice they'd never had before. Men who'd scoffed were now listening.

"I'm sorry," I said again. "I wish I'd known at the time."

"What could you have done about it?" she asked unhappily.

"I'd have told Aunt Peg." I didn't need to detail the kind of mayhem that would have ensued.

"I like to think that's true," Mattie said. "But I guess we'll never know. Victor left the club not long after that, so then I didn't have to worry about him anymore. I pitied the women who went on to join his new club, though. I hope one of them set him down good."

"I do too," I agreed.

"So that's why I'm here," Mattie announced. "Maybe I'm older and wiser now. Or maybe I just feel more empowered. But when I look back on that time in my life, it makes me sad. I let Victor take advantage of me. I let him make me feel like I was less of a person than he was. Something bad was happening and I did nothing to stop it. Well, not anymore."

I nodded.

"Look at this place," she said. "Something bad is happening here too. Puppies are being sold like chewing gum. People take a dog home, having given no more thought to the purchase than they did when they bought their coffee. It's abhorrent. Last time, I felt like I didn't have a voice. Now I refuse to shut up."

"Good for you," I said heartily.

"Good for me and good for the puppies," she replied. "Victor isn't going to get away with mistreating them the way he mistreated me. I'll make sure of that."

It wasn't until I was in my car on my way home to Connecticut that I began to wonder just how forceful Mattie's newfound sense of empowerment truly was. And what else it might have caused her to do to have her revenge on the man who'd wronged her.

• • •

I chose a route back from Tarrytown that took me through back country Greenwich. Since it was the afternoon before a dog show, I knew just where I would find Aunt Peg. Her young Standard Poodle bitch, Coral, was entered Saturday in White Plains. Today there would be plenty of preshow grooming to be done.

Coral had been shown in the puppy trim the previous summer. Now, as an adult, she was wearing a continental clip. A large mane coat covered the front half of Coral's body. There were rounded rosettes over her hip bones, bracelets of hair on her lower legs, and a pompon on the end of her tail. Her face, feet, and the rest of her body were all shaved to the skin.

Aunt Peg would have clipped Coral earlier in the week. Today was bath day. After that the Poodle's long hair would be meticulously blown dry.

Aunt Peg was the one who'd come up with the idea for her and Davey to team up and finish Coral's championship together. She did the majority of the pre-show prep work; then Davey took over Coral's care and management on show day. The two of them were still working on ironing out the kinks in that relationship.

Aunt Peg liked to micromanage every aspect of her dogs' lives—and her relatives' too, when she could get away with it. So things hadn't proceeded entirely smoothly thus far. But Coral had ended the summer having accumulated five points toward her championship and we were all pleased about that.

Coral's coat had been growing out for nearly five months. Tomorrow's show would be her adult debut. It felt like a long time since we'd had a Poodle in the show ring. We were all impatient to get back to it.

I didn't bother knocking on Aunt Peg's front door. I knew she'd be downstairs in her grooming room. With the big, freestanding dryer blowing at full strength, she wouldn't be able to hear me anyway. Her dogs heard my arrival, though. Zeke and Beau appeared in the hallway as I entered the house. I hung up my coat, then let the two Poodles escort me down the stairs.

Aunt Peg looked up as I entered the well-lit room. Coral was lying on top of a rubber-matted grooming table. Her eyes were closed—she was probably asleep. Coral's mane coat was already partly dry. The rest of it was covered by a damp towel, waiting to be dealt with shortly.

Aunt Peg was working on a small section, straightening the hair by sweeping her pin brush through it as a stream of hot air blew the coat dry. She didn't turn off the dryer. We would have to talk over it.

"This is a pleasant surprise," she said. "Have you come to work?"

"No way." I hoisted myself up on a low counter that was meant to hold grooming supplies. My grooming technique wasn't nearly as good as Aunt Peg's—and she never let me forget it. "I've come to watch *you* work. And to talk."

"That will do." Her gaze dropped to Coral, who'd lifted her head when we spoke. Aunt Peg smoothed the Poodle back into place and continued brushing. "You may entertain me."

One could only hope.

"How much do you know about the Pooch Pub?" I asked.

"The name sounds regrettably familiar," she said. "Is that Victor Durbin's place of business?"

I nodded.

"Then I know very little about it. And I'm profoundly grateful that I don't know more. Why?"

"Sam and I met one of Victor's partners at your seminar last Sunday. A man named Clark Donnay."

"Tall?" she asked. "African American? Sitting in the front row?"

"Yes, that's him."

"He introduced himself to me too. He complimented me on my speech. I had no idea he was a friend of Victor's."

"I'm not sure how friendly they actually were," I told her. "But they owned the Pooch Pub together. And now that Victor's gone, Clark has inherited the entire business."

"How very fortunate for him." She smiled speculatively.

"There are complications with that."

Aunt Peg's smile widened. She loved complications.

"Do you remember Larry Bowling?"

"Only the name. Isn't he the man Louise sent you to?"

"Precisely. Larry lives in Cross River and he's a member of the Empire Poodle Club. Louise said something about a dispute over unpaid stud fees. But Larry's problem with Victor turned out to be much bigger than that."

"Oh?"

"About two years ago Victor and Larry made a deal to start producing Mini and Toy Poodle puppies to sell at the Pooch Pub. Victor supplied the champion stud dog—"

"*Champion* stud dog?" Aunt Peg sounded shocked.

I nodded. "Victor thought the title was a good selling point."

"Selling point," she echoed faintly.

Aunt Peg looked ready to throttle someone. Hopefully not me.

"They used Victor's dog and Larry's bitches," I continued. "Larry also raised the resulting litters. In exchange for his time and effort, Victor offered Larry eight percent of the Pooch Pub's profits."

"Eight percent sounds like a lot," Aunt Peg

commented. "How many litters was Larry breeding in a year?"

"I didn't ask. But it doesn't matter. Because what Victor offered turned out to be a moot point. Larry was never paid anything."

Aunt Peg repositioned the towel, uncovering a new section of damp hair. Then she resumed straightening the coat. "Let me guess. Larry didn't think to ask for a percentage of the gross, and Victor told him that there were no profits to be divvied up."

"See?" I said happily. "You caught on right away. But Larry didn't. If he was as smart as you are, their feud and his lawsuit could have all been avoided."

"So Larry Bowling was suing Victor?" she asked with interest.

"Technically he's still in the threatening-to-sue stage. It didn't sound as though he'd gotten very far yet."

"He doesn't appear to be the brightest bulb in the box," Aunt Peg mused. "I wonder if his lack of legal redress left him feeling angry and frustrated. What sort of man was Mr. Bowling? Maybe the type who might have been tempted to take matters into his own hands?"

Chapter 18

I should have seen that question coming. Aunt Peg loved to leap ahead and draw conclusions before I'd had a chance to finish speaking. She was also sure that virtually everyone was capable of murder given enough provocation.

Which was a sobering thought even on a good day.

"Possibly," I told her. "But he's not the only one. Besides, Larry scoffed at the very idea of Westminster. He said he was nowhere near the show on Tuesday night."

"Oh pish," Aunt Peg replied. "Of course he said that. Even an idiot would know better than to admit to being in the vicinity of the body of a man he'd wanted to harm."

Once again, she moved the towel to expose a different area of the mane coat. Coral didn't even notice the change. Her lips ruffled as she blew out a breath. Her toes were wiggling too. I wondered if the Poodle was chasing a rabbit in her sleep.

"A man named Manny Garza made a similar arrangement with Victor," I said. "He was also supplying him with puppies."

"More Poodles?" Aunt Peg sighed.

"Not entirely. Manny's were Poodle mixes, Schnoodles and Cockapoos. But he was smarter than Larry. His deal included part ownership of the Pooch Pub."

"More complications." Now she sounded pleased.

"Yes, but Victor never paid him anything either."

"I'm not surprised. Who else?" She peered at me from across the table. "Victor was the kind of man who made enemies. I'm assuming there must be others who were nursing a grudge."

"Were you aware that Louise Bixby and Victor had a very public argument at the Empire specialty?"

"You mentioned something about that the other day," Aunt Peg said. "But I didn't want to hear details at the time. Now you can tell me all about it."

"Unfortunately, I don't know much. Bertie and I were too far away to hear what was being said. But Victor suddenly came stalking across the room and accosted her. That was how it started."

"I wonder what put a bee in his bonnet," Aunt Peg mused.

"According to Hannah Bly—she was the steward on that day—Louise had sent Victor a note."

"What did it say?"

I just shrugged. If I'd known that, I would have started with the information.

"Well that's not useful," Aunt Peg huffed.

"You and Louise are friends. Why don't you ask her yourself?"

"Louise and I are cordial acquaintances," she corrected me. "But I just might do that. Perhaps I'll run into her at tomorrow's show."

Perfect, I thought. That would give Aunt Peg something to do while Davey and Sam were readying Coral for the ring. Preparations always proceeded more smoothly when she wasn't hovering over Davey, critiquing every move he made.

She stood Coral up, then laid her back down on her other side. Now the right side of the Poodle's body was on top. Since that side faced away from the judge in the ring, it was always last to receive attention.

"Is that all?" Aunt Peg inquired, once she'd started brushing again.

"No. I saved the most interesting person for last."

"Who's that?"

"Mattie Gainer."

Aunt Peg looked up, surprised. She knew Mattie quite well. "Really?"

"Really. I ran into her earlier this afternoon at the Pooch Pub."

"How unexpected. What was Mattie doing *there?*"

"Apparently she was engaged in an undercover mission to gather evidence that would enable her to get the place shut down."

"Mattie told you that?" Aunt Peg's lips pursed. I think she was trying not to laugh. "Surely she was pulling your leg."

"She seemed serious enough to me. She was even wearing a disguise."

"A disguise?" She stared at me in disbelief. "A fake nose and a Groucho moustache perhaps?"

"Well, no," I admitted. "But Mattie did have on a baseball cap. And the collar of her jacket was pulled up over her face."

"I see." Aunt Peg was laughing now. "A baseball cap. That's what passes for a disguise these days? In my time, we were more creative when we wanted to remain undetected."

I didn't even want to think about the kinds of shenanigans Aunt Peg might have gotten up to when she was trying to remain unseen. I hadn't known her in her youth. But based on her behavior now, almost nothing would have surprised me.

"I'm not asking," I told her.

"Good, because I'm not telling," she said. "Let's get back to Mattie. But first, tell me about the Pooch Pub. Is the place a dump?"

"No. I wish it was, but it's not. The place is bright and clean, and the coffee is good. And while I despise the situation for the puppies' sake, their care seems to be decent enough."

"I guess that's something," Aunt Peg muttered. "In that case, Mattie will have her work cut out for her. She's a dear person, but sometimes I think she lets her enthusiasm override her good judgment."

"There's something else," I said. "It turns out that Mattie and Victor have a history."

Aunt Peg looked up. Her hand stopped moving. "What kind of history?"

"An unfortunate one. And one that took place right under our noses. Back when Victor was still a member of PPC."

"Years ago, then." She didn't sound mollified. "Mattie was new to the area. She'd just joined the club herself. I doubt that their memberships overlapped for more than a few months."

"Apparently that was enough time for Victor to corner her at meetings and put his hands on her."

Aunt Peg opened her mouth. Then closed it again. She looked utterly shocked. Her hand remained still, brush hovering above the damp hair. She should have redirected the dryer's nozzle when she stopped brushing. But obviously she wasn't thinking about what was best for Coral's coat.

"Are you sure you're right about that?" Aunt Peg demanded.

"That's what Mattie told me."

"I never noticed a thing."

"Me neither. Victor probably orchestrated things that way on purpose. He must have waited until we were all occupied elsewhere before making his move."

Aunt Peg glanced downward and frowned. She immediately went back to work. "Mattie was quite reserved when she first joined the club. You know what PPC is like. We have some strong personalities and nobody is shy about speaking her mind."

Certainly not Aunt Peg, anyway.

"I thought perhaps Mattie was intimidated by us," she mused. "I hoped she'd grow more comfortable, and more outgoing, as time went on. As indeed she has done."

"That's probably why Victor chose her to be his victim. He realized Mattie would be too cowed to say anything about his bad behavior to the rest of us."

"Damn the man!" Aunt Peg swore. All around the room, Poodle heads lifted. Coral's was among them. Aunt Peg barely seemed to notice. "Now I wish Victor was still around, so I could have the pleasure of punching him in the nose."

Aunt Peg seldom truly lost her temper—but when she did, watch out. I knew she would feel guilty that Mattie had suffered in silence. And that Victor had been allowed to harass the poor woman at her club—and on her watch.

"What if Mattie wasn't the only one?" she asked abruptly. "You don't suppose there were others, do you?"

That thought should have occurred to me too. "I hope not," I said fervently.

"Perhaps I'll make some discreet inquiries at tomorrow's show."

Louise Bixby's transgression was forgotten. Aunt Peg had a new mission now. More power to her, I thought, as I slipped down off the counter.

"It's been a couple of days," I said on my way out. "Have the police been back in touch?"

"No," Aunt Peg replied. "I haven't heard a blessed thing."

"Maybe that means you're no longer a suspect."

"That would be ironic, wouldn't it? Now when I suddenly have a reason to want to murder the man."

"I wouldn't go around saying that in public if I were you."

Aunt Peg just smiled and waved me out the door. I hoped she wasn't planning to stir up too much trouble.

Saturday's dog show was just twenty minutes away in White Plains. That, combined with the fact that Standard Poodles wouldn't be judged until afternoon, meant that we all had a chance to sleep late on Saturday morning.

Unfortunately Kevin didn't get the memo. He came flying into Sam's and my bedroom before seven a.m. Bud was with him. The two of them jumped up on the bed without breaking stride.

I managed to duck just in time. Sam's a heavy sleeper. He woke up with a loud "Ooof!" when Bud landed on his stomach.

"Time to go to the dog show!" Kevin announced.

"Not yet," I grumbled. I balled up my pillow and placed it over my head. "Go back to sleep."

"Can't. Bud woke me up. He wants to go to the show too."

I shifted the pillow to one side. "Sorry, sweetie, Bud can't come to the dog show with us. He's not entered."

"You could enter him." Kevin was undeterred. "Put him in a class for dogs with spots."

"I'm afraid that's not how it works," Sam said. He was holding one hand over his stomach. Bud weighed twenty pounds and was shaped like a football. My husband was going to be sore later.

"I see lots of dogs with spots at the shows," Kev said.

Of course he did. He stalked the Dalmatians. And sometimes the Pointers and English Setters.

Kevin sat down on the comforter. He crossed his arms over his chest. He was working himself up to a good sulk. "It's not fair. How come Davey gets to show a dog and I don't?"

"Because Davey's older than you are—"

"I'm *almost* five!"

"That's a great age," Sam told him. "And you have a birthday coming up. Lucky you."

Kev refused to be distracted. "Can I show a dog when I'm five?" he demanded.

"No—"

"Six?"

"Ummm . . ."

"*Seven?*" Kev's voice rose.

The Poodles were flattening their ears against their heads. I didn't blame them. If I'd been able to, I would have done the same thing.

"Look on the bright side," Sam told me. "At least Kevin can count."

In my opinion, nobody should be that cheerful before they've had their first cup of coffee.

"Bright side," I huffed. I slipped out of bed and headed for the bathroom. "Why don't you and Kevin go downstairs and let the dogs out? While you're doing that, you can finish explaining to him why Bud isn't coming with us."

"I'll put on the coffee too," Sam said to my departing back.

"Good idea."

Kevin was still sitting on the bed with his arms crossed. "Bringing Bud to the dog show is a *good idea* too."

I didn't turn around. Instead I shut the bathroom door behind me and headed for the shower stall. Sam would cope. He always did.

The venue for the dog show was a big concrete building with Ionic columns and wide front steps. Its interior arena was spacious and brightly lit. Best of all, there was plenty of parking out back.

Aunt Peg was bringing Coral to the show. We were schlepping the rest of the stuff we'd need: a grooming table, a big crate, and a tack box filled with grooming supplies. We'd done it many times before. It didn't take us long to unload.

Davey took the table, and Sam maneuvered the crate. I carried the tack box in one hand and a small cooler in the other. Kevin had a bag full of Legos that would keep him entertained for at least a couple hours. Teamwork, family style.

Once we were inside the building, Kevin ran on ahead. I was pretty sure he was searching for dogs that looked like Bud. Luckily for us, he ended up in the handlers' section.

Bertie saw us coming through the wide doorway. She lifted a hand and waved us over. The grooming area was crowded, but she'd saved us some space next to her setup. With just the one dog to prepare for the ring, we didn't need much.

"I can't believe you actually beat Peg to a dog show," Bertie said as we drew near. She had a Border Collie and a Samoyed out on her two tabletops. "That has to be a first."

"Kevin got us up early," I grumbled.

"Way to go, Kev!" she said. "Nice enthusiasm."

Bertie and Kevin high-fived. I guessed I was the only grouch who didn't like early mornings.

Aunt Peg's timing was perfect. As soon as we had everything set up, she arrived with Coral. She hopped the Standard Poodle up onto the table, then slipped off the collar and leash. Aunt Peg barely spared us—her family—a glance. She

222

was already scanning the rest of the big room to see who else was in attendance at the show.

"Get to work," she said to Davey. "I'll be back later to see how things are coming along."

Aunt Peg went marching away from the setup. Bertie stared after her thoughtfully. Davey was busy unpacking the tack box. Bertie turned and looked at him.

"How come Peg is trusting you to get Coral ready for the ring by yourself?" she asked. "What's up with that?"

Davey shrugged. "No idea. But it works for me."

"Aunt Peg is on the warpath," I told Bertie. "She has places to go and people to see."

Bertie enjoyed a good dustup as much as the rest of us. She grinned at that news. "Excellent. I want to hear all about it. Come and talk to me while I work."

I glanced at Sam. He shooed me away. As always, I wasn't indispensable to the process.

Besides, I'd already filled him in on what Mattie had told me. Also, this wasn't the kind of conversation the boys needed to overhear. So I set Kevin up on top of the crate with his plastic blocks. Then I walked around to the far side of Bertie's setup so we could talk.

She noted my new position. "A secret, then. That's even better."

I scooted up onto an empty table. "Do you know Mattie Gainer?"

"Well enough to say hello. We've crossed paths outside the Mini ring, but I don't think we've ever had a real conversation. Why?"

"Mattie had a problem with Victor Durbin."

"Like that's news." Bertie smirked. "Lots of people had problems with Victor."

"Her problem was a little more personal than most. Victor had a habit of cornering her at the PPC meetings and making rude advances."

"Yikes." She considered that with a frown. "It must have happened a while ago. Victor's been gone from PPC for years, hasn't he?"

"Yes, and good riddance. Even so, when Aunt Peg found out, I thought she was going to blow a gasket."

"I can imagine. PPC is her club."

"Now she's determined to find out if Mattie was the only one."

Bertie was brushing the Border Collie. She stopped and looked up at me. "Good luck with that. Even now, with more women opening up, it's still not the kind of thing most of us want to admit."

"Admit?" I was surprised at her choice of words. "The women aren't the ones who've done something wrong."

"True, but somehow it doesn't feel that way. Logically you know it's not your fault, but at the same time you can't help blaming yourself for letting it happen."

Bertie was one of the strongest, most independent women I knew. But before she got together with my brother, she'd been involved in an abusive relationship. One that she hadn't managed to escape until her ex-boyfriend had become violent. I knew she was speaking from experience.

I slipped down off the table. "Give me a hug."

Bertie extended her arm and pointed the pin brush at me, holding me at arm's length. "Stay back. I'm working over here."

"I don't care." I gathered her in my arms anyway.

After a few seconds, Bertie pulled away. "Don't embarrass me," she said. "It was over years ago."

"And yet you haven't forgotten how he made you feel."

"No, and I probably never will. But I learned something from the experience too. Nobody's ever going to make me feel that small, or that powerless, again. I won't allow it to happen. And as for you"—she cocked a brow in my direction—"have at it."

"At what?"

"Oh please," Bertie scoffed. "You think I don't know you're trying to figure out who killed Victor Durbin? I hope you find the guy. And when you do, I hope someone gives him a medal."

Chapter 19

Back at our setup, Sam and Davey had everything under control.

Coral was once again being brushed. When that was done, Davey would put in her topknot and spray up her hair. Then Sam would scissor the final finish to the Poodle's trim. My presence was utterly superfluous.

"I'm going to go wander around the show," I said. "Kev, do you want to come with me?"

He pushed his blocks to one side and jumped down off the crate. I reached out and wrapped my hand securely around his. Kev loved to slip away whenever there were spotted dogs nearby.

"If you see Aunt Peg, whatever you do, don't send her back here." Davey flashed me a grin. "We're doing fine without her help. Coral is going to look great in the ring."

"I'm sure she will," I agreed. "But this is only her first show as an adult, so don't get your hopes up too high."

"We won the last two times I showed her in the Puppy class," Davey said, sounding cocky. "Now that she's grown more hair, we're ready to pick up where we left off."

"It doesn't usually happen that way," I told him. "There's less competition in puppies than in the Open class, where you'll be today. And some of those bitches will be a lot more mature than Coral. To the judge, they'll look like more deserving winners. Coral is a very pretty Standard Poodle but she's still young, and showing in Open is a whole new ball game."

Sam was thumbing through the catalog. "Not to mention that there will be four professional handlers, including Crawford, in your class."

"Davey's going to win," Kev said firmly.

He had joined Davey and Coral in the ring when the puppy's picture was taken after her last win. The resulting photo was hanging on his bedroom wall. Now he wanted to do it again.

"Davey and Coral are going to have fun today," I said with equal firmness. "That's the goal."

"Fun?" Davey groaned. "You're missing the point."

"And you," I said, "are beginning to sound like Aunt Peg."

Kevin shrieked with laughter. Davey looked chagrinned. I knew he wouldn't like the comparison. But it served to make my point.

"Speaking of Crawford, where are he and Terry set up?" I asked.

"Over there." Bertie gestured toward a recessed alcove I hadn't previously noticed. "I didn't see them when I came in; otherwise I'd have been next to them."

Professional handlers, with multiple dogs to

prep and show, arrived at the dog show grounds as soon as they opened. This morning, Bertie had probably already been hard at work when Sam and the boys and I were home eating breakfast. As if to illustrate that, she swept the Border Collie off its tabletop and went striding toward the ring.

"You said we were going somewhere." Kevin tugged on my hand impatiently. He was staring in fascination at the nearby Springer Spaniel ring.

"Go." Sam motioned us away. "Davey and I have work to do."

We stopped at the Springer ring on our way to say hi to Terry and Crawford. That didn't take long. This show, falling a week after Westminster, didn't have a big entry. There were only a handful of Springers to watch.

"I like Bud better than those dogs," Kevin said at the end.

"That's a good thing, considering he's yours. Bud would be very disappointed if you found another dog you liked better."

Kevin shook his head. "Bud's the best. We should buy him a new toy." There was a row of concession stands along the far wall. They offered everything a dog owner could possibly need or want. "Something with a big squeaker in it," he added.

Sure. Because we wanted Bud to be able to make more noise.

Kevin looked up at me imploringly. I sighed.

"We'll take a look at the dog toys afterward," I told him.

Terry saw us coming. He leaned down and opened his arms. Kev dropped my hand and took off running. I was afraid he would bowl Terry over but the handler was rock steady. He planted a kiss on Kevin's nose.

"How's my favorite five-year-old?" he asked.

Kev giggled. "I'm only four. I won't be five until next month."

"Really?" Terry looked him up and down. "You're so big I thought you might be turning six."

That made Kevin shriek with delight. More than anything, he wanted to be a big kid.

Terry rose to his feet. I didn't get a kiss. Not even a hug. I guess he'd used up my family's quota on my son.

"I see we're up against Coral in bitches," he said to me. "How does she look?"

"Pretty . . . but maybe a little immature."

"Good. A win today would finish Crawford's bitch and he's hoping to get it done."

I glanced around. Several Standard Poodles, including their Open bitch, were out on tabletops in various stages of grooming. There was no sign of the handler, however. "Where's Crawford?"

Terry waved vaguely toward the other end of the room. "At the Pom ring. He'll be back in a bit."

"Your hair looks pretty, Terry," Kevin said.

Terry leaned down again, so he could talk to Kevin eye to eye. "Thank you. I'm glad you like it."

"I'm surprised to see it's still purple," I mentioned. "I thought that was a Westminster thing."

"It was. But then I decided I liked it. So I kept it this way."

"Are you going to change it back before the wedding?"

Monday was Valentine's Day. And dog show people were always busy on weekends. So Monday was the perfect day for Terry and Crawford to get married.

"We'll see." Terry's eyebrows waggled up and down. Thankfully they weren't purple too. "It annoys Crawford so much that I'm tempted to leave it. Just imagine the wedding pictures! You know me. I hate to get lost in a crowd."

As if anyone believed that could ever happen.

"How's the wedding planning coming along? Is everything all set?"

"I should hope so. It's only two days away."

Terry didn't sound concerned in the slightest. I couldn't decide if that was a good thing or a bad thing. Terry possessed many admirable traits but a gift for organization wasn't among them. As long as he and Crawford ended up married to each other at the end of the day, I supposed that was all that mattered.

"I was hoping you'd ask me to help out with the cake testing," I said.

His eyes skimmed up and down my body. "You don't need the extra calories."

That comment was rude. I really wanted to call him out on it. And I would have if it wasn't true.

"What about the decorations?" I asked instead. "Bertie's expecting big red hearts, and lots of little cupids running around."

"That sounds like fun." Terry grinned. "You can volunteer Kevin. We'll dress him up in a tiny toga, give him a bow and arrow, and let him terrorize the guests."

My son with weaponry? Definitely not a good idea.

Kevin had been amusing himself with a glossy dog magazine he'd found on top of a nearby crate. Now he heard his name and looked up. "Me?"

"No, not you. Another Kevin," I told him. That's what's called a mother's lie. It's like a white lie, but more benign. We've all used them. "Keep reading, honey."

I turned back to Terry. "You're not even going to give me a hint what to expect? Will there be dancing Poodles? A full symphony orchestra? Will you be carried down the aisle to Crawford in a sedan chair?"

"Oh *please*. A sedan chair?" Terry could scoff all he wanted. I could have sworn he looked intrigued. "Credit me with some taste."

"Says the man with purple hair."

He reached up and touched his aubergine locks. "I like my purple hair. And as for the wedding, you and Sam will just have to come and see."

"We wouldn't miss it," I said.

I glanced back over my shoulder, Crawford was nowhere in sight. And Kev was still looking at dog pictures. That meant I still had a few minutes to talk.

"I want to ask you about Victor Durbin," I said.

"Of course you do," Terry replied. "I figured that was why you came over here."

Ouch. I frowned at him. *"Really?"*

"For Pete's sake Melanie, the man died at a dog show. Does anyone doubt that you're going to get in everyone's business about it?"

Apparently not.

"Just one question. You told me you'd heard that Victor was going to be stepping down as president of the Empire Poodle Club. Did you ever find out why?"

Terry shook his head. "I didn't even try. After what happened, I figured it didn't matter anymore."

"You said you thought it must be bad, though. What if it was something that led to Victor's death?"

"At a Poodle club?" Terry sounded skeptical. He picked up a slicker brush and began to rake through a brown Mini's back bracelets.

"I heard that Victor was falsifying the club's membership records. He'd gotten EPC accredited under false pretenses."

"That's interesting," Terry glanced up. "I can see how that would make the other members mad enough to want him to step down. But it doesn't sound like grounds for murder."

He was probably right.

"Who told you that?" Terry asked.

"Hannah Bly. She's the club treasurer."

"She was also the steward at their specialty last weekend," he said. "You know, the woman who was standing in the ring trying to look like she was just about anywhere else when Victor and the judge went at it?"

"You saw that?"

Terry grinned. "Everybody saw it. How could we help it? We were hanging around waiting for the Toy judging to start."

"Did you hear what the two of them were arguing about?"

"I wish! But sadly, no. I was at the ring a minute earlier picking up our armbands. But by the time the fracas started, I'd returned to the setup."

"I asked Louise Bixby. She said it was just a misunderstanding. And that Victor was the kind of guy who liked to draw attention to himself."

"Well, sure. But at his own show? That seems like an odd choice." Terry sounded skeptical again. Once again, I couldn't blame him.

"When I was talking to Hannah, she told me that Louise sent Victor a note. And that was what had brought him storming over to the ring."

"Hmm," said Terry.

"What?"

"You know I said I'd just been at the ring to pick up our numbers?"

I nodded.

"There was a bit of a backup, and several of us were there waiting. Hannah was busy at the other end of the judge's table writing something. Then she folded the paper and handed it to someone outside the ring."

That was interesting. "Who?"

Terry shrugged. "I don't know. I wasn't really paying attention. It didn't matter at the time. I just wanted my armbands."

"Hannah could have been writing it for Louise," I mused. "Maybe that's how she knew there was a note." Except that Hannah had also told me she was just as baffled about the cause of the argument as I was. It was all very confusing.

"This is boring," Kevin announced. He'd finished thumbing through the magazine and set it aside. "I thought you said we could buy Bud a toy."

"We're going to," I said. "Any minute now."

Then I saw Crawford making his way back from the ring with the Pomeranian under his arm. It looked like it was time for me to get moving.

"We'll see you at the Standard ring," I told Terry.

"You'll understand if I don't wish you luck," he said with a wink.

"Ditto," I shot back.

Kevin led the way to the concession stands. When that child wanted something, he had a one-track mind. The first booth we came to sold a variety of canine supplies. I was happy to see there was a large selection of squeaky toys for him to choose from.

Kev bypassed the bin of fuzzy toy mice. He ignored the long cloth snake with beady eyes. Instead, he went straight for a big yellow rubber chicken that was hanging from a hook. He took the toy down and squeezed it to see what would happen.

The squeal that chicken emitted was loud enough to make me jump. Kevin just grinned. "This one."

"You're sure?" I uttered a silent prayer. There was always a chance he could change his mind.

"This one," he repeated.

"Bud's a little dog. That chicken is pretty big."

"He can drag it," Kev said happily. "Bud won't mind."

I dug out my wallet and paid for the toy. Kevin declined the salesman's offer of a bag to put it in. Instead, as we stepped away from the concession stands, he clutched the rubber chicken in his hands and squeezed it again.

Every dog in the vicinity whipped around to have a look. Even those in nearby rings. *Oops.* The handlers looked at us too. Actually they glared. They were not amused.

"I'll take that." I lifted it out of his hands. "You can have it back when we get home."

When we got to the setup, Coral was standing up on her table. Her topknot was in. Her mane coat had been sprayed up. Sam was watching as Davey used a pair of large curved shears to perfect the finish on her trim.

Even from afar, Coral's balance, her lovely hindquarter, and her pretty face were evident. But when I compared her to Crawford's Open bitch, Aunt Peg's Poodle looked young. And perhaps not quite as ready to win as she would be in a few months' time.

"Mom bought me a chicken!" Kevin cried gleefully.

More heads whipped around. Davey barked out a laugh. Sam looked appalled. He couldn't seriously believe . . . ? Apparently he did.

Give me some *credit,* I thought. Besides, where did he think I was going to find a chicken at a dog show?

I held up Bud's toy. "It's rubber," I said.

"Thank God for that," Sam muttered.

"You might not say that after you hear how much noise it makes."

Davey carefully lifted the shears away from

Coral's coat. He motioned to his little brother. "Go ahead."

I snapped my arm upward, beyond Kev's reach. "Not here. We nearly caused a riot over by the rings. You can hear what it sounds like when we get home."

"Who caused a riot?" Aunt Peg asked, coming up behind us. Her gaze swung my way. "You?"

"Not on purpose. The rubber chicken was the real culprit."

She leaned down and examined Kev's purchase. Her fingers poked the chicken's bald yellow body. "My dogs would tear that ugly thing to pieces," she said with a sniff.

"Ours probably will too," Sam agreed.

"It was Kev's choice," I told them. "It's a new toy for Bud."

"Good." Sam brightened. "He can drag it under the couch and leave it there."

Aunt Peg propped her hands on her hips. She looked around the setup. "So now I see what happens when I leave you lot to your own devices. Why is everybody standing around here talking about rubber chickens when the judging starts in five minutes?"

Chapter 20

That got us all moving in a hurry. Aunt Peg let Davey unwrap Coral's ears, hop her down from the table, and then walk her to the ring without any interference on her part. Maybe she was learning something, I thought. Maybe we all were.

Sam took Kevin's hand. The two of them led the way, clearing a path so that no one would jostle Davey's ring-ready Poodle. I fell in behind with Aunt Peg.

"What did you find out?" I asked.

"Not as much I wanted to. Unfortunately, this isn't a large show. Louise isn't here at all. I found a number of people who knew who Victor was—which isn't surprising considering the current situation. But only a few of them had actually known him when he was alive."

"Were any of them women?"

"Four, which is a regrettably small sample. And none had anything useful to say." Aunt Peg sighed. She didn't deal well with frustration. "I poked and prodded to no avail. I couldn't come up with a single complaint about Victor's behavior."

"I assume your questions weren't too subtle?"

Aunt Peg slanted me a look. One I'd seen many times before. That was a hard no.

We reached the Poodle ring. The Open Dog class was already being judged. There were just two in it. Sam went to get Davey's number from the steward. Davey was standing off to one side with Coral. One of his hands held her balled-up leash, and the other was cupped around the Poodle's muzzle. The two of them looked totally relaxed.

"Just because none of the women would confess to you doesn't mean nothing happened," I said.

"What is that supposed to mean?" Aunt Peg demanded. "Why shouldn't they talk to me? I'm a perfectly lovely conversationalist."

Who sometimes left people feeling like they'd been run over by a Mack truck. Delicate subjects were not Aunt Peg's forte.

"I was discussing the situation with Bertie earlier," I said. "She reminded me that many women are embarrassed to admit they've let themselves be taken advantage of. They think it makes them look stupid, or that people will think it's their fault it happened."

Aunt Peg reared back. Her expression froze. "*Bertie?* How would she know anything about that?"

Abruptly I realized what I'd said. A quick change of subject was needed. "Oh look! Winners Dog is being judged."

Aunt Peg flicked a glance toward the ring. "The

Open dog will win," she said as if any idiot could see that. "Now back to Bertie. Talk to me."

"Umm . . ."

Not only was I the idiot in question, now I sounded like one. Inside the ring, Aunt Peg's prediction quickly proved true. The Open dog took the points.

"Don't you want to wish Davey good luck?" I asked.

"Davey already knows he has my felicitations." She glared down at me. "Quit stalling and tell me what happened."

I was about to try another dodge when fate lent a hand. The sole entry in the Puppy Bitch class was absent. I gestured toward the ring. "I can't talk now. The Open bitches are going in."

This time I was successful in diverting Aunt Peg's attention. Immediately our conversation was put on hold. As the four bitches filed into the ring, she and I moved up to stand beside Sam and Kevin at the rail.

Terry was holding Crawford's specials dog. He came over to watch with us. "There were two points in dogs," he said in a low voice. "That would be enough to finish Crawford's bitch. Praise the Lord!"

I turned and stared at him. Terry wasn't a religious person. The comment seemed quite out of character.

"That bitch is the bane of my existence," he

muttered. "She chews her hair and barks all night. The sooner we can zip off her coat and send her home, the happier I'll be."

Aunt Peg watched as the judge sent the four Standard Poodle bitches around the ring together. "Mr. Kenny would have to be blind not to put up Crawford's bitch," she decided. "And, unfortunately for our chances today, he is not."

"What about Coral?" Sam asked.

Aunt Peg paused briefly. She considered her own bitch with an impartial eye—her judge's eye—before responding. "Coral looks well in there. Quite lovely, really. She makes me proud to be her breeder. And Davey's doing a very creditable job. But today, she lacks the other bitch's maturity—and her abundant hair. And of course Crawford can handle rings around everyone else. No, I would say that today belongs to his bitch."

None of us were surprised when once again Aunt Peg's prediction was spot on. Crawford's bitch won the class. Coral and Davey placed second. Since Open was the only bitch class with an entry, Crawford's Standard Poodle was automatically Winners Bitch. Davey and Coral were Reserve Winners.

"Praise the Lord!" Kevin cried out as the judge handed Crawford two ribbons, one blue and the second one purple.

It appeared to be our day to draw startled

glances—including one from Crawford. Sam was biting his lip to keep from laughing. Terry lost that battle. I heard a loud guffaw come from behind us.

I leaned down and quickly shushed Kev as Terry hurried over to the gate to switch Poodles with Crawford. The handler would show his champion in the Best of Variety competition. Terry, as assistant, would take the Winners Bitch.

"Not yet," I told Kev. "She still needs to go Best of Winners."

Davey exited the ring with his ribbons. He stared at us, his family, with a mixture of annoyance and embarrassment. Briefly it looked as though he might try not to acknowledge our presence. Then curiosity won out, and Davey brought Coral over to where we were standing.

"Praise the Lord?" he said incredulously. "What was *that* about?"

"I'll explain later," I told him, eyes still on the ring.

Aunt Peg patted her chest and Coral jumped up. Her front feet nearly reached Aunt Peg's shoulders. Peg ruffled her hands through the Poodle's coat. Coral was finished showing for the day. It no longer mattered if her hair got mussed.

"Sorry," Davey said. He handed Aunt Peg the two ribbons.

"Don't be silly," she replied. "You have nothing to be sorry about. You did a fine job of handling

242

her. Coral looked good and so did you. Best of all, the two of you are becoming an excellent team."

"But we didn't win."

"So what? You were beaten by a more deserving bitch. There's no shame in that."

Davey's eyes widened. He turned to look at me. *No shame in that?* he mouthed silently.

I understood his confusion. Aunt Peg was a fierce competitor. She was never complacent about a loss. But she was also honest enough to acknowledge when her Poodle had been fairly beaten.

Or maybe she was just mellowing in her old age.

Crawford won Best of Variety with his champion. Terry handled the Winners Bitch to Best of Winners. As he stood in the ring waiting to receive his ribbon, Terry clasped his palms together. His fingers pointed upward as if in prayer. He looked disappointed that Kevin didn't treat him to a repeat performance of the invocation.

Crawford and Terry stayed behind to have pictures taken with the judge. The rest of us headed back to the setup. Aunt Peg waylaid me along the way.

"Bertie," she said again in a tone that brooked no argument. "Tell me."

I seldom kept mum about confidences I learned

from suspects. But I never spilled my friends' secrets. Not even within the family.

I shook my head. "I can't. It's not my story to tell. It's up to Bertie. You'll have to ask her."

"If she wanted me to know, I presume she would already have told me."

"Precisely," I said.

"Just tell me one thing." Aunt Peg laid a hand on my arm. She pulled me to a stop. "If the culprit is your brother—my nephew, Frank—there's going to be hell to pay."

Thank goodness, that question was easy to answer.

"It wasn't Frank," I said.

"Victor?"

"No, not him either. It was something that happened years ago."

Aunt Peg looked pensive. Like me, she'd known Bertie for a long time. "I shall have to think about that."

Good. Maybe that would keep her busy for a while. And the rest of us could have some peace.

Or not.

Aunt Peg called early the next morning. Sunday morning. When Sam and I had once again had every expectation of sleeping in. And again, it didn't happen.

Sam picked up the phone. He opened one eye to squint at the caller's name. "It's for you," he said. He handed me the phone, turned over, and promptly went back to sleep.

"I had a perfectly marvelous idea," Aunt Peg announced.

Early on a dark Sunday morning in February, it was hard to think of any idea as marvelous. I levered myself up into a sitting position anyway. I was awake now.

Faith jumped up on the bed to join me. She liked to listen while I talked to Aunt Peg. More than my husband did, at any rate. I buried my fingers in the Poodle's thick coat and massaged her shoulders.

"If this is still about Bertie, I'm not discussing it," I said into the phone.

"Certainly not," Aunt Peg replied. "That's yesterday's news. Bertie and I had a long conversation last night. Today you and I are going to visit Olivia Wren."

"We are?"

"Of course we are. Olivia and Victor's mother are the closest of friends. I'm sure Olivia will have spent the last week comforting Bonnie in her time of loss. Who knows what tidbits of useful information she might have picked up."

Aunt Peg was right. That wasn't a bad idea at all.

"When are we going?" I asked.

"How would I know that?"

"I thought you had a plan."

245

"No, I had an idea. The two things are entirely different."

I sighed under my breath. "Are you going to make a plan?"

"Of course." She sounded surprised that I even had to ask. "I just have to confirm things with Olivia. Goodness, Melanie, it's not even seven o'clock yet. On Sunday, no less."

"You noticed," I said drily.

"Give me a couple of hours. I'll call you back."

Abruptly the connection severed. I set the phone down on the night table.

"Aunt Peg has a plan," I told Faith. Her plush tail flapped up and down on the comforter.

"Peg always has a plan," Sam muttered from the other side of the bed. I guessed that meant he hadn't fallen back asleep. "It sounds like you're going out later."

"Apparently I am." I pushed back the covers and slid out of bed. "But first I'm going to make coffee."

Olivia Wren lived in Fairfield on a piece of property that had been in her family for six generations. The house was colonial in design, with a square center block that had been built in the mid-1800s. The roofline had four chimneys, one in each corner. An old barn out back looked as though it now served as a garage.

It was Sunday afternoon and Aunt Peg and I

arrived together in her minivan. She parked on the side of the gravel driveway and we both got out.

"Wow." I stood and stared at the house. Aunt Peg had filled me in on its history on the way there. "This place is amazing."

"It is indeed," Aunt Peg agreed. "Each time I visit I feel as though I'm taking a step back in time. Olivia's ancestors participated in the American Revolution. I believe they were acquainted with Paul Revere."

"I'm impressed," I said.

"As well you should be."

Olivia greeted us at the door with a warm smile. She was a small woman but she wasn't frail. Dressed in corduroy pants and a chunky fisherman's knit sweater, she looked casual and comfortable. There were cozy shearling slippers on her feet.

"How lovely of you both to drop by," Olivia said as if she'd been the one to initiate the invitation. Two Toy Poodles, one silver and one white, were dancing around her legs. Their tails were wagging like mad. "Please come in. I don't believe you've met Winkie and Charles?"

As she closed the door behind us, I squatted down on the wide-plank floor and held out my hand. Charles, the silver Toy, immediately came over to say hello. Winkie was busy checking out Aunt Peg's boots.

"Charles is the official greeter." Olivia gazed

down at the pair fondly. "He loves everybody at first sight. Winkie prefers to wait and see if you pass muster before offering you her friendship. They are the last of my Toy Poodle line. When they're gone, I don't know what I will do."

"Hopefully that won't happen for a long time," Aunt Peg told her. "But when it does, let me know. We'll think of something together."

Olivia led the way into a spacious living room dominated by a stone fireplace that looked big enough to roast a pig in. Once again, I stopped and stared.

"That's original to the house," she said. "As are the interior beams, most of the flooring, and even some of the furniture."

We all chose seats. Olivia sank down on a plush couch. "Of course, not the pieces in this room," she added. "Here, I've decorated entirely for comfort—a concept that would have been foreign to my early ancestors."

She patted the cushion beside her. Winkie bounced up in the air and landed on the couch. Charles had deserted me. Now he was lying down beside Aunt Peg's foot. It figured.

"We wanted to talk to you about Victor," Aunt Peg began.

"So you said on the phone. And while I'm always happy to see you, Peg, I'm not sure I have anything to tell you that you wouldn't already know."

"You mentioned at the seminar that you're friends with Victor's mother," I said. "How is she doing?"

"Not well." Olivia sighed. "Victor's death was a huge shock. Bonnie lost her husband more than a decade ago, so she's coped with loss before. But a parent never imagines that she will outlive her child."

"Was Victor an only child?"

"Yes. And Bonnie is the first to admit that she spoiled him terribly. Perhaps that's why he grew up believing that everything he wanted was his by right. Victor wasn't an easy man to get along with. But murder?" Olivia shook her head in disbelief. "I could never have foreseen something like that."

"Have the police been in touch with Bonnie about their investigation?" Aunt Peg asked.

"No, but she and I arranged things that way on purpose," Olivia told us.

"Oh?" Aunt Peg said with interest.

"As you might imagine, Bonnie is not at her best right now. She didn't want to have to devote her limited energy to keeping abreast of new details and developments. She asked if I would mind stepping in to act as her intermediary with the authorities. Of course I wanted to help in any way I could, so I acquiesced immediately."

"Well done, you." Aunt Peg sounded impressed. "I wish I'd thought of that."

Right. Like that would have worked.

"You don't know Victor's mother," I pointed out. "And besides, the New York police view you as a suspect."

Olivia looked appalled. "Surely not!"

"Someone at the Empire Poodle Club informed the detectives that Victor and I were mortal enemies," Aunt Peg told her.

"That's ridiculous," said Olivia. "Who would do such a thing?"

Aunt Peg cocked her head to one side. "Actually I was hoping you might be able to tell me."

Chapter 21

M e?" Olivia's voice faltered. "How would I know?" Yes, how would Olivia know? I wondered. I glanced at Aunt Peg. What was she up to now? And why did she never warn me about these things in advance?

"You've been a good friend to Bonnie for many years," Aunt Peg said. "And at one time, you were quite close to Victor too. I believe he was your godson, wasn't he?"

Olivia nodded. Her hand reached for the Toy Poodle at her side. She cradled Winkie close.

I knew that move. I'd used it often enough with Faith. The older woman was seeking comfort from her dog. Wherever Aunt Peg was going with her questions, she was on the right track.

"Perhaps you might have even played the role of his fairy godmother?" she queried.

"I'm afraid I don't understand," Olivia said.

"I've spent quite a bit of time thinking about Victor Durbin over the last few days," Aunt Peg told her. "More time than I've devoted to him in years. Certainly more time than he deserved."

I tamped down a smile. Not that it mattered, no one was looking at me. But I knew just how she felt.

"Victor was a man whose ideas were always

251

more grandiose than his resources," Aunt Peg continued. "So I found myself wondering where he might have found the money to open his own business. Even with a partner, that had to have been an expensive undertaking. Then I remembered something you'd once mentioned when we were talking about investments. Victor used your seed money to open the Pooch Pub, didn't he?"

For a moment, I thought Olivia was going to deny it. Then her spine stiffened. She gazed calmly across the room at Aunt Peg. "At the time, I thought I was doing a good thing. Victor came to me with the idea. He'd written up a proposal for me to read. It was all very professional. He wanted me to invest in his vision—but quietly, behind the scenes."

Of course he would set it up like that, I thought. Victor always did want to have things all his own way.

"Meaning that you wouldn't have any say in the operation of the café?" Aunt Peg asked.

Olivia nodded. "In the proposal, the puppies were homeless dogs in need of rescuing. Victor told me he would get them from the pound and local rescue groups. There was certainly no mention of breeding Poodles—much less Poodle mixes—to be offered for sale. I would never have condoned that."

"When you discovered what Victor actually

intended to do, did you try to withdraw your investment?" I asked.

"Of course I did. I didn't want any part of it. Victor just laughed. He told me I was lucky to be involved with someone who could spot up-and-coming trends. He treated me like I was a dotty old woman who didn't have a single sensible thought in her head."

"I'm sorry that happened to you," said Aunt Peg. "It must have been a terrible way for you to find out just how nasty Victor could be."

"Maybe I am a dotty old woman," Olivia said unhappily. "Because it never occurred to me that Victor would betray me like that. I'd known him since he was a child. I was well aware of his faults. But previously, he'd always treated me with respect. I had no idea he thought so poorly of me."

She looked so dejected that I couldn't help but feel sorry for her. "You aren't the only person whose investment in the Pooch Pub brought them nothing but grief," I said.

"Perhaps that should make me feel better, but it doesn't." Olivia sighed. Then she turned back to Aunt Peg. "Victor and I were no longer close at the time of his death. In fact, quite the opposite. My relationship with Bonnie is very precious to me, but I had distanced myself from her son. So I'm afraid I wouldn't have any idea who was telling tales about you behind your back."

"I can appreciate that," Aunt Peg replied. "What will become of your investment now that Victor's gone?"

"It looks like I'll never see a penny of it back." Olivia lifted Winkie into her lap. Her fingers stroked the Toy Poodle's feathered ears absently. "My accountant is talking about a write-off."

"Have you met Victor's partner, Clark Donnay?" I asked. "He now thinks he's the sole owner of the Pooch Pub."

At least that was what he'd told me. But at this point, who knew if anyone was telling the truth?

"That man." Olivia's eyes narrowed. "I told the police they should focus their investigation on him."

"Why do you say that?"

"Clark and Victor were always at loggerheads over something. Even before the Pooch Pub opened, there were problems between them. Then working together every day led to even more friction. Victor often complained about him to Bonnie. If someone was angry enough at Victor to want to kill him, it was probably Clark."

"Plus, he's a man," Aunt Peg pointed out.

Olivia's gaze cut her way. "I'm surprised at you, Peg. I would think you, of all people, would believe that women are capable of doing everything men can do."

"We never heard any details about Victor's death," I said. "All we know is that he was stabbed during the dog show. It seemed like something that might have been easier for a man to accomplish."

Olivia digested that. "If you'd like to hear it, I'll tell you the rest," she said. "It's not for the faint of heart, though. Are you sure you want to know?"

Aunt Peg and I both nodded. I tried not to look too eager.

"Victor was stabbed in the stomach. It appeared that his assailant must have taken him by surprise because there were no defensive wounds on his hands. The only sign that there might have been a struggle was that Victor had a very badly bruised finger."

Abruptly I gulped. Aunt Peg and I shared a look. With everything that had happened since, I'd almost forgotten about Aunt Peg's encounter with Victor outside Madison Square Garden the night before he died.

"You don't say," Aunt Peg remarked.

"The autopsy did turn up something unusual, however," Olivia added.

She had our full attention.

"Victor had a very high level of THC in his blood when he died."

"THC?" I frowned. The letters didn't mean anything to me.

Aunt Peg was quicker on the uptake. "As in marijuana?"

Olivia nodded. "Bonnie and I were as surprised as you are. The detectives questioned us both about it. They wanted to know if Victor was a habitual user."

"Was he?" I asked, still reeling from this latest revelation.

"No. In fact, I can't imagine anything less likely. Victor was a man who wanted to control any situation he was in. To do that, he needed a clear head. He didn't drink to excess and he certainly wouldn't have used drugs."

"What did the police say to that?" Aunt Peg asked.

"It's possible he could have been given the drug without his knowledge. Perhaps someone convinced him to ingest something that contained it. The dose was quite large. That much THC would have made Victor drowsy and confused. He also might have felt weak or dizzy."

Now *that* was interesting.

"Those things would have made it easy for someone to overpower him," I pointed out.

"The police concluded the same thing," Olivia told us. "The crime could have been committed by almost anyone, as long as he or she had sufficient motivation to get the job done."

"Quite so," Aunt Peg agreed. "Do they have any suspects?"

"Other than you?" Olivia asked mildly. "I do know there's a list. The detectives are not inclined to tell me who's on it. All I know is that Bonnie is anxious for them to finish their investigation so she can lay her son to peace."

"Amen to that," Aunt Peg said quietly.

"What do you make of that?" I asked Aunt Peg on the way home.

Her gaze slid across the front of the minivan to focus on me. Considering the rate of speed at which we were traveling, I'd have preferred if she'd kept her eyes on the road. "Which part?"

"All of it, I guess."

Olivia had given us a lot to think about.

"The discovery of the THC in Victor's blood is puzzling to me," Aunt Peg said. "I quite agree with Olivia that Victor was all about being in charge. I don't doubt for a minute that he would shun the use of recreational drugs."

"So someone slipped him something."

"It appears so. I'm guessing it was someone he knew. I doubt Victor would have accepted the food or drink otherwise."

"The drug could have been put in his drink when he wasn't looking," I pointed out. "Westminster was very crowded. Maybe Victor was socializing in one of the bars. Someone steps over and jostles him . . . and voila."

"It would have taken planning to pull that together." Aunt Peg was thinking out loud. "And probably someone who was familiar with Victor and his habits. Let's not forget that having drugged him, the killer would then have needed to maneuver Victor away from the crowds to a secluded area. Even if he was feeling fuzzy—perhaps especially if he wasn't quite right—Victor wouldn't have gone with someone he didn't trust."

"Speaking of trust," I said, "I feel sorry for Olivia. She tried to help Victor. Then he used her money to create something he knew she would be morally and ethically opposed to. That must have come as a real blow."

Aunt Peg slanted me another look. "Are you trying to make a case for adding her to your list of suspects?"

"No." I frowned. "Not really. You?"

She shook her head. "Aside from the fact that Olivia doesn't have the physical strength to accomplish what was done, I have known her for years. Olivia doesn't have a devious bone in her body."

"You say that now," I retorted. "I nearly fell off my chair when you accused her of knowing who had given your name to the police."

"I just wanted to shake things up a little, that's all."

"Well, you succeeded in that."

Aunt Peg looked inordinately pleased with herself. "I'd say this was quite a successful outing. Tomorrow we'll regroup and try again."

"Tomorrow?" I said, surprised. I had plans for the next day. Plans I had no intention of changing. "What are you talking about?"

"Crawford and Terry's wedding, of course. I'm sure the event will draw quite a crowd. Who knows who might turn up?"

"You're not going to interrogate the guests," I told her.

"Why not?"

"Because it's a wedding. A celebration of Crawford and Terry's long relationship and their devotion to one another. It would be horribly rude if talk of Victor's death were to intrude on their happiness."

Seriously, did I even have to point that out?

"Oh pish," Aunt Peg said. "Crawford and Terry will never know. They'll be busy doing wedding things. Toasting, and dancing, and whatnot. They won't have the slightest idea what you and I are up to."

"What *you* are up to," I corrected. "I plan to be a proper guest. I'll be toasting and dancing, and enjoying myself, along with everyone else."

"So you say now." Aunt Peg smiled. "We'll see how long that lasts."

"I've never been to a wedding before," Kevin said that night as I was putting him to bed. "What will I do there?"

Kev was bathed and his teeth were brushed. He

had his pajamas on and he was in bed. Bud was under the covers beside him. The two of them had listened to three stories. I had put down the last book and was about to turn off the light.

So of course Kev had chosen that moment to ask his question.

"You don't have to do anything," I told him. "You're a guest. First we'll watch Crawford and Terry get married. Then there will be a reception afterward. You'll probably have something to eat."

"Davey says the getting married part is boring."

"It's only boring if you don't care about the people who are doing it," I told him.

"I care about Terry," Kevin said. "He's my friend."

"Terry cares about you too. That's why he invited you. You want Terry to be happy, don't you?"

Kevin nodded gravely.

"Marrying Crawford is going to make him very happy. The two of them have been together since before you were born. It's wonderful that they are finally able to make their relationship official."

Kevin counted back and frowned. "That's more than five years. What took them so long?"

"They had to wait for a law to change."

"A marrying law?"

"Yes, a marrying law." I reached for the light switch once more.

"But you and Dad got married a long time ago."
He was supposed to be nodding off. Instead,
Kev's busy brain was keeping him up.

"Our situation was different," I told him.

"That's silly," said Kev.

"I agree."

He didn't speak for a minute. I thought we were
finally finished. I turned off the light. The room
settled into darkness.

"A girl in my preschool has two dads," he said.
"Will Crawford and Terry have children too?"

"I don't know. We'll have to see."

"I'll ask Terry tomorrow," Kevin decided
sleepily.

That would certainly liven up the proceedings,
I thought. Between Kevin and Aunt Peg,
tomorrow's wedding could turn out to be a
memorable event. Even without dancing dogs
and armed cupids.

Chapter 22

I can't think of a better way to spend Valentine's Day," I said happily the next afternoon.

The whole family was in Sam's SUV. We were on our way to Bedford. Both the wedding, and the reception that followed, were going to be held at Crawford and Terry's home.

"I can," Davey grumbled from the back seat.

"Oh?" Sam glanced at him in the rearview mirror. "Did you have a hot date planned for tonight?"

"Nooo!" Davey's cheeks reddened. He was friends with plenty of girls but he had yet to go on his first real date. "But this will just be a bunch of people standing around talking. There's nothing interesting about that."

"Most of them will be dog people," I pointed out. "It will be like going to a dog show."

Davey wasn't impressed by that logic. "Except without the dogs," he said. "And they're the best part."

"You can hang out with me." Kev reached over and patted his brother's arm. "We'll have fun together."

"Oh yeah? What are you going to be doing?"

"I'm not sure," Kevin considered. "I think mostly eating cake."

Crawford's Bedford Kennels was located on a quiet country lane that was bordered on both sides by mature trees and crumbling stone walls. Though the most recent snowfall had been plowed away, low drifts on either side of the road narrowed the approach to the driveway. Fortunately, traffic was only heading in one direction.

Crawford and Terry's house was a classic two-story colonial set in the middle of a spacious piece of land. Since Terry had been cutting my hair for years, I visited often. Behind the house was a matching kennel building, also painted white with black trim. Usually when I arrived, the dog runs were filled with happy canines. Tonight they were empty and quiet. The main event was about to take place, and the dogs had already been put to bed.

When Sam turned in the driveway, we joined a line of cars that were slowly inching toward the turnaround in front of the house. A team of valets was waiting there to whisk the vehicles away. It was already dusk, but the home before us glowed. Its eaves and windows were lit with hundreds of twinkling fairy lights. Even Davey, who was determined not to be impressed, stared wide-eyed from the back seat.

The brick walkway that led to the house had been shoveled and sanded. Massive arrangements of yellow and white roses flanked both sides of the front door. As soon as I stepped out of the car, their heady aroma gratified my winter-starved senses. The flowers wouldn't last long in this cold, but in the meantime they would delight everyone who walked by.

Once inside, our coats were quickly dealt with. Then we were directed across the front hall to the living room. Other guests were already gathering there. Furniture had been removed from the room. In its place, rows of white, cushioned chairs had been set up on either side of a wide center aisle. At the head of the aisle, a raised dais was decorated with more glorious blooms.

Lighting in the room was subdued. Rows of candles flickered atop the mantelpiece and on each of the windowsills. Graceful floral boughs, fashioned of greenery and white roses, were draped from the intricate crown molding. In a back corner, a string quartet was quietly tuning their instruments.

I didn't see a single big red heart anywhere. Instead, I was awed by the elegant ambience of the room. Terry and Crawford had waited a long time for this. Now that their chance had finally come, I was overwhelmed by the quiet beauty of the setting Terry had created to celebrate their union. The ceremony hadn't even started yet and already I could feel tears pricking at the corners of my eyes.

A single violin began to play. People began to

find their seats. Sam led the way to some empty chairs in the third row.

The four of us had just sat down when Bertie slipped into the seat beside me. She looked lovely in a gray velvet wrap dress that set off her long auburn hair beautifully. My brother, Frank, took the chair on the aisle next to her.

"Just in time," Bertie said. She sketched a quick wave at the kids and Sam. "You try getting out of the house quickly when two kids don't want you to leave." Then she looked at me and frowned. "Wait. Are you crying?"

"Not yet," I replied. A loud sniffle escaped.

"You *are* crying," she marveled.

"I always get emotional at weddings."

"No, you don't."

She was right about that. So I changed the subject. "You could have brought Maggie and Josh with you." I'd already taken a look around the room. I was happy to see that Davey and Kevin weren't the only children in attendance.

"You're kidding, right? It's Valentine's Day. And Frank and I haven't had a night out in weeks. This wedding was the perfect excuse to ditch the kids and go somewhere where we could act like adults."

"Hi, Frank." I leaned around Bertie and greeted my brother.

Frank was four years younger than me. He and I shared the same light brown hair, hazel eyes, and determined chins, but other than the physical similarities we'd never had much in common. For much of my early life he'd been the bane of my existence.

Marriage to Bertie had matured my brother, however. Or maybe I was the one who'd grown up. Either way, our relationship now was better than it had ever been.

"Nice to see you, Mel." Frank stood up, leaned around his wife, and planted a kiss on my nose. "Now quit sniffling. You'll embarrass the rest of us." He waggled his fingers at Sam and the boys, then sat back down just as the string quartet began to play.

While we'd been talking, a pastor had taken his place on the dais. A door in the side wall opened. Gabe Summers, Crawford's adult son, came in and stepped to one side of the low platform. He was Crawford's best man.

We'd all met Gabe the previous summer. At the time, his relationship with Crawford had been a secret. Now it looked as though that cat was out of the bag.

Still there was no sign of Crawford. Or Terry, for that matter.

There was a quiet rustling sound as people began to shift in their seats to face the back of the room. The double doors that led to the hallway had been closed. Now they opened, and a tiny girl in a white dress walked down the aisle.

Her blond curls bobbed around her head as she enthusiastically scattered rose petals from a beribboned basket held over her arm. When she reached the dais, her mother took her hand and led her to one side.

The music paused briefly. Then the quartet broke into a new song. This music was rousing, and joyous, and unlike any bridal march I'd ever heard. Beside me, Kev began to dance in his seat. The song was familiar but I couldn't quite place it.

Then abruptly I forgot about that because now Crawford and Terry both stood framed in the open doorway. Both were wearing immaculate dinner jackets with satin lapels and black bow ties. Their white shirts were crisply pleated, their patent leather shoes were polished to a high shine. Terry's hair was back to its natural shade of dark blond. But best of all were the smiles on both men's faces.

Briefly Crawford appeared to be listening to the music too. He waited until it built to a high note, then he offered his arm to Terry. Arms linked, the two men walked down the aisle together.

As they passed us on their way to the dais, I suddenly realized the name of their processional. When I did, I almost laughed. The song was by Stevie Wonder. It was called "Signed, Sealed, Delivered I'm Yours."

Well done, Terry.

The ceremony that followed wasn't long, but it was filled with emotion. Crawford and Terry had each written their own vows. When Crawford paused to look into Terry's eyes before promising to cherish him, I started to grow misty eyed again. Then Terry promised to love, honor, and cook for Crawford for the rest of his life, and I ended up laughing along with the other guests instead.

When the pastor pronounced them married, the couple was treated to a sustained round of applause. Crawford looked faintly embarrassed by the enthusiastic response. Terry grinned and took a small bow. Then he waved to Kevin, who was bouncing up and down in place.

Terry had chosen a more refined piece of music for their triumphant stroll from the room. The stirring sounds of Beethoven's "Ode to Joy" followed them back down the aisle.

"That was wonderful," Bertie said as we gathered up our things. I could have sworn she was sniffling herself.

"Stevie Wonder." Sam smiled. "That was perfect. It has to have been Terry's choice. Crawford looked surprised when he heard it."

"Crawford looked happy," I said. "They both did. What a great day."

Terry and Crawford had had their pictures taken before the ceremony. And Terry flatly refused to take part in a receiving line. So when the two men simply walked across the hall to the dining room, where a buffet dinner was set out on the table, the rest of the guests stood up and followed.

A set of French doors on the side of the room opened up to a paneled library with a bar. There was plenty of room for everyone to move around. Crawford and Terry were immediately mobbed with well-wishers, so Sam and I decided to wait a few minutes before paying our respects. In the meantime, Davey offered to fix plates of food for Kevin and himself. Sam went to get a drink.

I looked around for Aunt Peg. I'd seen her earlier, shortly after we arrived, but she was standing in the middle of a group of people. Later she'd ended up seated on the other side of the living room. If I could locate her, I had something interesting to say.

I started to take a glass of champagne from a tray held by a passing waiter. Then I saw Aunt Peg gazing out the bay window in the library and took two instead. I crossed the room and offered one to her.

"This is a lovely house," she said, accepting the champagne flute from my hand. "Look here. Crawford has built a reading nook beneath this bay window. It must be a wonderful place to sit and read on a cold winter's day. Especially if you have a Poodle in your lap."

"You should tell Crawford you approve."

"Crawford certainly doesn't need my approval," Aunt Peg replied. "After today, I suspect he has just about everything he's ever wanted out of life."

"He's a lucky man," I agreed. "He and Terry both are."

She took a sip of her champagne. "I meant to work the room, you know. I'm sure there must be people here who have useful things to tell us. But the ceremony was so beautiful that I find myself reluctant to break the mood. I'm quite content to simply enjoy the moment."

"Good for you." I paused to sample my champagne too. "Let me know when you're ready to start feeling useful again."

"Oh?" Aunt Peg swiveled my way.

Her self-styled repose hadn't lasted long. They never did.

"With regard to Victor Durbin," I said. "I think I have an idea."

"You might have started by telling me that," she chided. "Rather than letting me stand here waxing maudlin like someone who's never watched dear friends get married before." Aunt Peg upended her flute and emptied it. "There. I'm ready now. Let's hear it."

Again, a waiter appeared with a tray. He offered her another glass of champagne. She waved him away impatiently. So much for enjoying the moment. The Aunt Peg I knew and loved was back.

"You know how sometimes you're thinking

270

about something, but you don't know the answer? Then you go to bed, and your brain keeps working on it overnight while you're asleep, and when you wake up, your subconscious mind has sorted it out for you?"

"No. Does that really happen to you?" Aunt Peg appeared bemused by the idea. "I can't imagine solving problems in my sleep. I prefer to be fully alert and tackle things head on."

Of course she did.

"Okay," I said. "Moving on. Yesterday when we were talking to Olivia, she mentioned Victor's bruised finger, which reminded me of your encounter with him outside the Garden last Monday night."

Aunt Peg nodded. "Odious man," she muttered under her breath.

"Then she told us about the THC that had been found in Victor's blood during the autopsy. And that brought to mind something else. When Victor accosted you that night, something fell out of his pocket."

She thought back. "You mentioned that at the time. I didn't see a thing myself. What was it?"

"I'm not sure," I admitted. "It was dark, and he moved very quickly to pick it up and put it away. It appeared to be some sort of little baggie. I thought it might have had white powder inside."

"Powder?" Aunt Peg frowned. "Are you implying it was a drug of some sort?"

"It might have been. As you recall, we were in a hurry to get inside. So I didn't stop and think about it at the time. But now, looking back, I'm wondering if that's what it was."

"I'm not terribly conversant with illicit drugs," Aunt Peg said. "What would a packet of white powder be, cocaine?"

"I was thinking more of something like a roofie."

Aunt Peg was shocked. "Isn't that the substance that's known as the date rape drug?"

"Exactly."

She wasn't as uninformed as she thought. Aunt Peg was, however, beginning to look ill. I was glad she hadn't accepted that second glass of champagne.

"Think about it," I said. "Remember how insistent Victor was that you accompany him to a bar for a quick drink?"

"A celebratory quickie, he called it." Aunt Peg grimaced. "Do you think he was planning to put something in my drink?"

"I think it's possible."

"I just thought Victor was trying to delay me," she said. "I assumed he wanted to make me late for my judging assignment. But if your guess is correct, he had something else in mind entirely. He intended to ensure that I never showed up at all."

Chapter 23

Aunt Peg was outraged by the thought. "That man was nothing but a rat bastard."

Her tone was enough to make several heads turn in our direction. I hoped the other guests hadn't been able to hear what she'd said.

"You won't get any argument from me," I said.

"Victor must have realized that the only way he could get the better of me was to make sure I was incapacitated," she growled. "He intended to ruin the most important night of my career."

"It could have been worse than that," I told her.

"Worse? What could be worse . . . ?" Her voice slowly faded away. "Oh."

"Oh, indeed," I replied. "It makes me reconsider what Mattie told me. What she described was bad enough. But what if he did more than she was willing to let on?"

Aunt Peg nodded. "You're quite right to worry about that. It's beginning to look as though I had a narrow escape."

Another waiter was circling the library. My champagne flute was nearly empty. I traded it for a full one. Aunt Peg helped herself too.

The champagne was having a mellowing effect on me, and probably Aunt Peg too. Considering where we were and what we were discussing, that was a good thing.

"And then there's Louise Bixby," I said, when the waiter had moved away once more.

"What about her?"

"I told you she was behaving oddly at the Empire specialty. Her judging was all over the place. And then she and Victor had that argument."

Aunt Peg nodded. "We still don't know what that was about."

"Now I'm wondering if Victor had something to do with all of Louise's issues that day," I said. "Maybe he had attempted to slip her something too. Or maybe he succeeded."

Aunt Peg's brow rose. "Not another roofie?"

"That's just one possibility. Don't forget that when Victor died, he'd recently been exposed to marijuana."

Aunt Peg had taken a sip of her champagne. Now she nearly choked on it. "Don't tell me you think Louise might have been *stoned* when she was judging Poodles?"

I shrugged. "All I know is that something strange was going on. When I asked Louise about her argument with Victor, she said that her lunch must have disagreed with her because she didn't feel well all afternoon."

"That could explain why she wasn't acting like herself." Aunt Peg still wasn't convinced by my version of events. "If Victor did drug Louise, what could he have been hoping to accomplish? That was the first Empire Poodle Club specialty. It was Victor's opportunity to showcase the kind of event his club was capable of hosting. It was in his best interest for everything to go perfectly."

"Except . . ." I said.

Aunt Peg gave me a beady-eyed glare. "Now what?"

"Terry heard that Victor was stepping down as president of the club."

"I don't believe it," she said firmly. "Why would he do that?"

"Possibly because of irregularities in the EPC's membership roster."

"Oh pish. No club's records are perfect. You'll have to come up with a better reason than that."

I thought it was a perfectly good reason. But *whatever.*

"Keep thinking." Aunt Peg reached over and patted my arm. "I'm sure you'll come up with something. In the meantime, I'm going to circulate."

Having been ditched by Aunt Peg, I went to check on the boys. I found them on the dais in the living room along with a handful of other kids. The group was engaged in a lively game of Twister. Kev was happy, and Davey looked like he had everything under control.

I was on my way back to the dining room to

look for Sam when I saw Crawford at the other end of the center hall. Seeing me, he disengaged himself from the couple he'd been speaking with. For a moment I thought he meant to duck out in the other direction. Sadly, over the last half year our relationship had deteriorated that much.

But to my surprise, Crawford headed my way. I stopped and waited for him. He was smiling as he approached. I tried not to read too much into that. Both he and Terry had been smiling all evening.

"Congratulations," I said. Crawford didn't protest when I drew him into my arms for a hug. "That was a beautiful ceremony. I couldn't be happier for both of you."

"Thanks." His gray eyes twinkled. "It's been a long time coming. Who'd have thought that at my advanced age I'd still be marriage material?"

Crawford was in his sixties, but showing dogs had kept him fit. He still had the physique and the skills of a younger man.

"Everyone," I told him. "Terry is lucky to have you."

"I was lucky to have found him. Terry planned this entire event. All by himself. He said he wanted to surprise me. And boy, did he. I wasn't expecting something quite so . . . dignified."

"I'm sure he wanted you to have a ceremony you'd be proud of," I said. "Even though I was hoping to see a few dancing Poodles myself."

"Hunh." Crawford chuckled. "Dancing Poodles. Try to show a little restraint, Melanie."

He glanced at someone over my shoulder. I knew other guests were waiting to speak to him. He and Terry were the men of the hour. Everyone wanted to offer their congratulations.

It wasn't fair of me to monopolize Crawford's time. But there was one more thing I still needed to say. "About what happened last summer—" I began.

Crawford lifted a finger and placed it on my lips to stop me from talking. He hadn't accepted my apologies before. This time I was determined to make him listen.

I reached up and folded his hand inside both of mine. Then I lowered our joined hands and pressed them against my chest. "Please, Crawford. Let me tell you how sorry I am. I know what I did was wrong. You were right to be angry. But I truly hope you'll be able to forgive me."

"That was a very pretty apology." Unexpectedly Crawford smiled. "But you should have let me stop you when I tried."

My heart dropped. "Does that mean you still won't forgive me?"

"No, it means it wasn't necessary." Crawford took his hand back from mine. He extended his left arm and pushed back the sleeve of his dinner jacket. A new gold watch circled his wrist.

"Terry gave me that earlier today," he said. "It was his wedding present to me."

"It's gorgeous," I told him.

"Do you know what he wanted from me on this special day?"

I shook my head.

"Just one thing. Terry told me he needed me to forgive you. He wanted things to go back the way they were. He wanted you and me to be friends again."

"Oh." I swallowed heavily. "Oh my." My breath caught in my throat. I couldn't seem to be able to say anything else.

This time it was Crawford who reached over to take my hands in his. "Terry had a point. It was time to let bygones be bygones. Besides, it's hard to stay mad when it was your meddling that led to this day. I'm standing here tonight, a newly married man—and I'm the happiest I've ever been."

I just looked at him. I still couldn't manage to say a word.

Crawford leaned closer. He whispered in my ear, "And you and I are good. Is that okay?"

I nodded. Then I brushed away a tear.

He turned me around and pointed me toward the bar. "Go get yourself a drink, Melanie. You look like you could use one."

When I tried to look back at him, Crawford was already gone, quickly absorbed into a new group of people. Instead, I saw Davey and Kevin heading my way.

Davey took one look at me and frowned. "Geez, are you crying again? What's the matter now?"

"Nothing." I quickly scrubbed my hand across my face. "I'm just happy, that's all."

"Happy." Davey snorted. "I'd never have guessed."

"I'm happy," Kevin announced. "Terry told me it's almost time for cake."

The wedding cake was two tall tiers of devil's food covered with buttercream frosting and decorated with a cascade of edible flowers. Crawford and Terry held the knife together when they cut the first piece. Each fed the other a small bite. Then they handed out the first plates to the children who'd gathered around them.

Davey nabbed two plates, one for him and one for his brother. They went and sat down in the nook beneath the bay window. Sam and I got cake for ourselves and hovered nearby. The library was filled with candles too. Like in the other rooms, the romantic lighting made the space seem to glow.

"I talked to Crawford," I told Sam. It wasn't often that I saw my husband dressed up. He looked very handsome in his suit and tie. I reached up and wiped a small bit of creamy frosting off his lower lip.

"Everyone has talked to Crawford," Sam said. "It's his wedding."

"No, I mean . . . *really* talked. And we're good."

"It's about time."

"What's about time?" asked Bertie. She and Frank came over to join us.

"Crawford and I are friends again," I said. Just the thought made me smile.

Frank looked confused. "You're here at the guy's wedding. Why wouldn't you be friends with him? What did you do now?"

I rounded on my brother. "Why does everybody always assume everything is my fault?"

"Well . . ." said Sam.

Okay, in this case, maybe. But not *always*.

Bertie slipped an arm around her husband's shoulder. "I'll fill you in later," she promised.

We chatted for a few minutes; then I spotted Aunt Peg in the dining room. She was standing with Louise Bixby. I excused myself and went to join them.

"Good evening, Melanie," Louise said. "Peg and I were just talking about what a lovely occasion this is."

"Terry did a wonderful job," I agreed.

"We were also talking about Victor's specialty," Aunt Peg said. "And Louise's judging."

"Perhaps it wasn't my finest hour," the other woman admitted. "Although thankfully I did manage to find Crawford's Mini special, who went on to place in the group at Westminster under Peg."

Sure, for the variety. It didn't seem advisable to mention that she'd put the Toy Poodle over him for Best of Breed.

"Topper's a very nice dog," Aunt Peg agreed smoothly. "Melanie mentioned earlier that you hadn't been feeling well that day. I was sorry to hear that. What a shame not to be on top of your game at such an important event."

"These things happen." Louise shrugged. The small movement made her sway slightly on her feet. She was holding a highball glass. It was half full with what looked like whiskey. It probably wasn't her first drink of the night. "There will be other shows."

Her cavalier attitude made me wince. Especially since it came from a judge. What a slap in the face to the exhibitors who'd gone to a great deal of effort to show under her, and who should have won, but had instead gone home empty-handed.

"I heard you and Victor had a rather prickly relationship," Aunt Peg mentioned casually.

"Prickly?" Louise retorted. "That's a nice way of putting it. I hated the man's guts."

"Really?" To her credit, Aunt Peg managed to sound surprised. "What did he ever do to you?"

"To me?" Louise blinked. Abruptly she seemed to catch herself. When she spoke again, she chose her words with more care. "Nothing. I was just speaking generally. You knew Victor, Peg. He was a horrid man. Everyone thought so. Even the members of his own Poodle club didn't like him."

Louise turned her whole body to look at me. "I told you that a week ago."

"Yes, you did," I said. "You sent me to talk to Larry Bowling."

"And did you take my advice?"

"I did."

"There you go," Louise said with satisfaction. "I'm sure he told you the same thing." She peered at me over the top of her glass when I didn't immediately reply. "He did, didn't he?"

"Yes," I agreed. "Larry also thought Victor was a horrid man."

Aunt Peg was now behind Louise. She rolled her eyes at me. I tried not to laugh.

"Last week at the specialty, did Victor give you anything to eat or drink while you were judging?" I asked Louise. "Or maybe before?"

"No." She fortified herself with another sip of whiskey. "Why would he have done that?"

So much for that theory. I tried another tack.

"Did anyone at the show bring you something to eat or drink?"

Louise laughed lightly. "Are you worried that Victor's show committee didn't take good care of me?"

"Yes," I fibbed. "That's it exactly."

"Never fear. Hannah was on top of her duties all day."

"Oh?" Aunt Peg rejoined the conversation. "She was your steward, wasn't she?"

"Yes, that's right. When I arrived she had a cup of hot coffee and a brownie waiting for me on my table."

Aunt Peg and I exchanged a look.

"How nice of her," I said.

Louise nodded. "The brownie was delicious. Hannah told me it was homemade. I offered to share but she said she'd already eaten one she'd brought for herself."

Hannah? I thought. I was probably frowning. I knew she'd had her own reasons for being mad at Victor. But it didn't make sense that she would try to get even with him by sabotaging his show. After all, it was her show too. She was also an officer of the Empire Poodle Club.

I closed my eyes briefly. This conversation was making my head hurt. Or maybe I'd had too much champagne.

"Louise, dear," Aunt Peg said brightly. "Tell us about the note. What did it say?"

"Note?" The woman stared at her muzzily. "What note?"

"The one you sent to Victor," I told her. "The one that brought him running to your ring."

Louise's face was a mask of confusion. "I have no idea what you're talking about."

"My mistake," I said easily. "Perhaps Hannah was the one who did that."

"Hannah? Sent Victor a note?" Louise was still bewildered. She took another gulp of whiskey. I doubted that would help her figure things out. "Why would she do that?"

"We were hoping you could tell us," Aunt Peg said.

"I'm sure I don't have any idea. Victor and Hannah?" Louise shook her head. Just looking at her made me dizzy. "Those two didn't get along at all. Even at their own show, they were barely civil to each other all day. I can't imagine Hannah wanting Victor anywhere near the ring. You must be mistaken."

And there we were. Smack up against another dead end.

I glanced around the room and saw that Sam was holding Kevin now. Kev's arms were around Sam's neck and his head was resting on Sam's shoulder. My younger son had fallen asleep. It was time for us to go. I left Aunt Peg with Louise, checked in with Sam, then went to find Terry.

"You're leaving already?" he said after I'd congratulated him and thanked him for a lovely time. "The night is still young."

"Not for people who have children in preschool. Plus, I have to work in the morning." I leaned in and gave him a hug. "Everything was beautiful,

Terry. You did a wonderful job. And you and Crawford make the best couple ever."

He arched one brow. "Better than you and McDreamy?"

"Okay." I grinned. "Second best."

Sam had taken the boys and gone to get the car, so I had another minute or two to spare. "Thank you for fixing things between me and Crawford," I said.

"You know it was the least I could do."

"Still," I told him, "I'm grateful."

Terry nodded. "That's the theme of the night. Gratitude. Crawford and I never thought we'd get here. That we would ever be *allowed* to get here—but somehow we did. Now give me a smooch, doll. Then go find that family of yours. It's been one heck of a day, hasn't it?"

It had indeed.

Chapter 24

The next morning Aunt Peg called me at work. Again. Luckily I wasn't tutoring a student at the time. Or maybe it wasn't luck. Maybe Aunt Peg has figured out a way to hack into the Howard Academy computer system and check my schedule.

Nevertheless, even Faith looked on with disapproval when I opened the desk drawer and pulled out my phone. "It's Aunt Peg," I told her.

Usually that fixes things. This time it didn't help. Faith still walked back to her bed, where she lay down and tucked her muzzle neatly between her paws. Some days everybody's a critic.

"You're not supposed to call me while I'm at school," I said into the phone.

"Oh pish," Aunt Peg replied. "How is it my fault where you are when I want to talk to you?"

If there was a correct answer to that question I had no idea what it was. "Last night was a bust," Aunt Peg continued flatly.

"What, the wedding? I thought it was beautiful."

"Sure, that part was very nice. But what did we find out? Nothing except that Louise Bixby can't hold her liquor. Hardly useful information. It's been a whole week."

As if I didn't know that. I'd been counting the days too.

Victor Durbin had died the previous Tuesday at Westminster. And what had I managed to learn in the meantime? That everyone who knew the man didn't like him. That was hardly news.

I figured Aunt Peg had called to berate me for not having answers yet. But it turned out she was mad at someone else instead. *Yippee.*

"I called that New York detective who came to see me last week," she said. "I also reminded him that a week had passed. I asked if he and his cohorts had managed to solve the crime yet."

"Cohorts?" I swallowed a laugh. "You actually called them cohorts?"

"I don't know why not. That describes their relationship perfectly. More important than what I called them was his answer. Which was no."

"I think we'd have heard something if it was yes," I mentioned.

Aunt Peg didn't dignify that comment with a reply. "I asked him what was taking so long. And do you know what he said?"

"I haven't a clue."

Waiting for her to answer, I shifted in my seat to angle my body away from the door. I could hear movement in the hallway outside. The pitter-patter of student feet. At least I hoped that's what it was. I really didn't want Mr. Hanover to catch me bending the rules again.

"He had the nerve to tell me that he and his men are very busy. That parts of Manhattan are high crime areas, especially for tourists. 'People visit the city from places where life is slower and easier and they don't know enough to put their guard up,' he said." Aunt Peg's voice rose in outrage. "As if everyone who lives outside the five boroughs is a country bumpkin."

"That's just silly," I said.

"Not only that, but he left me with the distinct impression that solving this murder wasn't a high priority. As far as they're concerned, Victor Durbin is just another out-of-town visitor who turned into a statistic. As you might imagine, when I finished talking to the detective, I was feeling quite motivated."

Presumably Aunt Peg meant she was motivated to call me. Not to do the legwork herself.

"It's time for us to get back to basics," she told me.

"Which means what . . . exactly?"

"Who had the most to gain from Victor's death?"

"That's easy," I said. "Clark Donnay. When Victor died, he inherited ownership of the Pooch Pub."

"Then you'd better go talk to him again," Aunt Peg decided. "See if you can shake loose something useful this time."

Even though she couldn't see me, I grinned

anyway. "You want to show up the Manhattan PD."

"No," she replied. "I want to know who killed Victor Durbin."

I learned a long time ago that when Aunt Peg tells you to do something, it's easier just to do it. Even Sam agreed with me about that. He didn't protest when I asked if he could pick Kev up at preschool because Faith and I had a stop to make on our way home.

"Will you be home in time for dinner?" he asked. Married to me, Sam has become adept at preparing for all contingencies.

"I hope so," I told him. But who knew? Aunt Peg might call with another assignment. I figured I'd better leave my options open.

The last time I'd visited the Pooch Pub, I'd left Faith behind. This time, I hadn't had a choice. But when we arrived, I had bad news for her.

"You have to wait in the car," I told her. "This is not the kind of place for you."

Faith didn't believe me. Actually, she wasn't even looking at me. Instead she was standing on the seat, staring into the Pooch Pub through its large front window. A plethora of puppies was gamboling around inside. I knew she wanted to be part of that. I was equally sure she wasn't going to be.

"I'm sorry," I told her.

Faith's tailed whipped madly from side to side. *Look! It's dog friendly!*

"Those puppies are only there because they're for sale," I said. "Plus, who knows what shots they may or may not have had?"

I can play with them anyway!

"No you can't," I said firmly.

There was a rawhide bone in the glove compartment. I kept it there for emergencies. This definitely qualified. I took it out and offered it to her.

Faith looked down at my extended hand. She knew what that meant. Her tail drooped. *Not going with you?*

"Not this time," I said. "I won't be gone long."

Faith delicately took the bone from my fingers. With a resigned sigh, she lay down on the seat. It was a good temperature inside the car, but I cracked the windows anyway to keep the air fresh.

So. Aunt Peg's plan had gotten me to the Pooch Pub. But in true Aunt Peg fashion, she hadn't told me how I was supposed to inveigle a second meeting with Clark Donnay once I was here.

My previous conversation with the Pooch Pub's owner hadn't gone perfectly. Nor had it ended on a high note. Now I wondered how I was going to get him to talk to me again.

In the meantime, I walked up to the counter and ordered a mocha latte. Then I found a seat at a table by the window. The pub wasn't as crowded as it had been the last time I was here. With only a few tables in use, there were half a dozen puppies wandering around the room looking for something to do. When I lowered my hand toward the floor and snapped my fingers, two puppies quickly came running over.

One was black and white, the other cream colored. Both were fluffy and bright eyed. I decided I was probably looking at a pair of Cockapoos. Possibly littermates. Probably less than three months old. As every puppy seller knew, these guys were at their most adorable stage. No doubt they'd be gone in a matter of days.

I reached down and lifted the cream girl into my lap. She immediately jumped up and tried to lick my chin. The boy puppy attacked the zipper on my jacket, which was hanging over the back of my chair. At least this pair was well socialized.

"Good afternoon, Melanie Travis."

I'd been concentrating on the puppies and hoping that Faith wasn't watching us through the window. So I hadn't noticed Clark's approach. Apparently I wasn't going to have to seek him out after all. Nor did I have to offer him a seat. Before I even had a chance to speak, Clark pulled out the chair opposite me and sat down.

Well then. It looked as though we both had something to say.

Clark glanced at my latte. Then at the puppy in my lap. "I see you're still sniffing around. Unless you'd like to try to convince me you stopped in today because you were thirsty?"

There didn't seem to be much point in equivocating. "No, I came because I wanted to talk to you."

Clark sat back in his chair. He crossed his arms over his chest. He ignored the black and white puppy who was trying to climb up his leg. "Talk."

His appearance had taken me by surprise. I hadn't yet had a chance to prepare what I was going to say. So I led with the first question that came to mind. "Larry Bowling's lawsuit, are you worried about that?"

"No. Not in the slightest."

I lifted up the cream puppy and placed her on the ground. "Why not?"

He peered at me intently through his black-framed glasses. "Let me turn that around. Why should I be?"

"Because the Pooch Pub is yours now. And litigation could interfere with its successful operation."

"Frivolous litigation," Clark replied. "My lawyer has already contacted Mr. Bowling and his merry band of litigants. Their lawsuit—such as it is—has no merit. Their quarrel was with Victor, not me."

"Their quarrel had to do with ownership of the

Pooch Pub," I pointed out. "And while Victor may be gone, he was your partner when their agreements were made. That's probably enough for them to be able to make life difficult for you."

"Ahh," Victor said softly. "Now I see."

"See what?" I sputtered.

"You and your associates have joined forces with them, haven't you?"

"No." The answer was automatic. I still had no idea what he was talking about.

Clark straightened in his seat. "I think you're lying to me, Melanie Travis."

"I'm not—" I began. Then I thought about what he'd said. "Wait—what associates?"

"Your fellow Poodle club members. That's what this is actually about, isn't it? You've come to spy on me, too."

Now I was way past sputtering. I was dumbfounded. And utterly silent.

That was such a rare event in my life that Sam would have laughed to see it. Except that suddenly it felt as though nothing about this conversation was funny.

I swallowed and caught my breath. Then I put down my latte and said, "Maybe we'd better start over."

"That depends." Clark braced his hands on the edge of the table. He looked as though he was about to rise.

"On what?"

"On what you're doing here." He glared at me across the tabletop. "This time I want the truth."

"I'm trying to figure out who killed Victor Durbin." I opened my mouth and blurted out the answer. After the fact, even I was a little surprised by what I'd said.

I expected Clark to be offended. Perhaps to bluster about his innocence. He did neither. Instead, to my surprise, he appeared to relax. "Go on," he said.

I shrugged. "That's it."

"You're not trying to shut down the Pooch Pub?"

"No. Why would I want to do that?"

"Your friends seem to believe I'm doing something nefarious because I'm helping these puppies find good homes."

I gave him a level look. Clark wasn't the altruist he wanted me to believe he was. But maybe I didn't have to get into that right now.

Instead, I finally connected the dots and said, "Mattie Gainer."

"Yes," Clark replied. "Mattie Gainer. You were talking to her at the seminar in New York. Then I saw you two sitting together here, last week after we spoke in my office. At the time, I didn't know who she was. Unfortunately for me, that state of blissful ignorance didn't last."

"Wait a minute," I said. "Now you're the one who's talking about spying on people. You *saw* me?"

Clark gestured upward toward a small camera mounted near the ceiling. I hadn't noticed it before. Now I felt like it was pointing right at me.

"Security cameras, Melanie Travis. Most businesses have them. I see everything that happens in here."

Why did Clark keep calling me by my full name? I had no idea. It was kind of making me nuts.

"Melanie," I said. "My name is Melanie. Or if you prefer, Ms. Travis. Take your pick."

"Your name is the least of my concerns." His lips quirked. "Particularly since I don't expect our association to continue for much longer. I saw you come in today, look around, and take a seat. I assume you know that I put a stop to Ms. Gainer's laughably transparent snooping over the weekend. I will also assume that having been ejected from the Pooch Pub herself, Ms. Gainer sent you here in her stead."

It took me a minute to process that. Then I stopped trying and just focused on the most important part. *"You ejected Mattie from the Pooch Pub?"*

It really wasn't funny. I heard myself snicker anyway. Poor Mattie. She was no Mata Hari.

"That amuses you?" Clark asked.

"Well . . ." I had to press my lips together to keep from laughing again. "Yes."

"I see."

"Mattie means well," I told him.

"I don't care," Clark replied. "She was bad for business."

"You shouldn't take it personally. Mattie was very angry at your partner, Victor."

"Former partner," he corrected me. "And that's not surprising. Apparently many people were angry at Victor. But it doesn't change the fact that I'm not going to let her succeed in shutting down the Pooch Pub. Nor you either, for that matter."

"That isn't my intent," I said.

Clark tipped his head to one side and studied me. "Is it your intent to see me arrested for Victor's murder?"

"Did you do it?" I asked.

"No, I did not."

"You had a good motive," I commented.

"I also have a good alibi," Clark replied mildly. "The police have verified it. That was the first thing they asked me about."

Damn. Suddenly I felt like an idiot. A smarter sleuth would have asked that question sooner.

"If Ms. Gainer had a problem with Victor, she should have taken it up with him while he was still around to defend himself," Clark said. "Lord knows she wouldn't have been the only woman to do so."

I'd finished my latte and started to stand up. I thought I was ready to leave. Now I sank back down in my seat. "There were others?"

"Victor was never shy about chronicling his romantic exploits," Clark told me with obvious distaste. "He thought of himself as a Casanova. What the women thought, I can only imagine. Well, except for one. She showed up here."

"Here," I repeated.

"Not in the pub. In Victor's office. Uninvited. When he and I were trying to work. I didn't care what he did on his own time, but Victor had no right to bring that kind of trouble to our place of business."

"What kind of trouble?" I asked. I was beginning to feel like a ventriloquist's dummy.

"I don't know. And I don't want to know. When she started screaming threats at Victor, he shut his office door. Whatever had gone on between them, he never should have let things reach that point."

"When did this happen?"

"More than a month ago. Maybe around Christmas. Before the door slammed, I heard her say something about a holiday party. I didn't catch most of what she said. All I know is that she was very, very angry."

Maybe angry enough to kill?

"The woman you saw with Victor. Do you know her name?"

"No, I'd never seen her before." Clark shrugged. He didn't care.

"Can you describe her?"

"She was tall. He stopped and considered. "Taller than you, and maybe a couple of years older. She had very short dark hair. And sharp features. I think she was another Poodle club lady."

From the physical description I thought I knew whom he was talking about. But his last sentence clinched it. The woman who'd been screaming threats at Victor was Hannah Bly. It had to be.

Chapter 25

Kevin came down for breakfast the next morning dressed entirely in red. He had on a red turtleneck and red overalls, paired with matching red socks. Bud, who was with him, had a bright red ribbon tied to his collar.

"Those aren't the clothes I laid out for you on your bed," I told him mildly.

Of course, we were running late. I had four bowls lined up on the kitchen table. I was busy pouring Cheerios into all of them. When I finished doing that I planned to plop a carton of milk on the table and tell my family that breakfast was served.

"Nope," Kev replied. He reached into the basket in the middle of the table and snagged a banana. "Bud didn't like the clothes you picked."

In this house, we all talk to our dogs.

"Oh? What was wrong with them?"

"They weren't red."

Davey came skidding around the corner into the kitchen. He tossed his heavy backpack on the floor. It slid for several feet, ending up next to the dogs' water bowl. Faith and Eve just watched the commotion, but Tar jumped up to investigate. I hoped he wouldn't tip the bowl over onto the backpack. With Tar, you never knew.

"Hey squirt, nice outfit," Davey told his brother. "You look like a tomato."

"Yay!" Kevin said. Sarcasm went right over his head. Plus, he liked tomatoes.

"Today's a red day," Kev announced solemnly. He eyed my outfit from top to bottom. I was wearing gray corduroy slacks and a Fair Isle sweater. "You should change."

"I don't have time to change." I pulled out a chair and got him in it. "Have some cereal."

Kev stared at the bowl in front of him. "It's Cheerios again."

"You like Cheerios."

"I like tomatoes better."

"That's on you," I told Davey.

He held up his hands in a gesture of innocence. "I don't know how you figure that. I didn't dress him."

Davey picked up a bowl, splashed some milk into it, then tipped the bowl to his mouth and drank his cereal down. Kevin watched in fascination. Actually I was kind of fascinated myself. Davey finished the whole bowl in a few quick gulps without spilling a single drop. He walked over and placed the empty bowl in the sink.

"At dinner, I'm going to expect better manners," I informed him.

"At dinner, I won't be in such a hurry." Davey slipped his jacket off the back of a chair. Then he reached around Tar and grabbed his backpack. Surprisingly, it was still dry.

"Did you finish your homework?" I asked as he headed for the back door.

"Mostly," Davey told me over his shoulder.

"When are you going to do the rest?"

"On the bus." The door opened and shut and he was gone.

A moment later Sam appeared. He was wearing a red flannel shirt. Before I could comment on that, he looked across the kitchen at the back door. "Did Davey already leave?"

"You just missed him," I said. "We're running late."

"So I see." He eyed the two remaining bowls of cereal. "That's breakfast?"

"Unless you want a banana."

"Or a tomato," Kevin added. Suspiciously his bowl was already half empty. And Bud was under the table chewing something.

Sam looked at me. "Do we have tomatoes?"

"No, but Kevin decided it's a red day."

Sam gestured toward his shirt. "I heard about that earlier. It looks like you're the only one who didn't get the memo." He pulled out a chair and sat down. Then he reached for a cereal bowl and filled it with milk.

"You need to change your clothes," Kevin reminded me.

I sighed and pulled over the last bowl. I dug

301

my fingers into the mound of cereal and scooped up a handful. It was quicker if I ate my Cheerios dry. Hopefully my manners would be better by dinnertime too.

"So what's on the agenda for today?" Sam asked.

"School!" Kev told him gleefully. At his age, school was still a treat.

"For me too," I said.

Sam wasn't fooled. I'd been MIA a lot recently. He suspected today might not be any different. And he was right.

"And after that?" he asked.

"I want to go to the police station in New Canaan and have a chat with Detective Hronis. I'll drop Faith and Kevin off at home on my way, assuming it's all right if I leave Kev with you?"

"Sure," said Sam. "That works. Hronis is the guy you met in December when Claire had that problem?"

Claire was Davey's stepmother. She was married to my ex-husband, Bob, and the two of them lived on the other side of Stamford. During the holidays, Claire had worked as a personal Christmas shopper, and "that problem" referred to the fact that one of her clients had been murdered. Neither Sam nor I had any intention of elaborating in front of Kevin.

I nodded. "He and I didn't get along in the

beginning. But eventually we figured out how to tolerate each other well enough."

At least nobody else had ended up dead. I counted that as a plus.

"I thought I might run a couple of theories by him and see what he thinks."

"Detective Hronis is in New Canaan," Sam pointed out. He was well aware of the circumstances surrounding Victor's death in New York.

"He's in law enforcement," I said. "That's close enough for me."

Kevin had been listening to our conversation while he polished off his cereal. "Does he wear a uniform?" he asked.

"I'm afraid not," I told him. "He isn't that kind of policeman."

"Too bad." Kev considered. "Maybe he'll get a promotion. And then he'll get a uniform to wear."

Sam grinned. Since he thought it was funny I figured I'd let him explain. Meanwhile I needed to run upstairs and change my sweater. It was a red day, after all.

The New Canaan Police Department was housed in a large brick building with four tall columns flanking the front door. Located on South Avenue between the Merritt Parkway and downtown, it was easy to find. There was even plenty of parking out front.

I hadn't called for an appointment but Detective Hronis and I had just met in December, so I was pretty sure he'd remember who I was. I was counting on his curiosity to get me a meeting. That and the fact that when it came to crime fighting, New Canaan was generally a pretty dull town.

Once I'd parked, I sat in the car for a few minutes to organize my thoughts. I expected the detective might be skeptical about what I had to tell him. So I needed to be as clear and as concise as possible.

Looking back, I realized that when I contemplated all the things people had told me about Victor, it was the women's voices that resonated the loudest. It was too bad it had taken me so long to actually hear what they were trying to tell me. Early on, Olivia had referred to Victor as a cad. Then Louise had issued a similar warning. It wasn't until Mattie disclosed her story that I'd finally started to pay attention to what really mattered.

Then I'd talked to Clark. Based on what he'd told me, I now suspected that what mattered most of all was what Hannah Bly had *not* said.

Hannah belonged to Victor's Poodle club. The fact that she was also on the board of directors meant she would have spent a significant amount of time in his company. But in hindsight, her complaint about Victor seemed relatively minor compared to some.

Unless she hadn't told me the truth. Or at least not all of it.

According to Clark, Hannah was angry about something that had happened at a Christmas party. That wasn't a likely place for a dispute over membership irregularities to have come to a head. But in that rowdy social setting, I could well imagine something much more sinister happening between Victor and Hannah.

Hannah was strong, and fit, and felt capable of handling herself in any situation. Victor liked to take advantage of women, and he carried a packet of powder that ensured he never had to take no for an answer. If Victor had attacked Hannah and she'd been unable to fight him off, it wasn't a stretch to think that the consequences of that forced encounter could have proved disastrous.

Victor had had a significant amount of THC in his blood when he died. Now I was pretty sure I knew how it got there. With marijuana being legal in nearby states, it wasn't difficult to come by. Hannah would have been able to finesse that part of her plan easily enough. I was betting she'd plotted a revenge that followed Victor's lead.

The note whose trail I'd been following was just a red herring. Hannah had been two steps ahead of me all along. She'd concocted that story to throw me off the right track. And I'd fallen for it, just as she'd wanted me to.

Meanwhile, what Hannah hadn't wanted me

to figure out was that she'd put something in Louise's food at the specialty. Perhaps that had been a trial run for what she was planning next? Victor had drugged Hannah at the Christmas party, and then she'd retaliated in kind at Westminster. After that, it was payback time.

It was a good working theory—but even I had to admit that it still contained a few holes. I hoped Detective Hronis would be willing to hear me out, and maybe offer some input of his own.

As I got out of the car I realized that I was feeling conflicted. I genuinely liked Hannah. Even now, I wasn't entirely sure whether I wanted Hronis to agree with me—or laugh me out of his office.

Inside the building, I gave my name to the receptionist and took a seat. The detective didn't keep me waiting long. Hronis was in his forties and had the kind of face that had already settled into permanent lines of disgruntlement. He wasn't tall, but somehow he took up a lot of room. He walked with the deliberate stride of a man who was ready to defend his territory.

The detective's gaze skimmed around the reception area and he gave the woman behind the desk a fleeting smile. Then his eyes settled on me and the smile died. "Ms. Travis," he said. "This is unexpected."

I stood up and held out my hand. Hronis hesitated only a moment before reciprocating.

His large hand engulfed mine and gave it a hearty pump.

"To what do I owe the honor?" he asked.

"I need help."

A bushy brown brow lifted. "Police help?"

"Yes."

I could have sworn he almost sighed. Then the detective shook his head slightly and said, "You'd better come with me."

His office was on the second floor and had a window that overlooked the heavily wooded residential area behind the building. At other times of the year it must have been a lovely view. Now, between the gray February sky and the tangle of barren tree branches, it just looked stark and cold.

"Take a seat," Hronis said. "And tell me what this is about."

Aside from the chair behind the desk, there was only one seat in the room. The chair he directed me to was metal, straight backed, and hadn't been designed for comfort. I took off my down jacket and balled it up in my lap. I might have been stalling for time while I figured out how to get started.

Hronis, meanwhile, leaned back to perch on the front edge of his desk. He stared down at me, then crossed his arms over his chest. He was waiting.

"A man named Victor Durbin was killed in New York City a week ago," I said.

He dipped his head in a small nod. "Friend of yours?"

"More like an acquaintance. At one point we both belonged to the same Poodle club."

"A Poodle club?" he repeated. "That's a real thing?"

"Yes. It's an association for people who breed and show Poodles."

He looked bemused. "Like with a clubhouse? Maybe a pool and tennis courts?"

We were in Fairfield County—so deep in country club territory. That made his confusion understandable. And actually kind of funny. I was careful not to let a single hint of humor show on my face.

"Not exactly. It's more like a business organization or a social group. We hold monthly meetings to talk about our Poodles. Sometimes we host dog shows or other kinds of performance events."

Hronis stared past me. Presumably he found the jumbled bookshelf against the wall fascinating. "The world is full of wacky people," he muttered to himself.

"You would know," I replied smartly.

That snapped his gaze back to me. "Excuse me?"

"I meant your job. Being in law enforcement. I'm sure that puts you in contact with lots of crazy people."

"I hope you're not being sarcastic, Ms. Travis."

"I wouldn't dream of it," I told him. "I need your help."

"So you said. Perhaps you could move this story along?"

It wasn't me who'd derailed the conversation. But okay.

"Victor Durbin was murdered," I said. It didn't seem as though we'd moved much past that point.

"In New York," Hronis replied. "Fifty miles from here. Was he a New Canaan resident?"

"No," I admitted. "He lived in Peekskill."

"Then maybe I'm a little confused as to why you're here."

"I think I have an idea who killed him."

Hronis frowned. Now he was staring at the ceiling. "Why am I not surprised?" Then his gaze lowered and fixed on me. "You should talk to someone in that jurisdiction. . . . You said it happened in the city. Which borough?"

"Manhattan. Midtown. Madison Square Garden."

"Probably Midtown Precinct South," he considered. "I could get you a name."

"I don't want to talk to someone I don't know. It will just be some random person in a huge police station who won't pay any attention to what I have to say. I already have a name. Yours."

Hronis sighed. "Is there any connection between this crime and the town of New Canaan?"

"Yes," I told him firmly. "The woman who killed Victor lives here."

"Okay." The detective walked around the back of his desk and sat down. He picked up a pen and grabbed a sheet of paper. "That's a start. What's the woman's name?"

Of course it wasn't that simple. Now that Detective Hronis was finally listening to me, I had to start by giving him the details of Victor's murder. I followed that by telling him about the people Victor associated with whom I'd spoken to. I lined up the clues I'd unearthed in a way that I hoped made sense.

Hronis took notes as I talked. Occasionally he stopped to ask a question, but mostly he just nodded and let me keep going. At one point he said, "I suppose there's no point in my asking how you came to be involved in this?"

"It just happened. I knew Victor. And then my Aunt Peg ended up being a suspect."

That took us off in a whole new direction. I described Aunt Peg's encounter with Victor the evening before he died. I made special mention of the packet that had fallen out of his pocket when he'd jerked away.

Detective Hronis grimaced at that. At least I thought he had, until he said, "You really broke the guy's finger?"

"Of course not. It was only bruised. But I needed to do something to make him release her. Don't you think the white powder was suspicious?"

"Maybe," he allowed. "It would be more suspicious if I knew what it was. For all you know, it could have been powdered sugar."

I stared at him across the desk. "Do you really believe that?"

"No. But I'm just trying to stick to the facts."

"The facts are that Victor was a horrible man who wouldn't keep his hands to himself. One woman has admitted that she had problems with him. Several others have implied as much. And the woman who lives here in your town was overheard screaming at him about an incident that happened not long before his death. There was a witness who heard her threaten him."

He glanced down at his notes. "Clark Donnay. The business partner."

I nodded. "I think the powder Victor was carrying was Rohypnol. And that his encounter with Aunt Peg wasn't the first time he'd planned to use it."

"Do you have any proof of that?"

"Not exactly," I admitted. "But there's something else."

"I'm all ears," Hronis said. I was pretty sure that was sarcasm.

"According to the autopsy, Victor Durbin had a lot of THC in his blood when he died."

"So maybe he smoked some marijuana."

"Or maybe Hannah slipped him the drug without his knowing it—just like he'd done to her. She gave Victor something laced with enough THC to make him dizzy, and maybe nauseated. Then she volunteered to help him find a men's room. In his impaired state, it wouldn't have been hard for her to overpower him once they were inside."

"And you think this woman"—he glanced down at the paper—"Hannah Bly did that?"

"Yes."

"Why her? Why not one of those other women who were all supposedly mad at him?"

"Because I believe she used the same drug on someone else two days earlier at Victor's dog show."

That assertion led to even more explanation. By now, Detective Hronis was looking increasingly skeptical. I wasn't even sure I blamed him. All these arguments had sounded better in my head. Out loud, they seemed pretty flimsy.

"So that's it?" he said when I was finished.

I nodded.

Hronis was staring down at his notes. And frowning again. His fingers had begun to drum a steady tattoo on the desktop—as if he hoped that action might drum up some additional evidence for him to peruse. I was beginning to feel the same way.

"You don't believe me, do you?" I asked.

The detective raised his head to look at me. "Let's just say I think it's an interesting story. But I'm not entirely convinced. And I have to repeat what I told you earlier. None of these things you're talking about happened in my jurisdiction."

He was right. But I still couldn't bring myself to give up.

"Will you at least talk to Hannah Bly?"

"I don't see how I can do that," he said. "You've got plenty of conjecture here, but you haven't offered me much in the way of proof."

"But—" I began.

Hronis held up a hand for silence. I quickly complied.

"Here's what I will do. I'll get in touch with my counterpart at the Manhattan precinct and pass along your information. Will that make you happy?"

At this point, that was probably as good an outcome as I could hope for.

"I guess so," I replied. "Thank you for listening."

"Let me walk you out." He came around his desk and waited in the doorway until I'd pulled on my jacket and preceded him into the hallway.

"One more thing, Ms. Travis," Detective Hronis said. "Let's not make a habit of this, okay?"

There was only one answer I could give to that. "Yes, sir."

Chapter 26

Bertie called while I was on my way home.
"Where are you?" she asked.

"In my car." I checked the rearview mirror and moved into the outer lane.

"No, like where specifically?"

"On the Merritt Parkway, just about to get off my exit. Why, where are you?"

"I'm sitting in your driveway. I had a doctor's appointment in Greenwich and I stopped by to say hi on my way home." Bertie and Frank lived in Wilton, which was on the other side of New Canaan.

"A doctor?" I frowned as I pulled onto High Ridge Road. "Is everything all right?"

"Sure. It was just a normal checkup. No big deal."

"Then what . . . ?" Abruptly I laughed. "Oh wait, I get it. Frank's at home watching your kids, isn't he? And you're in no hurry to get back and relieve him of dad duty."

Bertie laughed too. "As long as I stay away, I have the whole afternoon off. That never happens so I'm taking advantage of it. Let's do something fun."

"Great idea. I'll be there in five. And for Pete's

sake, don't wait in the driveway. Why hasn't Sam let you in?"

"Nobody's home," Bertie told me. "Just a bunch of barking Poodles trying to sound like fierce watchdogs. Faith looked through the window and saw it was me. If she could turn a knob, she'd have opened the door, but no such luck."

By the time she finished explaining that, I was almost there. A black Jeep Wrangler was parked near the garage. Bertie hopped out as I approached. On a rare day off, she was wearing jeans, tall Dubarry boots, and a woolen peacoat. Her knotted cap had a bright red pom-pon on the top. Bertie and I exchanged hugs and she followed me inside.

As soon as we walked through the door, Bertie was mobbed by the canine welcoming committee. She squatted down to greet each dog by name. Eve and Augie nudged their way to the front of the pack, only to be pushed aside by Tar, whose exuberant greeting nearly knocked Bertie over. Bud took advantage of that to wriggle his plump body between Bertie's legs.

I stepped around the commotion and hung up my jacket. "Sure, forget all about me just because we have a visitor," I grumbled to the Poodle pack. None of them took any notice of me. They were still busy assuring Bertie that she was the best guest *ever*.

"What can I say? Dogs love me." Bertie rose to her feet. She pulled off her coat and hat and threw them on a nearby chair.

The canine crew continued to crowd around as she led the way to the kitchen. I stopped to read a note Sam had left me on the hall table. It said that he and Kevin were out running errands. I hoped that meant they were bringing home something good for dinner.

Bertie ducked into the pantry, then passed out peanut butter biscuits. I refilled the dogs' water bowl, then got two bottles of green tea out of the refrigerator. When I opened the back door, all the dogs went racing outside except for Faith, who opted to remain with us. She wasn't young anymore and it was cold out there.

As I sat down at the kitchen table, Bertie emerged from the pantry a second time. Now she had a bag of Oreos. She was squinting at the wrapper, looking for a freshness date. "These were hidden way in the back. Are they old or new?"

"If they're here, they're new," I said. "Oreos never have a chance to go stale in this house." Bertie tossed the package on the table between us and I nabbed an Oreo for myself. "Sam probably hid them from Kevin. That child would live on cookies if we let him."

"He must have inherited Aunt Peg's sweet tooth." She pulled out a cookie, twisted it apart, and licked off the cream filling. "So what have you been up to today? And what are we going to do for entertainment next?"

"About that . . ." I said.

Bertie looked up. "Uh-oh."

"What?"

"Why does that sound ominous?"

"It doesn't."

"Oh, please. How many years have I known you? I recognize that tone of voice." Abruptly her eyes narrowed. "You're going to talk about Victor Durbin, aren't you?"

"You asked what I'd been up to," I pointed out. "As it happens, I was just in New Canaan talking to Detective Hronis about the investigation."

"What investigation? Not his." Bertie was well aware of the circumstances surrounding Victor's death. And where it had taken place.

"No, actually mine."

She sighed. Then she reached for another cookie. "So?"

"He didn't believe what I told him. I mean, he thought it was an interesting story, but he didn't see why it should have anything to do with him."

"I think I agree," said Bertie. "Why should it?"

"Because the woman whom I'm pretty sure killed Victor, lives in New Canaan."

Her hand stilled in the air. "Woman?"

"Hannah Bly. Remember her?"

She frowned. "No, but the name sounds familiar."

"Hannah was the steward at the Empire specialty last week."

"Oh, that's right. She was the one trying to keep Louise Bixby from looking like an idiot."

"Actually, I'm pretty sure you have that backward," I said. "I believe that Hannah was the cause of Louise's crazy behavior."

"Really?" Now Bertie sounded curious. She fished two more cookies out of the bag. "Tell me about it."

By the time I got to the end of the story, Bertie was totally absorbed in what I had to say. We'd also managed to finish most of the Oreos between us. Hopefully Sam and Kevin were bringing home a new supply.

When I finished speaking, I got up and let the dogs inside. Tar's plush black coat was covered with snow. He must have been rolling in the stuff. Before I could grab a towel to dry him off, the big Poodle bounded into the middle of the room and shook vigorously. Droplets of melting snow went flying everywhere.

Seated nearby, Bertie shrieked and jumped to her feet. I didn't even try not to laugh.

"You're right," I said. "Dogs do like you. That's why Tar wanted to be right next to you when he shook."

Bertie snatched the towel I'd retrieved from the laundry room and used it to dry her hair. "Everyone thinks you're so meek and unassuming, but I know the truth. You have a mean streak."

"Me, meek and unassuming?" I gulped. That wasn't at all how I saw myself.

She slanted me a look. "You let Peg walk all over you."

"Not all the time."

"You're better about standing up for yourself than you used to be," Bertie allowed. "But still. You need to learn to fight back."

I opened my mouth to defend myself, then shut it again without saying a word. Instead I sat back down at the table.

Bertie tossed the damp towel on top of the washing machine. Bud followed her into the laundry room and took a look around. He was ever hopeful he might find food in unexpected places. Nothing in the small room must have smelled promising because I saw him eye the dangling end of the towel. In another minute, he'd have it on the floor.

Or maybe I was just fixating on that because I didn't want to think about what Bertie was saying.

She returned to the table, pulled out her chair and took a seat too. "Peg uses you," she said. "Shamelessly."

I shook my head. "Aunt Peg and I work on things together." Even as the words came out of my mouth, I knew they weren't entirely true.

319

"That's not how it looks to the rest of us," Bertie replied. "I've always wondered if it weren't for Peg being so nosy—and then prodding you to find out what she wants to know—whether you'd even get involved in solving mysteries at all."

"I would," I replied quickly. "Of course I would."

Bertie didn't look convinced. She peered at me across the space between us. "All I'm saying is that Peg needs to learn to respect you. You know you're allowed to say no to her, right?"

"Since when?" I laughed.

Bertie didn't join me. She didn't think it was funny.

Come to think of it, maybe I didn't either.

"Basically, you're telling me to grow up," I said.

"Or to grow a pair. At least where Peg is concerned." Bertie picked up the Oreo wrapper and shook it to see if it was empty. A lone rattle sounded from within. She fished out the last cookie. "I'll split this with you."

"Is this the point where I'm supposed to get really firm and demand that you give me the last Oreo?"

Okay, that did get a laugh.

It did not, however, get me a whole cookie. Bertie still twisted the Oreo into two pieces. She paused and looked at the two halves. One had cream filling on it, the other didn't.

I lifted a brow and waited for her to choose.

After a moment, she handed me the cookie with cream.

"Thank you," I said.

"I figured it was only fair since they were your cookies to begin with." Bertie paused, then asked, "Are you mad about what I said?"

"No."

"Are you sure?"

I told her the truth. "No."

Bertie nodded. She'd expected that. But she still wasn't about to apologize. Instead she said, "Let me make it up to you."

"How?"

"This is my afternoon off, but you get to choose what we do next. Anything you want, I'm in."

"Okay." I grinned. Bertie might end up regretting that impulsive offer. "I want to go talk to Hannah Bly."

Her face fell. "You're kidding."

"Nope."

"Why would you want to do that? And before you answer, let's both bear in mind that you think the woman might be a murderer."

"Which is precisely the point."

Bertie still looked reluctant. So much for anything I wanted.

"This confronting a killer thing is your gig," she said. "Not mine."

"Who said anything about confronting her? I just want to talk."

"Really?" she asked skeptically. "And say what?"

"I want to tell Hannah about the people I've spoken to, and the conclusions I've drawn based on what they said. Then I'll let her know that I've spoken to the police, and I'll encourage her to turn herself in."

"Like that's going to happen," Bertie scoffed.

"It could."

"What if she laughs at you instead?"

I shrugged. "Then at least I'll know I tried."

"Fat lot of comfort that will be when she pulls out a knife and tries to stab you."

"Hannah won't have a knife," I told her. "She'll be out in the middle of the woods. Hannah and her dog, Izzy, hike a couple of miles in Waveny Park every afternoon. Faith and I went with her one day last week. She invited me to join her anytime."

"And you want me to come too," Bertie said.

"You offered," I pointed out.

"Apparently that was a dumb idea."

"Whether or not you come with me, I'm still going," I said.

"That's an even dumber idea. It seems to me that we both need to stay out of the Waveny woods."

"Didn't you just tell me that I need to stop letting people boss me around?"

Bertie scowled. "I was talking about Aunt Pcg,

not me. Besides, I'm not telling you what to do, I'm trying to make you see sense. Think about it. You've told the police everything you know. The sensible thing now is to sit back and wait for them to make their move."

"The New Canaan police have no moves," I told her. "Detective Hronis said as much when I was there. Besides, once I've explained things to Hannah, she'll realize that I'm not a threat to her. The police didn't believe me. They're not following up on what I told them. So unless I can convince her to confess, everything I've done turned out to be useless."

Bertie reached across the table and took my hand. Her fingers squeezed mine. "You're not useless."

"Come with me." I could see she was wavering. "You can be my bodyguard."

She withdrew her hand and sat up straight. "I thought we were going to do something fun."

"You love the outdoors. A hike in the woods will be great fun."

Bertie sighed. She pushed back her chair and stood up. "Here goes nothing."

"I hope not," I said.

Chapter 27

I sent Hannah a text asking if she wanted a walking buddy and got back an immediate reply.

"Great idea," she wrote. "You caught me just in time. Izzy and I are on our way to Waveny now. See you there in ten minutes."

"We need to hurry." I showed Bertie the text. As she read it, I rinsed out the green tea bottles and tossed them in the recycling bin.

She looked up from the screen. "We're really doing this?"

"Yup." I went to the closet and exchanged my shoes for boots. Then I wound a scarf around my neck and grabbed a warm parka. "You'll like Hannah. She's a nice person."

"Sure." Bertie muttered. "Until you accuse her of killing Victor."

The dogs had followed us out to the hallway. They danced around our legs with excitement. They were hoping we were all going for a walk.

Reaching for a pair of gloves, I paused. "What if I'm wrong about Hannah?"

Bertie was zipping up her coat. She stopped too. "In that case, we can abort this whole mission."

"No, we have to go. At the very least, I need to tell her what I know and give her a chance to explain herself."

The Poodles were still crowded around us, waiting to see what would happen next. "Pick a dog," I said to Bertie.

"What?" She looked at me, surprised.

"Pick a Poodle. Hannah will have Izzy with her, and the Waveny trails are great for dog walking. We'll take a couple along with us."

I looked at Faith. She swished her tail back and forth. I didn't need to ask the question. Faith has always been able to read my mind. "You know how cold it is out there," I told her.

Faith woofed in reply. *Coming anyway!*

"Okay," I said to Bertie. "Faith is with me. Who do you want?"

She glanced downward at the Poodle pack. "Who's the biggest one?"

That was easy. "Tar."

"Who's the scariest one?"

Seriously, was that a real question? Gazing around I saw only grinning canines and wagging pom-ponned tails.

"Umm . . . none of them?"

Bertie grabbed a leash from the hook on the closet door. "Tar it is, then. At least he looks like he could knock someone down if he had to."

"Nobody's going to be knocking anybody down," I said.

Least of all Tar, I thought. That big Poodle loved everybody.

"We're just going to talk to Hannah."

"You never know," Bertie told me darkly.

We quickly loaded the two Poodles into the back of the Volvo and got under way. Taking the back roads between Stamford and New Canaan, we made it to Waveny Park in twelve minutes. As I drove up the rear driveway past the early nineteenth century Tudor mansion that was the park's centerpiece, Bertie looked around avidly.

"Wow," she said. "This place is gorgeous."

I glanced over at her. "You've never been here before?"

She shook her head.

"They do the best Fourth of July fireworks in the area."

"Not better than Calf Pasture Beach." Bertie was still gazing around. The wide fields on either side of us were blanketed with crusty snow. Trees flanked the long driveway. Their naked branches twisted in the air above us. "I'm surprised it's so empty, though. Where are the people?"

"Home for the winter," I told her. "In two months this place will be crazy busy again. Which also means that in two months we won't be able to walk the dogs off-leash. Enjoy it while you can."

Hannah and Izzy were waiting for us in the small parking lot near the carriage house. When I performed the introductions, Bertie didn't step forward. Instead, she remained standing beside the Volvo. Her wariness was palpable.

Hannah, however, nodded and smiled as soon as I said Bertie's name. "Sure, I know who you are. I've watched you handle dogs in the ring. You do a great job."

"Thank you." Bertie smiled in spite of herself. I saw her shoulders relax a bit. The three Poodles were circling around us, getting acquainted. "Izzy's beautiful. Is she a champion?"

"A third generation homebred," Hannah replied proudly. "Add partly owner-handled to her title. She's a dog who loves to stay active. I'm thinking about doing agility with her next." She gestured toward the open trail. "Everyone ready to move out?"

"Let's go," I said.

The three big Poodles, two black and one white, dashed on ahead of us down the path. Faith and Izzy already knew what to expect. But the wide trail that led through the woods was a revelation for Tar. He raced back and forth, bounding through the snow as he tried to see everything at once. Faith and Izzy followed at a more sedate speed.

As she'd done the previous week, Hannah set a strong pace. Bertie and I both kept up easily, but I was pretty sure I'd be tired later. We'd gone about fifty feet down the trail—far enough to be surrounded by the densely packed trees—when Hannah turned to face me.

"So, you're back," she said. "What's that about?"

"Maybe I enjoy the exercise," I replied brightly.

Hannah wasn't fooled for a second. "Or maybe you kept asking questions after we spoke last week. Everybody knows that about you, Melanie. You never know when to leave well enough alone."

Okay. She meant for our conversation to get straight to the point. So I followed Hannah's lead. "That's the problem. Things weren't *well enough*. A man has been killed."

"You mean Victor?"

I certainly hoped there hadn't been another death. "Yes, Victor."

Hannah shrugged. "No great loss. I'm sure I'm not the only person who told you that."

"He had a lot of enemies," I agreed. "Many of them were women."

"You don't say," Hannah muttered.

"Your problems with him went way beyond his falsifying club records, didn't they?"

Abruptly she stopped. "Who told you that?"

"No one. I figured it out for myself."

"Oh." Hannah put her head down and started walking again. "Well, you're wrong."

Bertie had remained silent until now. She'd been watching the dogs play in the snow and following half a step behind us. Now she caught up and said to Hannah, "Do you know a guy named Kenny Boyle?"

The dog show community wasn't huge.

After a while, almost everyone began to look familiar. And everybody recognized the big name handlers—no matter what breed they showed.

Hannah considered only briefly before nodding. "Tall, good looking guy, right? Professional handler, mostly working breeds?"

"Yeah, that's him," Bertie said.

I turned and stared at her. I never heard her mention Kenny's name. I was surprised to hear her do it now. She didn't meet my gaze.

"Friend of yours?" Hannah asked.

"No." Bertie's tone was flat. "Although at one time he and I were close. At least I thought we were. It turned out I was wrong. Kenny isn't the kind of guy who knows what to do with real emotion. Mostly he just enjoys manipulating people—and getting his own way."

Hannah nodded. She was listening. And maybe thinking of someone she knew who fit the same description.

"Kenny thought he was the most important guy in the world. When we were together, he had me believing that crap too."

"But then you came to your senses," I interjected. "And you left him."

"I did," Bertie acknowledged. "But not soon enough. Not until he'd banged my head against a wall, given me a black eye, and threatened me with much worse."

Hannah sucked in a breath. "I'm sorry."

"Thank you," Bertie said softly. "But the really crummy thing about the whole experience was that even after I'd left Kenny, I couldn't put it behind me. For a long time I was convinced that everything that had happened was my fault. That there was something wrong with me that made Kenny act that way."

"That's not true," I said.

"I know that now." Bertie looked over at Hannah and me. "But back then, nobody ever talked about this stuff. You were just supposed to pretend everything was fine and go on with your life. Because the alternative—the idea of admitting that you'd allowed some guy to turn you into a victim—was too embarrassing to contemplate."

Hannah scowled. "You should have fought back."

"You're right, I should have," Bertie agreed. "But I was younger then, and a lot less experienced. I didn't even realize how he was molding me into what he wanted until it was too late—and then I didn't possess the tools to fight back. Kenny was older, bigger, and stronger than me. When he told me I was worthless, I believed him."

Faith had gotten tired of racing around with the two younger Standard Poodles. Panting happily, she dropped back to my side. I took off one glove and curled my fingers through her hair. Izzy and

Tar, meanwhile, were dodging in and out of the trees ahead of us, engaged in a lively game of tag.

Hannah turned to Bertie. "Why are you telling me this stuff?"

"Because it sounds like you also got involved with a man who took advantage of you. Someone who made you feel powerless, just like I did with Kenny."

"Dammit," Hannah swore. She rounded on me. "I never said anything like that. What have you been telling people about me?"

"It wasn't what you said when we spoke before," I told her. "It was what you didn't say. Especially when I considered everything else I learned about Victor."

"Like what?"

"It appears that he intended to drug Aunt Peg right before she was due to judge the group at Westminster."

Hannah's eyes widened. "What are you talking about?"

I described the encounter that had taken place between them. Her face grew pale as I spoke. She sputtered a harsh laugh when I admitted that I'd nearly broken Victor's finger.

"Serves him right," she said.

The three of us smiled in complicit agreement.

"That wasn't the first time Victor tried to get away with something underhanded," I continued.

"Mattie Gainer complained about him cornering her at club meetings. Louise Bixby told me he was trouble. And even his godmother, Olivia Wren, called him a cad."

I paused to let that sink in, then said gently, "Victor did something to you too, didn't he?"

Hannah didn't answer. Instead, she jammed her hands in her pockets and strode quickly up the trail, leaving me and Bertie behind.

"Now what?" Bertie asked under her breath.

I shrugged. "Now we catch up."

"I know you're the one who sent the note at the specialty that started the fight between Victor and Louise," I called after her.

Hannah spun around to face us. "Why would I do that?"

"Maybe because you wanted to make Victor look like an idiot at his own show?" I guessed.

"Victor didn't need me to make him look like an idiot," she snapped. "He was fully capable of managing that all on his own."

"Louise told me she didn't feel well that afternoon," I pressed on. "And her judging certainly reflected that. She said the only things she had to eat or drink at the show were the coffee and brownie you brought her. You put something in her food, didn't you?"

"Why would I care how Louise felt?" Hannah demanded. "Maybe she was coming down with the flu."

"The flu," I mused. "That's a good excuse. Is that what you told Victor when he began to feel queasy after you drugged him on Tuesday night?"

"I don't know what you're talking about," Hannah snarled. "This stuff you're saying is crazy."

"I don't think it is," I said quietly

Hannah's angry gaze flicked between Bertie and me. "You can think all you want, but you know nothing. I can't believe you came out here pretending to be sympathetic, acting like you care about what happened to me, when all you really want is to trick me into blurting out something I shouldn't." Her voice rose sharply. "Are you listening to me? You know nothing!"

"Bertie and I are both listening," I said. "Tell us what we don't know."

Hannah's face was mottled with outrage. Her hands curled into fists at her sides. For a moment I thought she was going to turn away from us again. But then a sob rose up from deep in her throat and suddenly her eyes looked haunted. It was as though a wall had crumbled inside her, and then the words came pouring out in a rush.

"Victor Durbin raped me," Hannah snapped. "He roofied my drink during the club Christmas party, took me into a bathroom, and raped me. Victor treated me like I was garbage, just a body he could use any way he wanted. And he made sure there wasn't a single thing I could do to stop him."

Her booted foot stamped down hard in the crusty snow. Faith jumped back as small shards of ice sliced through the air. I quickly shifted her behind me.

"Now you know the truth," Hannah growled. "And I hope you're satisfied. I know I am. Because I made sure that Victor got exactly what he deserved."

Chapter 28

The dense woods around us swallowed Hannah's angry words as if they'd never been uttered at all. But they had. Bertie and I had both heard them. And now I felt as though I'd been punched in the gut. This was the point where I was supposed to feel a sense of achievement. Instead, I was consumed by a deep well of sadness.

I had accomplished what I'd set out to do. I had found Victor's killer—only to realize that my sympathies lay with her rather than her victim. I couldn't bring myself to condemn Hannah for her actions. What she'd done was terrible, but she'd lashed out in anger to right a wrong. And the world was a better place without Victor Durbin in it.

While I stood frozen in place, Bertie responded with compassion. She spread her arms open wide and walked across the small space that separated us from Hannah. I thought Hannah might turn away. Instead, I watched as her angry defiance crumbled. When Bertie wrapped her arms around Hannah, the other woman let herself accept the embrace.

For a minute Hannah's posture remained wooden. Her arms were stiff at her sides.

But Bertie simply continued to hold her and eventually Hannah relaxed. Then she gulped in several deep breaths, and her body began to shudder with heartfelt sobs.

Seconds later, I heard Bertie sniffle too. I reached up with a gloved hand to brush away the moisture coating my own lashes before it could begin to freeze. Beside me, Faith whined softly under her breath. She wanted to offer comfort. She just didn't know where to start.

"It's okay," I told her softly. "Everything's going to be all right."

I hate it when I have to lie to a dog. But in this case the deceit felt justified. Faith needed to know that everything in *her* world would be all right. For now, that would have to be enough.

Tar and Izzy came circling back to us. The white Poodle looked around briefly, puzzled by the scene. Like Faith, she sensed something was wrong. Quickly Izzy scrambled through the snow to get to her owner. She tried to wedge her body between Hannah's and Bertie's legs.

The two women pulled apart fractionally. As Bertie's arms slid away, Hannah squatted down beside Izzy. She buried her face in the Poodle's warm coat.

Bertie returned to my side. She and I gave Izzy and Hannah a moment. We couldn't stand still for long, however. The wind had risen. The bare branches that formed a canopy over the trail were rattling above our heads. It was too cold not to keep moving.

Hannah must have realized that. She pulled away from Izzy and looked up at us. "So now what happens?"

"You need to talk to the police," I told her.

Immediately Hannah shook her head.

"You have to get a lawyer and turn yourself in."

Hannah levered herself to her feet. "How can you say that, knowing what Victor did to me? I acted in self-defense." Her gaze swung Bertie's way. "You of all people should understand that."

"I understand how you felt," Bertie said. "There were times when I thought Kenny deserved to die for the way he treated me. Maybe I even fantasized about killing him. But the difference is I didn't do it."

"Maybe you should have." Hannah's gaze glittered with malice. "I didn't just fantasize about it, I made a plan. And you know what? After all the things I worried about, all the pieces I put together so meticulously—securing the marijuana, perfecting the dosage before using it on Victor, scoping out the scene to find just the right place to take him—none of it proved necessary. Do you know why?"

Bertie and I shook our heads.

"Because when the time came, it was easy. Victor just about fell into my hands. When I offered to buy him a drink, he didn't hesitate to accept. When I told him I wanted to go someplace where we could be alone, he followed me like a stupid fool. Victor's ego was so huge that it never crossed his mind I wouldn't want to have sex with him again. He never suspected my motives for a second."

Thinking back, Hannah smiled with satisfaction. "The moment when hot-and-heavy Victor had to abandon his idea of why he thought we were alone, and realized what was actually happening to him? That was a real rush. I'm glad I decided to use a knife, because stabbing Victor made perfect sense. It was a violation of his body, just like he'd violated mine."

While she was speaking, I'd begun to shiver. I didn't know whether the sharp wind now whipping through the trees was the cause, or whether it was Hannah's dispassionate—almost disdainful—description of the deed that had chilled me to my core. But suddenly I was done listening. I wanted to be moving again.

"Let's go," I said sharply. "It's time to head back."

Bertie and I waited until Hannah started walking; then we both fell in behind her. The trail we'd taken formed a long loop. I figured we were about a mile away from the parking lot.

Faith and the other two Poodles skipped on ahead. When a squirrel popped out from behind a tree, all three dogs took off in pursuit.

Hannah watched them go, then glanced back at Bertie and me over her shoulder. She appeared to be taking our measure, attempting to decipher our reactions to the story she'd told. She had to be wondering whether or not she'd succeeded in convincing us that her actions had been justified.

We'd been walking only a minute or two when she opted to state her case again. "You both know Victor was a terrible person. And once I realized what he was capable of, I *had* to stop him. I couldn't let him do to anyone else what he'd done to me."

"I understand that." I was willing to say almost anything that would keep Hannah walking and talking.

"So we're all in agreement, right? What I told you is just between us. No one else needs to know."

Even after everything, I still liked Hannah. So I told her the truth. "I'm afraid that's not possible."

She stopped and turned around. "Why not?"

"It's too late. I've already told a couple of other people about my suspicions."

Her gaze narrowed. "Who?"

"Detective Hronis of the New Canaan PD, for one."

Hannah's nose was red from the cold. So when her cheeks blanched, the contrast was even more apparent. "You're lying."

"I'm not. I thought someone in authority should

know. But it turned out the detective didn't believe me."

"Smart man." Hannah nodded approvingly. "Who else?"

"Aunt Peg."

"Dammit!" She winced. "Not her."

I almost laughed. It appeared Hannah was more concerned about what Aunt Peg might do than she was fearful of repercussions she could face from the police.

"I'm afraid so."

"You can fix that," she said quickly. "Tell her you were wrong."

"She won't believe me."

"Sure she will," Hannah persisted. "Peg always thinks you're wrong about something."

"Only about things that don't really matter," Bertie put in. "Not a matter like this."

Hannah scowled at both of us. "I'm not going to jail. Not for doing what needed to be done. Everybody hated Victor. It's not my fault that I was the only one who was brave enough to act."

"You don't have to convince us," Bertie said. "Melanie and I aren't your judge and jury."

"But you do need to hire a good lawyer," I told her. "Someone who will go to the police with you and argue that there were mitigating circumstances surrounding Victor's death."

"I acted in self-defense," Hannah insisted. "Anyone can see that."

Anyone who chose to ignore the six weeks of waiting and planning between the time of Hannah's rape and the day she took her revenge, I thought. I opted not to mention that.

The Poodles had given up trying to catch their squirrel. All three came trotting back down the trail toward us. Hannah called Izzy over to her side.

I did the same with Faith. As she drew near, I watched the Poodle move and assessed her condition. She looked happy but her tongue was hanging out of the side of her mouth. I wanted to make sure she wasn't overexerting herself trying to keep up with the younger dogs.

Focused on Faith, I missed the moment when Hannah grabbed Izzy's collar and yanked the white Poodle sideways. The two of them leapt off the cleared trail and went running into the woods together.

"Hey!" Bertie yelled. "Come back here!"

I looked up then, just in time to see Hannah and Izzy disappear into the dense thicket of trees. "Let them go. It doesn't make any difference if Hannah runs away. If the police decide they want to talk to her, they'll be able to find her."

"I don't care about Hannah." Bertie had already hopped over the small drift of deeper snow on the side of the trail, preparing to follow in their wake. "I was calling Tar. He must have thought it was a game when Hannah and Izzy took off. Because he went with them."

Dammit, how had I missed that? I spun around, looking in all directions. Tar was nowhere to be seen. I called out the big black dog's name. There was no response.

I moved quickly to join Bertie. "Hannah's probably planning to cut through the woods to beat us to the parking lot. We need to catch up before she gets in her car and leaves."

Bertie was already forging a path through the heavy snow. "You don't think she'd take Tar with her, do you?"

"At this point, I have no idea what she might be capable of doing," I replied grimly. "And I'd just as soon not have to find out."

Faith immediately took the lead. The snow was deep, but the trio running ahead of us had left tracks for us to follow. The Standard Poodle hopped nimbly from one set of footprints to the next. Bertie and I had to work to keep up.

Even with the trail partially trampled flat, it was slow going. Tree trunks pressed close on either side. Underbrush clogged the gaps in between. It was midafternoon but the sun was already beginning to dip lower in the sky. Within the confines of the forest, it was hard to see even ten feet ahead.

When the trail of broken snow cut sharply to the left, I hoped we were still heading in the right direction. I paused to whistle sharply for Tar. Blowing heavily, Bertie stopped beside me.

"I'm not sure this is right," she said, gesturing back the other way. "I think the parking lot should be over there. I hope Faith hasn't got us following after a possum or a wolverine."

"There aren't any wolverines in Waveny Park," I told her. At least I hoped there weren't.

Bertie frowned. "Is there any reason why Hannah wouldn't take the most direct route to the carriage house?"

"I don't know. She hikes these trails every day. She must know the whole area really well. Maybe there's a creek in the other direction she doesn't want to ford. Or maybe she's trying to get us lost."

"Lost." Bertie blew out a derisive breath. "You can't get lost in New Canaan. Let's grab Faith and head back in the other direction. We've got boots on. I'm willing to plow through some water if it means we can beat her to the parking lot."

I was all for taking a shortcut if we could find one. We hadn't even been in the woods for ten minutes, but already it felt as though the shadows were closing in around us. I couldn't wait to leave the thick snarl of trees behind.

We struck out in a new direction. Every few steps, I paused to call out Tar's name. The lack of a response was disheartening. Tar wasn't the smartest dog, but he was still a Standard Poodle. He must have realized by now that he'd followed the wrong person. I kept expecting to see that big goofy dog come bounding back to us through the snow. But it didn't happen.

"Maybe Hannah's holding on to him," Bertie speculated.

I'd wondered about the same thing. My fingers curled around the unused leash in my pocket. "That's all the more reason to hurry up and find them."

Faith went trotting out ahead of us again. After a few seconds I could barely see the rounded pom-pon on her tail in the gloom. When she abruptly began to bark, that was all the impetus I needed to start running through the heavy drifts to catch up. Bertie was right behind me.

I stumbled awkwardly through a tangle of downed branches. When I finally made it out the other side and was able to look up, I could see the outline of the carriage house through the trees. The parking lot was no more than twenty feet away.

As Bertie and I struggled to reach her, Faith waited for us on the narrow strip of land between the macadam and the edge of the woods. My line of sight was still limited, but I didn't see Tar anywhere. Or Hannah and Izzy.

Hannah's small sedan and my Volvo were both still parked on the other side of the lot. I exhaled quickly in relief. But as I shoved aside a thorny bush and finally broke through the last line of trees, the sedan's lights came on and its engine rumbled to life.

I scrambled toward the parking lot as Hannah quickly reversed out of her space. When she turned the sedan to face the exit, she and I were opposite each other. I could clearly see Hannah sitting grim faced behind the wheel. Izzy was on the seat beside her. But there was still no sign of Tar.

Faith barked again. I was turning to tell her to stay where she was when I suddenly heard an answering yip. Tar's fuzzy black head popped out from behind the Volvo. I almost choked on a sob of relief. Maybe the big Poodle wasn't so dumb after all. Having become separated from us, he must have figured out that his best course of action was to remain beside our car.

"Tar!" Bertie cried out. "Good dog."

Tar was delighted to see us. He bounced up in the air and came flying out from behind the Volvo. His feet slid on the icy surface. As he bounded toward us, Hannah suddenly floored her gas pedal. The silver sedan shot forward. It was heading straight toward him.

"No!" I screamed.

Tar lifted his head in confusion. His steps slowed uncertainly. He was oblivious to the oncoming car. Now it was only feet away.

I didn't even stop to think. I simply began to run, sprinting across the space between us. Only one thing mattered—saving my dog.

Cutting in front of the sedan was a risky move.

I thought I had enough time to clear the car—
and to propel both myself and Tar out of the way.
Maybe if the pavement hadn't been slippery with
snow, I would have made it.

Instead, just as my hands reached the big
Poodle and shoved him back, I felt the impact
of a jarring blow resonate throughout my entire
body. My legs flew out from under me. Suddenly
I was flying through the air. I came down hard on
the Volvo's hood and a searing pain shot down
my side.

All the oxygen seemed to have vanished from
my lungs. My body shuddered, then lay still.
Somehow I'd lost control of my limbs. Unable to
prevent myself from falling, I slithered down off
the hood and landed in a heap on the pavement.

I'm in big trouble, I thought.

Stars came out of nowhere to dance in front
of my eyes. Then abruptly they disappeared and
everything went black.

Chapter 29

I woke up slowly.

It hurt to even think about opening my eyes. So for a minute I just lay very still and concentrated on breathing in and out. My lungs were working again. That had to be a good thing.

Gradually an awareness of my surroundings returned. The ground beneath me was cold. And wet. My whole body ached. One of my legs was bent back and there was a piercing pain in my ankle that made me think I should try to wiggle my toes. That was a big mistake.

I groaned softly. Then I realized that something big and warm was pressed against my chest. Probably Faith. When I made a sound, she quickly shifted around and began to lick my face. That helped.

Dimly I was aware that Bertie was nearby. It sounded like she was yelling at somebody. Possibly into her phone. I hoped she was calling for help because I knew I needed it.

I took a deep breath and tried opening just one eye. That seemed to work out all right. Except that the side of my head was pressed up against the Volvo's tire and I was staring down at the driveway. Not much of a view.

So I opened the other eye. And saw pretty much the same thing.

It felt like moving would require a lot of effort. So instead I just blinked. My vision cleared. Another good thing.

I turned my head slightly. Now I could see the woods. Nothing useful there. Then Bertie came striding into my field of vision. Finally, it felt like I was getting somewhere.

She squatted down beside me. "Melanie, can you hear me?"

"No need to yell," I croaked. "I'm right here."

"Thank God you're alive." She peered down at my face. "I thought you were dead. Or maybe dying. Don't try to move. I called nine-one-one. Help is on the way."

"I want to sit up," I told her. I lifted an arm and maneuvered Faith just slightly away. The Poodle immediately protested the distance between us. "Help me up."

"Are you sure that's a good idea?"

"It's got to be better than lying here squished up against a tire."

Gingerly, Bertie took my arm. She lifted and I pushed. A few seconds later, I was upright and leaning against the Volvo's fender. "That's better." I sighed.

Suddenly I looked around. That was another mistake. "Where's Tar?"

"He's fine. I locked him inside the car so he

couldn't get into any more trouble. I tried to put Faith in there with him, but she wouldn't listen to me."

I looped my arm around Faith's neck. "Good girl," I whispered.

Bertie glared at us. "Good girl, indeed. The two of you deserve each other. I've never been so scared in my life. What were you thinking, running in front of Hannah's car like that?"

"I don't know." I groaned again. "Maybe that I was faster than a speeding bullet?"

"It isn't funny," she snapped.

"I know. I'm sorry." My lower lip began to quiver. "You're right, that was a stupid thing to do. I wasn't thinking."

Bertie stared at me, her anger fading. Abruptly she became solicitous instead. "What's the matter? You're not going to cry, are you? Oh my God, are you in pain? Are you bleeding somewhere? What should I do?"

"Just stay with me," I told her. "I'm not going to cry. I think I'm just cold."

"Of course you're cold. You're probably in shock. And it's friggin' freezing out here." Bertie yanked off her coat and spread it over me.

As she straightened we both heard the sound of approaching sirens. More than one. Idly I wondered how many people she'd called. I hoped Bertie didn't have Aunt Peg on speed dial. That would really finish me off.

As the first of the official vehicles turned into the parking lot, Bertie looped a collar around Faith's neck. Over the Poodle's objections, Bertie put her in the car where she'd be safely out of the way. I knew it was necessary but I was sorry to see Faith leave. Without her warm body beside me, I quickly felt chilled again.

The New Canaan police station was just down the road from Waveny Park. Still, I was surprised when the first person to come walking around the Volvo was Detective Hronis.

He took in the scene, then carefully hunkered down in front of me. The detective's gaze roamed over my body before returning to my face. His expression revealed an emotion he'd never directed toward me before. He was clearly concerned.

I must have looked worse than I felt. And I felt pretty bad.

"What are you doing here?" I asked.

"Your friend called me. She said you mentioned me in a conversation you were having. She thought maybe I could help. You want to tell me what happened here?"

"Bertie's the woman who called you. She and I were out on the hiking trails, taking a walk with Hannah Bly."

His sympathetic countenance vanished. It was replaced by a scowl. "I assume that's the same Hannah Bly you just told me about earlier?"

I nodded.

"The woman you suspected of being a murderer?"

"Yes."

"You decided to go for a walk in the woods with her." Hronis closed his eyes briefly as if he couldn't believe what he was hearing. Or maybe he was praying for patience. In my diminished mental state, it was hard to tell. "Was there any particular reason you thought that would be a good idea?"

"I wanted to tell her that she should turn herself in to the police," I said.

"You couldn't have called her on the phone for that?"

Now there was a good idea. In hindsight, too bad I hadn't done so.

"I thought Hannah was a nice person. I felt I owed it to her to hear her side of the story."

"Her side." He frowned. "Does she have a side?"

"Yes. Hannah says she acted in self-defense. Six weeks before she killed Victor Durbin, he slipped a roofie in her drink at a party and raped her."

Hronis immediately zeroed in on the first part of what I'd said. "She admitted to you that she'd killed him?"

"She did." I sighed. "Bertie heard her too."

More flashing lights were spinning in the air

above me. Two paramedics appeared. I glanced up at them over the detective's shoulder.

"How bad are you feeling?" Hronis asked. "Do you think you need immediate medical assistance?"

"I'm not going to die anytime soon if that's what you're asking."

He turned to the two men. "Give us a minute, will you?" They both stepped back to give us some privacy.

"Then what happened?" Detective Hronis asked.

"Hannah asked us not to tell anyone what she'd done. I told her it was already too late for that." I gave him a wobbly smile. "That was where you came in."

"Right." He frowned again. At least that was a familiar expression. "You and I had our little chat, what . . . maybe three hours ago?"

"I guess so."

"Three hours, not even. That was all the time you were going to give me to look into what you'd said before you decided to take matters into your own hands?"

Put like that, it did make my actions sound precipitous. Maybe I could see why he might be upset.

"You said you didn't believe me," I told him.

"No, that wasn't it," Hronis stated. "I said we needed proof."

"And now you have it."

The detective shook his head. He was not amused. "I also have a woman sitting on the ground who's apparently been hit by a car. In case you don't realize it, Ms. Travis, there were easier ways to go about this."

Now it was my turn to scowl. "Believe me, Detective, I know that now. But when Bertie and I came out here earlier, I had no intention of getting hurt."

"Yet somehow you managed to get in the way of Hannah Bly's car."

"No, actually, my dog did."

"Your dog?" he repeated incredulously.

"Yes," I snapped. "But he's fine. Thank you for asking."

"Your dog," Hronis said again.

Rather than repeat myself, I gestured toward the car window above me. I knew that Faith and Tar would be standing on the seat watching us. No doubt two black noses were pressed against the glass. Even though the window was closed, I could hear Faith whining unhappily.

Hronis glanced upward, then back down again. "I'm glad your dog is fine," he said gruffly. "And I'm sorry you're not. As for Hannah Bly, I was already in the process of getting in touch with the Midtown precinct. I'll put a rush on that now. In the meantime, we'll pick her up and bring her in for questioning. Worst case, we can charge her for what she did to you."

"Thank you," I said. "Maybe you could ask the paramedics to give me some help?"

I leaned back and closed my eyes. Everything was out of my hands now. It was time for the authorities to take over. I couldn't even have made my own way to the hospital. The paramedics took care of that.

Bertie had called Sam and he met us at the entrance to the emergency room. I was still feeling fuzzy so Sam took over as I underwent a battery of tests. After that, the doctors decided to keep me in the hospital overnight for observation. I was pretty banged up but the consensus was that I'd been very lucky.

Hannah must have seen me at the last second and tried to avoid hitting me, as it appeared her car had delivered only a glancing blow. I had a concussion, and there were numerous unsightly bruises mottling various parts of my body. Beyond that, the only serious injury was to my ankle. My fibula had a clean break. I wouldn't be out running with the Poodles anytime soon, but eventually I could expect to make a full recovery.

Hannah took my advice and hired an experienced attorney. He accompanied her to the police station when she turned herself in. He stood by her side when she confessed to killing Victor Durbin.

Then Hannah's lawyer came up with a way to take a thorny legal problem, turn it around, and present it to maximum advantage. He characterized Hannah as both a victim and a heroine. She was hand delivered to the media as a crusader who'd fought for the rights of abused women everywhere.

I had mixed feelings about positioning rape as a justification for murder, but the press lapped up Hannah's story eagerly. With popular opinion solidly on her side, I suspected she'd wind up with a plea deal that would allow her to avoid jail time. At any rate, the news outlets' avid coverage would make it easy for me to keep tabs on future developments in the case.

Having lost both Victor and Hannah, the Empire Poodle Club didn't last long after that. Its inaugural specialty show turned out to be its swan song. To no one's surprise, the remaining board members were anxious to distance themselves from the double-edged scandal. That, combined with the AKC investigation, was enough to quietly close the club down.

I emerged from the hospital with my left leg encased in a medical boot and a pair of crutches under my arms. I quickly discovered that any sort of movement on my part was slow, awkward, and uncomfortable. I hadn't been a clumsy person before, but I was now.

On my first day home I tripped over Bud twice. Then I managed to sweep half the dinner dishes off the kitchen table with the tip of my crutch.

For some reason, my sadistic family found my struggles to adapt wildly amusing.

"It's not funny," I groused.

"Actually, it kind of is," Davey replied. "Cars are pretty big. I can't believe you didn't see that one coming."

Neither of the boys knew the details of my accident. And Sam and I had no intention of enlightening them. All they knew was that somehow their mother had ended up in the wrong place at the worst possible time. Since I'd declined to fill in the gaps in the story, Davey and Kevin figured the accident must have been my fault. *Of course.*

Sam had seen me through more than a few previous scrapes over the years we'd been together, so his sympathy was limited too. But I forgave him for that when he arranged for a couple of surprise visitors to drop by the house.

Crawford and Terry had returned from a brief trip to St. Lucia. They showed up on our doorstep on Monday afternoon, looking tanned, relaxed, and blissfully happy. Terry had a big smile on his face. Improbably Crawford was carrying a plate of brownies.

"Sam told us you needed cheering up," Terry said. "I can see why. You look terrible. Like you were run over by a truck."

"Thanks a lot." I shoved my crutches aside and

gave both men hugs. "It's great to see you guys. Come on in. You look wonderful."

Davey was still at school. Kev was on a playdate. So Sam only had to manage the Poodle pack. He put all the dogs out back—except for Faith, who hadn't left my side in days. Then he and I got our guests settled in the living room. The plate of brownies went on the table between us. They looked homemade and smelled delicious.

"How was the honeymoon?" I asked.

"Honeymoons are for young people," Crawford said. "We just had a nice little vacation."

"A post wedding vacation," Terry interjected. "You know, like a honeymoon." He was delighted to be married, and he wasn't going to let anyone forget it.

Crawford shook his head fondly. He lifted the plate and offered it to me. "Have a brownie."

"Thank you. Did Terry bake them?"

"Nope." Terry grinned. "Crawford did."

That was a surprise. Crawford didn't cook. Ever.

"Really?" Sam and I both looked at the handler.

He just shrugged. "Now that I'm married, I figured it was time to learn."

"What else can you cook?" I asked.

"Don't be so impatient," Terry chided me. "We're taking it in small steps. This week, brownies. Next week, maybe scrambled eggs."

Sam and I smiled together. "Tell us all about your trip," he said.

Terry happily recounted everything they'd done during their beach vacation. When he finally paused for breath, Crawford chimed in. Between beachcombing, deep sea fishing, and visiting an island brewery, the pair had found plenty of ways to entertain themselves. I was surprised to learn that Crawford was an avid snorkeler.

"What?" he said, slipping me a wink. "You don't think I have hidden depths?"

"I never doubted that for a minute," I replied, and we all laughed.

Later, when they were leaving, Terry pulled me aside. "It's great to see you and Crawford getting along again. I'm glad things are finally back to normal."

I felt the same way, but I couldn't let Terry have the last word.

"Normal?" I asked him, balancing on my crutches. "What's that?"

Books are produced in the United States using U.S.-based materials

Books are printed using a revolutionary new process called THINKtech™ that lowers energy usage by 70% and increases overall quality

Books are durable and flexible because of Smyth-sewing

Paper is sourced using environmentally responsible foresting methods and the paper is acid-free

Center Point Large Print

600 Brooks Road / PO Box 1
Thorndike, ME 04986-0001 USA

(207) 568-3717

US & Canada:
1 800 929-9108
www.centerpointlargeprint.com